A COLD BLUE

KILLER

Third Book in the Tom Curran Series

D1601381

JUNE 11, 2020

Tim Ramsey (cptramsey@yahoo.com)

Chapter 1

The gunman spotted Curran and twisted his body to keep the petrified coed he caught by the throat between them. A bolt of raw adrenaline shot through Curran's veins, but it didn't affect his action. He calmly raised his weapon, took careful aim at the crazed man's face, and fired. The man fell backward with his captive, out of sight behind the high library counter. Curran knew there was a second gunman and turned his aim at the open door. Suddenly a shot rang out. Curran turned around to see a gunman facing him, smoke emanating from the barrel of the pistol pointed at him.

"Awe, shit," he declared. "I always forget about that guy."

"How many times we do this one?" Caraballo asked, his best friend from childhood and a member of the team.

Curran didn't answer. Instead he holstered his weapon before looking behind him at the man controlling the computer-generated training scenario set in a near 360-degree circle around him. Instead of bullets, the gun fires a laser pulse detected by the video screens. The bad guys in the video are just that; video. Good thing. Curran would have been killed for the third time this morning.

"You're obviously distracted," quipped Caraballo.

"By what?"

"The prospect of a fishing tournament and the fact you'll be on the Jersey shore in a matter of hours."

Curran grinned while watching for the bad guy in the new training video, changing scenery flashing colors on his face. This time he successfully scanned behind him and finished the scenario.

Curran and Caraballo wrapped up their training at the CCBSC (Close-Quarter Battle Simulation Center) and were about to leave when one of the training officers came into the rather plush locker room. He found Caraballo relaxing in a thick brown leather chair as Curran stuffed his shooting gear into his range bag. He handed Curran a note.

"What's that?" Caraballo asked as Curran read the note.

"It's from Theresa," he said. He looked perplexed as he read. "It just says 'call me. All okay here. Urgent elsewhere."

"You gotta love her ability to be succinct."

Two hours later, thanks to the short flight from Arlington Virginia to Woodbine, New Jersey in Caraballo's Cessna 206, Curran and Caraballo found themselves at the home of Grace O'Reilly, mother of an old friend of theirs named Robert, whom they called Baba. Curran pulled up to a quiet little house in the woods. It seemed out of place; a seashore-style Victorian nestled among the trees in the Southern New Jersey Pinelands.

It seemed out of place because it was; fifteen years ago, her husband had it moved in two giant pieces from nearby Sea Island to its current location. It had no yard, just a perfect circular asphalt driveway arcing its way through the woods. Next to the house sat an old, faded, rust-spotted Ford pickup truck, the bed laden with floats, ropes, grey-weathered wooden poles with sturdy gaff hooks attached to the ends, a pile of rotting rubberized rain gear, and five gallon containers of 90-weight gear oil and diesel fuel additive. It was the only sign of the home of a fisherman. The siding and lattice work on the house appeared brand-new, and the roof was recently replaced. The house was immaculate. Next to it was a small Toyota SUV with a bouquet of fake flowers in the cupholder.

Curran and Caraballo stepped out of Curran's blue OJ-style Ford Bronco and breathed in the scent of the pine forest, feeling the slight breeze as it eased past, rustling the leaves on the scrub oaks at the fringes of the woods. Nearby, three steps led from the ground up to the front porch. Curran walked up the porch step, noting the brand-new composite decking and stainless fasteners. He stepped onto a brown straw fiber door mat with the words "Welcome Home" outlined in black. He rang the doorbell and waited. Moments later he saw someone moving behind the decorative translucent glass of the front door.

The door was opened by a woman about sixty-five years-old, fit, fairly tall, wearing blue pants, a flowered V-neck shirt, and white tennis shoes; a hospital volunteer's uniform. Their eyes met. Straight nose, angular jaw, deep-set blue eyes, and small ears holding small stud earrings, her strong Polish facial features and highlighted light-brown hair hinted at youth, but the slight neck waddle and freckled, pinkish skin on her chest sad she'd been around a couple years.

"Tommy!" the woman exclaimed. Her wide eyes beamed excitement at him. "Oh, my goodness!" she added as she walked out and wrapped her arms around Curran, one around the neck, the other under an arm. It was a good hug; one from someone you knew very well.

"Let me look at you," she said, her hands on his shoulders. "You look fantastic!" she added, a quick smile right before a tear came to her eye.

"You do too, Gracie," Curran replied.

"Oh," she said as she went back in for another hug. The hug felt different this time, as if she was relieved to see him. "Come on in!" she added, motioning him inside. "What can I get you? Iced tea? Some coffee maybe?"

"What are you having?"

"Well, I just got back from the hospital. I was cleaning the bathroom," a complete non-sequitur.

They moved from the foyer and walked through time. It was the same formal living room he walked through as a kid when the house was out on the island. Hardwood floors and ornate wainscoting lined every space, wrap every room, ran down every hall, and even climbed the stairs. White wainscoting under pale blue walls; it always reminded Curran of the street hockey rink at the park on Sea Island.

He followed the woman into the kitchen. A small square table sat off to the left, one side pushed against the wall, the top covered in mail over a white tablecloth with blue silhouette patterns of little girls in bonnets and puffy dresses, and baby ducks. The same blue pattern repeated in the wall border spanning the room near the ceiling, and on the wooden breadbox on the Formica countertop. The same white wainscoting surrounded the room, dipping under three windows half-hidden by loose white curtains. On a side table in the corner sat a bread mixer, a collection of wooden rolling pins, and stacks of cookbooks. In the other corner, near the end of the kitchen counter was the back door with a set of old wind chimes hung in front of the glass at the top. At the end of the counter was a stand-up five-gallon water cooler, and next to it a glass jar for making homemade iced tea. Curran noticed the familiar yellow lemons etched on the sides. Next to that was another familiar sight; a huge glass jar full of homemade pickles. If you could see a picture of that room from twenty-five years earlier, it would look exactly the same.

"Sit. Sit," she directed, pointing at a chair at the table. She pulled a tall glass from the white overhead cupboard and filled it with iced tea. No ice. There never seemed to be a need for it. She delivered it to Curran sitting at the table and took a seat to his right, almost blocking the path through the kitchen.

"It's about time you came to see me," she declared. Her motherly tone caused a twang of guilt in Curran. "How long has it been?"

"About ten years and about twenty pounds ago," he replied.

"More like twenty years. When my sister died, I finally decided to pay attention to my health. Well, that and Robert's father dying."

"I heard about that. I'm sorry."

"So how have you been? What have you been up to?" she asked, quickly changing the subject. "It looks like the army's been good to you."

"It has."

"I wish Robert stayed in instead of doing his combat tour and getting out."

"Everybody figures out how they do the army, and how the army does them."

"I guess. Tell me, have you been around the world?"

"A couple times. Not exactly tourism, but I've seen some things."

"Well, you were special forces, right? Did you spend much time in combat?"

"All in all, about ten years, but you know special ops; we're never really out of it."

"Well, I wish during all that time you would have come to see me."

"Yes ma'am."

"I remember when you were young. Robert's father really thought you were something. He always did. Never stopped thinking that."

"He was great."

"Yeah, so you're staying at the orphan home in Sea Isle?" she asked. This sort of jumping from subject to subject is normal, until you land on something that she really wanted to talk about.

"No, they knocked that down and sold off the property years ago. Condos are there now."

"So where are you staying?"

"At Annette DeFelice's house on fifty-second street."

"Who?"

"You know my friend Constantine, the guy outside, right?" he asked. She nodded in the affirmative.

"I was going to ask why you left him outside?"

"He had to make a phone call back to DC," Curran replied. It was a lie. Truth be told, Caraballo never really liked her son and never got to know his family like Curran. "The house is his mother-in-law's house."

"Oh yeah, I remember now. That's how you met; the orphanage summer house was on the same block."

Curran knew she was avoiding the topic at hand. She was the cause for the "urgent elsewhere" portion of Theresa's cryptic telephone message. He studied her face, posture, and general disposition for a moment.

"Gracie, what happened?" he said smoothly.

She looked at him pensively, mental gears turning. It wasn't suspicion regarding the question, or about how to phrase the answer.

She was genuinely avoiding the issue. Curran sipped his tea. After watching her for a moment, he continued.

"I half-expected to find him in his van somewhere waiting for the tide to come up. What happened?" he said, urging her to speak. After a moment of resistance, she broke into tears.

"Basically, he was beaten to death."

"What?" Curran said in disbelief. "In Sea Island?"

"No. Out on the boat?"

Curran was completely caught off guard. A mixture of shock and fright gripped him. He felt his hair bristle.

"Gracie, I'm not tracking. Tell me what you mean?"

"He said he was out on the boat and was told to stay out of an area. When he didn't turn around, two men came on another boat. They boarded his boat and attacked him. He came in and drove himself to the hospital."

"And that's where he died?"

"Yes, the following day."

"Jeez, Louise," Curran muttered in disbelief. "Did he say who did it?"

"He said he didn't know."

"Did he say where he was exactly?"

"No."

"Did he try to call the Coast Guard?"

"He said they smashed his radio."

"What about a cell phone?"

"You know him," she said disappointedly. "He still didn't carry one."

"Jesus," Curran replied. He had expected to hear a tale of how Baba died by accident or even took his own life, but not something like this. He was practically a case study in PTSD and twenty-one veterans still take their own lives every day, so this was as painful a surprise to Curran as getting your nuts caught in a bear trap.

"You know, I saw him a couple weeks ago," Curran added. "I stopped and saw him at the dock. He was getting the boat ready to go out again." Curran paused for a moment, remembering. He smiled. You know, he kept calling me sir." Tears welled in his eyes. One went down his cheek. A chill went down his spine. "I had to tell him to stop it."

"He told me," Grace said, sliding Curran's iced tea glass closer to him. Curran grabbed it.

"He did?"

Grace nodded. "He said you told him *you* should call *him* sir for receiving the Silver Star in combat," she added, chuckling.

"I did say that. I meant it too. It took balls of steel to do what he did. Say, where is he now?"

"Still at the hospital. The VA is supposed to come get him soon."

"Okay." Curran was starting to wonder why she seemed so resigned to his fate. How quickly things change.

"Know what the last thing he said was?" she asked, looking at him with a serious gaze and furrowed brow.

"What?" Curran asked, bracing himself.

"Tell Tommy."

Chapter 2

By the time Curran and Caraballo reached the house on Sea Island, Curran's brain was already torturing him with thoughts about Robert O'Reilly. To his friends, he was called "Baba." He had a love for the musical group "The Who" as a kid. Somebody realized the song "Teenage Wasteland" is actually entitled "Baba O'Reilly," and put two and two together.

Curran didn't sleep too well. First, he thought how sad and useless it was that a Silver Star winner died as result of an unnecessary beating. Then Curran's voracious reading habit made him think of the passage from Hemingway's *A Farewell to Arms* from 1929; "I was always embarrassed by the words sacred, glorious and sacrifice and the expression in vain. I had seen nothing sacred and the things that were glorious had no glory, and the sacrifices were like the stockyards at Chicago if nothing was done with the meat except to bury it." Curran pondered on the term "meat." He felt like that sometimes in the army. He tossed and turned until around 4 am.

When Curran got out of bed before dawn and a song by the 90's band Counting Crows popped into his head. One verse kept playing over and over; "If dreams are like movies, then memories are films about ghosts." He couldn't shake it, so he got Caraballo out of bed. The two skipped the boat trip and went straight to the beach down at the inlet on the south side of town for some fishing.

As the two walked over the dunes and across the beach to the water's edge on the west side of the bridge leading from Sea Island to Avondale, the next island south, big diesel sportfishing boats swooped past the beach, then through the open drawbridge section of the Inlet Bridge heading to the ocean. The boats were heading out for the final day of the South Jersey Marlin and Sailfish Open fishing tournament. The low rising sun reflects glare off the smooth hull sides of the boats and casts shadows from the bridge long across the water. Laughing gulls cry out in the cool morning air as the smell of salt marsh and seaweed drifts past.

"Pretzel King," Curran said out loud, surf rod in hand. On the teak-covered transom of the boat going past are the words "Pretzel King," written in gold script.

"Must be the Schaefer Pretzel guy's boat," said Caraballo. Schaefer's is the largest pretzel company in the Delaware Valley area; one look at his palatial bayside estate in nearby Avondale show's he's making some dough, all pun intended.

Another boat swung through the open section of the bridge right as the wake from the first boat broke in a knee-high wave in front of the two men. The boat's captain steered the vessel from his perch atop a gleaming tuna tower, a structure set twenty feet atop the vessel's flybridge.

"On a Roll," Caraballo said from nearby, his voice barely audible above the rumble of the nearby diesel engines. He turned to

Curran, one squinting eye caught by the glaring eastern sun. "That's the pork roll guy, right?" he asked.

The fleet of sportfishing boats roared past in a parade of monetary excess and wealthy pastime pursuit seen in places like Miami, Fort Lauderdale, and Palm Beach. There were boats from the Philadelphia pretzel king, the owners of a local hot sauce company, a chicken wing franchise, meat barons, sports team owners, a liquor distributor, a concrete company, a television evangelist, and the CEO of a chemical company.

Then a big, 39-foot center console with four huge outboard motors blew by, a crowd of twenty-something, bearded, tattooed guys hanging on for dear life as the driver barely missed a little runabout bobbing close to the bridge. It bristled with fishing rods and blasted rock and roll music so loud it would make you wonder if the bunch would end-up sterile by day's end. Down the side of the boat in huge neon-blue italic letters was the word FUUSGUS!!!...complete with three exclamation points. It was Colin Rafferty, the guy who parlayed a Wharton School of Business degree into an internet pornography empire. The name of the boat apparently means "Fuck You U. S. Government You Suck." Some say it was an improvement over the name of his first boat, "Mr. Stiffy." His parents must be so proud.

Curran moved a short way toward the curve in the beach that lead toward the inter-coastal waterway around the back of Sea Island. He casted his line and watched it sink as Caraballo moved closer to the bridge. Curran kept thinking about Baba. Why would someone come on his boat and beat him so badly he would die? Did he do something? Did he know them? What's going on? Thoughts ran thick through his head. Curran gazed around, thinking about how they just ended a rather strenuous mission in Central America and the team was exhausted. This was supposed to be down- time. But Baba was a childhood friend. Curran's cobbled-together family was coming "down the shore" as they say in New Jersey, and he didn't want to ignore them. But Baba told his mother to call him. Something was wrong.

Caraballo went back to the bait bucket after realizing his bait was gone. He retrieved two small mud minnows and placed them on the gold circle hooks on his surf rig while keeping an eye on Curran retrieving his sixth flounder of the day. Caraballo walked to the water's edge and eased himself into the cool water out to about knee deep. He refers to this water temperature as "tingly," saying "your legs don't mind, but your crotch will." After spying what he believed was a good eddy of water near the base of the bridge's northern drawbridge support, he gathered the determination required to make the long cast, flipped the bail on his big spinning real, reared back, and with a mighty heave, sent the line toward his target.

Or rather, he didn't; the line went off at a 45-degree angle and rocketed skyward toward the bridge. He jerked the rod in front of him and tried to close the bail on the reel, whipping the rod tip in the opposite direction of the cast. He looked up to watch the line barely miss the bridge. Sort of. Jutting from the roadway was a rusted, faded green, empty metal light bracket about two feet long. The line flew over the bracket, caught it, and the rig made about six rotations around the sad, lonely metal bar with complete, unfortunate abandon. When it stopped, two hooks, two minnows, and a three-ounce egg sinker dangled helplessly, yet tauntingly, hung-up on the bridge.

"Shit!" Caraballo blurted lowly. He stood testing the possibility of using a springing action with the rod to possibly un-wrap the rig. This was followed by a slight tug on the line, followed by a bit more pressure, and then some vertical rod whipping with slack line. He stopped and stood dumbfounded, staring at the bridge. He reeled-in and put good pressure on the line in the hope it would either pull the rusted bracket from the bridge or miraculously free the line; no dice. "Uh, Tom?" he said reluctantly.

A short way down the beach, Curran squatted in ankle-deep water releasing the flounder he had just caught while kept his eye on a dull grey commercial lobster boat that eased itself under the bridge. He recognized the man behind the wheel as someone from his past. He turned and looked at Caraballo through his blue-mirror sunglasses.

"I think I'm done fishing," Caraballo said. When Curran looked over at him, Caraballo sheepishly pointed to the fishing rig dangling off the bridge.

"How'd you do that?"

"I don't know," Caraballo said, aggravated.

"Well, you hooked it; reel it in," Curran said tauntingly.

Caraballo pulled back, putting a big bend in the rod, followed by tugging on it to create the appearance his quarry is fighting back. Curran started walking toward him.

"Caraballo's fresh catch of the day," Curran said in a pirate voice, paraphrasing a line from the movie "National Lampoon's Summer Rental."

"Lightly seasoned, fried to a golden brown," he replied; same movie.

"We'll take five!" the two said in stereo; same movie again.

"Reel in as much as you can and we'll cut it off," Curran directed.

"But that's the last surf rig."

"That's okay; we gotta go anyway. The girls should be at the house by now."

"Ah, the salad days…"

Caraballo reeled in as much line as possible, stretching the line straight to the bridge. When he had all he could get, Curran stepped in front of him and cut it with his fishing knife. Suddenly, with no tension on the line, the rig popped off the metal bracket 50-feet overhead and hurtled to the water, landing too far out to retrieve. The two men stood gobsmacked, and then started to giggle. After a moment, they tossed the remaining mud minnows into the water, gathered their gear, and walked off the beach. They traveled across the sand noticing their stubby shadows, the strong late morning sun shining high over the marshes and bay to their left, over pink tourists and lonely seagulls on the beach, casting a huge shadow under the bridge. They took advantage of the shade. Curran had caught nine fish while Caraballo caught three (Curran normally never counts while Caraballo counts everybody's catch) and they thoroughly enjoyed themselves here in the feel-good capital of the Jersey Shore.

"It's Miller time!" Caraballo proclaimed.

"Little early for me."

"So, how'd you do?"

"Six or seven I think," Curran said. "How about you?"

"I caught a bridge."

Chapter 3

Curran and Caraballo got back in Curran's old Bronco and traveled
north back to 52nd Street. As he slowed on the main street in
preparation to turn, something made Caraballo look over at him.

"What is it?" Caraballo asked, noticing the furrowed brow
atop Curran's green mirror sunglasses.

"Ah," Curran growled aggravatedly as he got off the brake,
checked his mirrors and made a U-turn. "I have to see something, he
added. He could feel the hairs on his arms standing up. He wanted
answers.

"I think I know what you're doing," Caraballo responded.
"Oh yeah?"
"Yeah. You know what Alexander Pope said."
"Yes, I do. Fools rush in where angels fear to tread."
The two men drove back down to the south end of town,
turned west on 82nd street and parked in one of the three spaces in
front of the small Coast Guard station on the bay. They walked
toward the pier looking for Baba's boat. Curran first noticed the
Coast Guard SAFE boat was not in its spot at the end of the pier.
Good, maybe they wouldn't be bothered. Then they spotted Baba's
lobster boat tied to the dock on the inside of the T-shaped pier on the
left, facing north.

"So, who are you today?" Caraballo asked. "Commander
Morrison? Detective Jameson?" he added.

"Today it's," Curran blurted before something caught his eye. He spied a Coast Guard officer approaching. "Well, today I'm Tom Curran," he said matter-of-factly. "That's Shane Rafferty right there."

"Is there *anybody* you *don't* know?" chuckled Caraballo.

"Hey, you got my twenty dollars?" shouted Rafferty as the three men converged. It was his normal greeting.

"Hey Shane," Curran said as the two shook hands. "You remember Connie," he added, pointing a hand toward Caraballo.

After greetings were exchanged and a short conversation about fishing and Rafferty's next promotion, Curran asked him about Baba's boat. Specifically, how did it get there?

"Mr. O'Reilly pulled up to the dock, claiming he had fallen and hurt himself," Rafferty reported. "We helped him off the boat, called the ambulance, moved his boat around to the inside of the pier and secured it after he was taken away."

Curran got the impression Rafferty didn't know Baba had died, thinking if he did know, then Rafferty would never let him on the boat since it would be secured for an eventual police investigation. That was only a matter of time. Curran told Rafferty he needed to check out Baba's boat. Rafferty was reluctant at first, with the Coast Guard being responsible for the boat while in their custody, but Curran reminded him of their friendship and promised to not remove anything without showing it to Rafferty.

It was your typical commercial lobster boat. About forty-four feet long, big open deck with space to hold stacks of traps, a small pilothouse forward. Behind the pilothouse midships sticking up through the extended roof was a dry-stack exhaust wrapped in an aluminum ventilated shield. To starboard was another helm station next to the block and line coiler for retrieving the traps, and near that was a combination sorting table and giant ice chest set under the extended pilothouse roof for keeping the bait or the catch. The inside of the boat, the pilothouse and decks were faded and worn, mostly a dull white in color, while the outside of the hull was a faded blue. The name on the back was "Crikey!" from the expression of the Australian wildlife expert Steve Irwin.

"What are you looking for?" Caraballo asked as the two climbed aboard.

"I don't know. What would piss you off enough to whoop someone's ass to death?"

"I don't know. Bad drivers. People stuck on their cell phones. People talking in the movies. Guys with man-scarves, liberals," Caraballo replied as he searched the pilothouse.

"Besides that," Curran said as he stepped down into the forward v-berth. He searched in the racks on the wall, under the mattress pads, and in the drawers.

"Gun control advocates, polluters, people that call Catholicism a "matriarchal religion.""

"The list is getting better," Curran quipped as he came back up into the pilothouse.

"People that force their opinion on you but don't respect yours. Bigots. Homophobes. People that say "eye-talian and eye-rackie.""

"What do you think?" Curran asked, changing the subject.

"Looks like a pilothouse to me. Nothing unusual."

"You're right. Let's check the back."

The two men searched the entire stern of the boat including inside the cooler box and under the deck in the lazarette and bilge spaces. Nothing.

"One more thing before we go," Curran said, looking at the boat's GPS unit. He turned it on and went through some chart pages before stopping on one screen.

"Look at that," Curran said, pointing at the illuminated screen.

"What's that?" Caraballo asked.

"That's the track of his last trip. He got to this point, stopped, and came right back," Curran said, finger touching next to a specific spot on the electronic chart.

"So, the end of that point is where he got boarded?"

"Looks like it," Curran said as he pulled a small notebook and pen from his cargo pocket.

"What's right there?"

"That's what we have to find out," Curran replied as he wrote the coordinates for the spot on the GPS in his notebook.

"So, we're doing this?" Caraballo asked cautiously. Curran looked him in the eye.

"Yep, we're doing this."

Curran and Caraballo returned to the house to find Mrs. DeFelice, Caraballo's former mother-in-law, and Theresa, her daughter and Curran's "significant other" putting groceries away. Curran stayed behind to visit with them and tell them what's going on as Caraballo left for the little general aviation airport about ten minutes away on the mainland.

Flying is one of Caraballo's passions. He used to be an army fixed-wing pilot. That ended when he did an aerobatic maneuver in a twin-engine executive aircraft with two general officers in the back. After that, he joined Special Forces to be with his best friend and went through training as a Special Forces medic. He took to the medical training like it was his calling. People tried to get him to go to medical school. He refused. He didn't want to leave the Special Forces or his best friend. After that came training as a Physician's Assistant. To the military, they're as well trained as any doctor, but better at trauma, combat medicine, and much more able to go to the far reaches of the world and provide medical care of all kinds to needy people, or the ones we want to have on our side. Caraballo is one of the best. He might go back to doing it full time. That's a secret he's only discussed with Curran. Covert operations don't let him be around it enough. Just don't call him 'Doc;' unlike most medics or even doctors, he doesn't like it.

Thirty minutes later Curran drives up the pine tree-lined access road to the Woodbine Municipal Airport, a small airfield five miles inland from Sea Isle City. The road ends at a small parking lot in front of the Fixed Base Operation (FBO), a small white building about the size of a double-wide mobile home that holds the airport office. To the left, a single-lane road travels toward a row of pale green aluminum hangars sitting alongside a side taxiway. To the right, a maintenance hangar sits next to a long set of connected airplane hangars that run along the main taxiway. Behind the hangars is an open tarmac used for single engine aircraft parking spots, and behind that, a perimeter road keeps the pine forest away from the airport. Curran pulled into the lot next to the FBO. The perimeter fence attaches to the sides of the building in front of him flush with the front, making the only way onto the airfield through the back door of the building or from the hangars, their access controlled by an electronic gate. To the right, on the other side of the fence, a single rusty gas pump dispensing 100 low-lead aviation gasoline sits perched alone on a cracked concrete pedestal. The pedestal is painted yellow, somehow streaked with rust stains, and set in the middle of a twenty-foot diameter concrete pad. Behind the building on the side of the airfield slightly to the left, sits the same dirty, algae-covered Piper Warrior airplane Curran saw last year when he was here. The grass is freshly cut around it, but tall around the landing gear. He wondered if you can call a perpetually broken airplane a "hangar queen" if it isn't in a hangar. Maybe it's a lawn ornament.

Curran glided his truck into a parking spot in front of the building. After grabbing a pair of binoculars from the bag in the back seat, he hopped out of his Bronco and headed inside the FBO. He opened the door to the rattle of little bells hung on the inside. Stepping inside, goose bumps popped up on his arms as the cold air conditioning washed over him. His eyes instantly met those of a large woman, mid-sixties, plump, silver hair. She sat at a small round table near the far-right window reading the newspaper.

"Wow, the a/c's really working, huh?" he said.

"Hey Tom, how ya doin?" the woman happily replied.

"Doing great Annie; yourself?"

"Heck, if I was doing any better, it would be illegal. Haven't seen you in a while," she adds. Her normal speech pattern is a few decibels above normal.

The radio on a small shelf behind her crackled to life.

"Woodbine radio, Cessna November one-three-one-three-one. Good morning."

Without getting up, Annie reached for an old-fashioned silver stand-up microphone on the counter behind her. Shuffling sideways in her seat, Curran noticed the full-length leg brace wrapped around her left leg. Seeing her leaning toward the microphone, he had a sudden flash of Roy Orbison go through his head.

"One-three-one, Woodbine, go ahead," she says into the microphone.

"Annie, I'm at hangar five, request taxi to the fuel pump, over."

"One-three-one, permission granted. Good morning Connie."

Annie set the microphone back down on the counter and spun back around to face the table. She sipped her coffee as she looked at Curran.

"I have a full cup of Wawa over there if you'd like some," she offered. Wawa is the convenience store chain that dominates South Jersey, named after the town of Wawa, Pennsylvania, which is named after the Ojibwe Indian word for the Canada Goose (bet you didn't know that!).

"No thanks. Connie made some a little bit ago." He looked around the room, feeling the time warp. The décor was straight out of the 60's; black and white pictures of vintage aircraft, dark paneled walls, art deco flyers for airplane services; pictures of stewardesses in their 60's uniforms; two Formica tables wrapped in stainless steel. Maroon vinyl seats. Glass case with aviation motor oil, shop towels and fuel sample cups near the counter. The room isn't just decorated like the 60's…it's *from* the 60's. Everything in it was at least thirty years old. The sound of a small aircraft taxiing started to rise.

"Speaking of Connie, there he is now," Annie said, gesturing out the window with her cup in hand.

A plain white Cessna 206 Stationair rolled down the taxiway in front of the FBO building. On the side in tall black letters was N13131. Curran thought how bizarre Caraballo got those registration numbers; 13 and 31 have always been lucky for Curran and have recurred many times over his lifetime. Before him, Father Duffy said those were his lucky numbers too. Duffy was the priest at the Philadelphia boy's home where Curran grew-up. It started when Curran was the thirteenth kid he took in and he lived in room thirty-one. Odd since there were only 15 rooms.

Caraballo pulled the airplane close to the fuel pump and killed the engine. He hopped out of the aircraft and threw the yellow wooden wheel chocks under the tire on the left side. After that, he walked around the plane and over to a large cable reel mounted on a stand near the gas pump and grabbed the grounding cable wound to it. He walked back to the plane as the reel payed-out the cable. Caraballo looked tentatively at the right aileron, then moved to the engine cowl, popped the latch, raised the cowl, and clipped the end of the cable on an internal engine mount. Grounding wasn't really necessary since the engine was off and the aircraft was on rubber tires, but the army taught him to ground everything when dealing with fuel, and he is a creature of habit.

Caraballo grabbed the small folding ladder hanging on a bracket next to the fuel pump and walked back to the plane. He set the ladder about three feet from the airplane door and stepped up on it. Reaching over the wing, he removed the cap to the starboard fuel tank as Curran reached him holding the fuel dispensing nozzle. Caraballo reached down and grabbed the nozzle. Curran pulled the hose further over and held it up to keep the pressure off his friend.

The aircraft came into Caraballo's possession by way of a U.S. Marshall's auction where an anonymous government agency submitted the paperwork to acquire the aircraft for surveillance work. After filing the appropriate papers, a private contractor called AMIGAS LLC took control of the Cessna and then hired Caraballo as the company pilot. On the surface, it's all perfectly legit. The truth is, the government agency was MacPherson (the team's handler), the private company is a front established by Curran, and if anyone ever asked what they do or what the name means, they can't tell anyone what they do, and the name is an acronym for "Ask Me If I Give a Shit." Some people think it's the small caps version "Amigas," meaning "girlfriends" in Spanish. No one cares. They set the whole thing up to help channel team expenses, but it worked out well since Caraballo wanted an airplane. The acquisition costs and expenses claimed by MacPherson are really money that funds the team and the aircraft was free due to seizure from drug runners. Taxpayers should feel better because Caraballo comes out of his pocket for all the expenses to run it. They apparently also "own" a Lear jet the team has never seen, and a King Air down in Homestead. Florida. The other expense picked-up by AMIGAS LLC is the hangar, a structure proving to be more and more useful in housing not just the airplane, but some team tactical and communications gear, a couple dirt bikes, and a healthy supply of weapons. It has some nice little renovations.

The two departed twenty minutes later. The plane banked easily over the pines and headed due east toward the coast. Caraballo reached the beach around 27th Street and turned south. The plane ran down the beach, passed the house at about three-hundred feet, and turned east again.

"Sharon and Theresa made the bakery run," Curran said over the airplane's intercom system. He saw them walking up the front steps.

"I hope they save me a sticky bun," Caraballo replied.

"Two white boxes; it looks like they bought out the whole supply."

The guys flew out to the spot of the GPS coordinate Curran took off Baba's GPS. They flew a slow, five-mile diameter circle looking for something. Anything. Instead, they find nothing.

"I'm going to increase the circle to ten miles, Caraballo announced.

"I'm surprised we didn't see anything yet. Not even another boat. No commercial boats, no recreational boats. Nothing.

"Oh boy, here we go," Caraballo said with a sense of foreboding.

"What?" Curran asked, looking down at the water.

"Right there, due south about level," Caraballo said, pointing a thick arm across Curran. Two distant grey dots seemed to be coming straight toward them.

"We're okay, dude," Curran said. "Fishing boats use small planes this time of year to spot schools of bunker and tuna."

"They're not spotter planes."

Thirty seconds later Curran realized Caraballo was right as two F-16's roared past, one pilot rocking his aircraft in recognition of Caraballo's airplane. It's sort of saying hello with a $50 million-dollar aircraft. It was the northeast fighter patrol from the National Guard unit out of Atlantic City International Airport.

"See," quipped Curran. Caraballo just nodded, taking a second to check his instruments.

"Was one of them Thunder 3?"

"Didn't look like it," Curran said nonchalantly.

"Armed?"

"Completely."

Caraballo made a few s-turns to check behind him for other airplanes.

"Clearing your tail?" Curran asked.

"Yep. Not a big fan of an AMRAAM up the ass," Caraballo said flatly.

"Go south. See that container ship way off in the distance?" Curran said, pointing over the dashboard around the right window pillar.

"What are you thinking about?"

"Not sure yet. I'm thinking several things; what if a container with classified cargo fell off a ship like that? Or something under the water got screwed-up. The mouth of the Delaware Bay has sensors and nav aids. About four months ago a ship coming out of Delaware Bay strayed a bit too north and skimmed the shoals about five miles from here," Curran said, looking at the color GPS navigation unit mounted among the myriad of other aircraft instruments. "I'm also thinking about the North Cape reef system out here. It all started with a barge called the Tin Man back in the fifties. Now there are a bunch of other boats sunk out there, along with concrete blocks, artificial concrete reef balls, and most recently, some army tanks."

"Why are you thinking about that?"

"The Tin Man is the only thing *not* deliberately put on the North Cape Reef. When the environmentalists decided to make an artificial reef, they figured the area near the Tin Man was as good a place as any; north of the ship channel, a few different depths, and mostly a sandy bottom for things to sit on. They put a bunch of old New York City subway cars out here."

"I'm still not tracking." Caraballo said.

"I don't know," Curran said dismissively. "I'm just thinking out-loud. Maybe it's my conspiracy theorist brain working overtime. You know, like drug runners dropped some stuff on the reef for someone else to pick up and Baba got too close."

"Wouldn't be too unreasonable. The biggest cocaine seizure in history *was* up the Delaware River in the port of Philadelphia."

"It was probably some other lobster fisherman pissed at Baba. I don't know.

"Maybe."

"What's that," Curran said, looking at a boat in the distance. Caraballo approached the area and maneuvered into a slow left-hand turn around the vessel. "Looks like a crab boat," he added, looking past Caraballo out the left window. It's a big working vessel with the house toward the stern, the whole thing painted royal blue with liberal application of rust on the deck and hull sides. On deck is what looks like a 40' shipping container.

"Look at that!" Caraballo shouts excitedly. "They have an ROV in the water," he added after noticing a yellow box-like object at the water's surface. ROV stands for 'Remotely Operated Vehicle,' an un-manned submersible controlled by a long cable that leads back to a control station on the boat. It reminded Caraballo of the remote-control P-51 Mustang model airplane he used to have.

"Must be hired for research."

"Yeah, put everything in a big container and off you go. Use any boat."

"Do research boats normally have an ASIS boat with them?

Curran looked down to see a black rigid hull inflatable boat tied to the opposite side from where the boat was operating the

ROV. "That's interesting," he said flatly. The way he drew out the words let Caraballo know he found it suspicious.

"Mark the location. It could be right over the North Cape Reef," Curran directed. Caraballo pressed a button on the GPS unit and a small x appeared on the electronic chart.

"Dude. Look at that," Caraballo directed as he pointed at the aircraft's GPS screen.

"Holy Smoke. It's right next to Baba's point," Curran responded as a chill ran up his spine.

Curran snapped a few pictures of the vessel with a small digital camera and wrote down
the registration numbers. "You see a name on that thing?" he asked.

"No; probably covered up by all the floats hanging on the ass-end."

"Okay. Tell you what; let's keep going to the canyon."

"You just want to see if anybody's catching anything in the tournament," Caraballo jibed.

"Yeah. I figure since we're out here," Curran replied, smiling.

The Baltimore Canyon is a 28-mile-long, 5-mile-wide major submarine canyon situated less than 70 miles off the coast of Maryland, along the edge of the Mid-Atlantic continental shelf. It's a major marine ecosystem in and of itself, attracting gamefish of all sorts, including marlins, tunas, wahoo, mahi-mahi, and more.

Curran and Caraballo fly out to the canyon and survey the area. Along the way, they spotted the fleet of boats involved in the sportfishing tournament. Once in the middle of the Canyon area, they circled overhead one boat watching them fight a big tuna the guys could see from the air. After watching for twenty minutes, they flew back to the spot where they saw the boat with the ROV near the North Cape Reef. As they approached the area, both men spotted something new on the horizon.

"I wonder what *he's* doing there," Curran said. A sportfishing boat had come alongside the salvage boat.

"What's up?" Caraballo asked as they passed over the two vessels.

"I know that boat. It's the only coral-colored sportfish in South Jersey.

"More like mauve. "So what?" Caraballo replied, not seeing the significance."

"He should be out fishing in the tournament with the others, not sitting there next to a salvage boat.

"Again, Bro, so what?" The two men turned and looked at each other.

A salvage vessel with a blacked out special ops boat tied to one side gets a visit from a boat that should be seventy miles away in a fishing tournament, and get this," Curran said, trying to pique Caraballo's interest.

"What?"

"The boat in question is owned by the CEO of a chemical company."

"Yeah, that's weird," Caraballo replied, a bit reluctantly.

"I can see that light bulb over your head," Curran said as he turned his head back and looked out the side window as they circled the area. Caraballo sat quietly flying the airplane and thought about current events.

"Dude," he said. "Dude," he repeated, getting Curran to look over at him. "It can't be this easy, can it?"

Curran paused for a moment. "Is it ever?"

"Well, why don't we just go brace that fucker and figure this whole thing out?"

Curran started to smile. "Man, I know you're the rock you want to break bad people with, but I have an idea."

You do?"

"Yep."

"That fast?"

"Yep."

Caraballo seemed to be waiting for more information.

"What? Is it the information or the decisionmaker that has you puzzled?" Curran said playfully.

"I'm good."

"Never fear, I think you'll like this one. We're going to need another man, so I hope Perez made it to town. Tell you what, let's fly north for a while and see what else we see, and then head for the barn."

"Sounds good," Caraballo replied before turning north.

About twenty miles due east of Sea Island, the guys noticed a huge commercial fishing boat. It's a purse-seine trawler lying in the water beside an enormous circular ring of buoys almost a quarter mile in diameter, the buoys suspending a net from the surface down to about fifty feet. In the center of the circle is a school of bait…all dead, floating on the surface.

"Isn't that interesting," said Caraballo.

"Yep, out here catching dead fish."

"I wonder if that's what they *came* here to do?"

"I don't know, but I recognize the boat. Mark it," Curran directed as he snapped some pictures.

"Whatever's killing those fish is only twenty miles off the coast. We get a good storm for a few days and that shit will be on the beach. What then?" Caraballo said.

"I don't know. That might have come from one of those huge factory ships just dumping stuff overboard. Who knows, but let's hope the weather holds," Curran responded. "Remember when you asked me if we were doing this?

"Yep."

"We're definitely doing this; it's not in our nature to let things slide, and something just feels hinky to me."

"Me too. But tonight, we have to give the girls some attention."

"You are correct Sir.

Chapter 4

Curran and Caraballo got back to the house in the mid-afternoon. Curran rounded-up Theresa and her two kids from her previous marriage and hit the beach. After swimming with the kids (Theresa's not much of a swimmer), throwing the frisbee, and collecting some seashells, Curran explored the peculiar beach pastime of allowing children to bury you in sand.

Caraballo and Angelina disappeared on their bikes up the boardwalk headed for the shops in the center of town. Around 5 pm, Perez arrived. Curran and Theresa found him in the kitchen with Mrs. DeFelice wearing a black apron with a red crab on the front over the words "Caution: the chef is feeling a little crabby." Formally Sergeant First Class Oscar Perez, Curran gave him the now standard handshake and one-armed hug. Perez used to be a hothead but mellowed after finding his place on the team years ago. Standing about five-foot ten-inches, Guatemalan, built like a concrete block stood on its end, dark, with a heavy Spanish accent, Perez found his niche as Curran's right-hand man. He decided long ago that he would be the one that assisted the team leader in everything. He speaks three languages fluently, about three more conversationally, is expert in weapons and communications, is tough as nails and loyal as a Rottweiler. When the situation calls, as it has in the past, Perez is also the team sniper.

Dinner was exquisite. It started with Festa Dei Sette Peschi and Caponata (the Feast of the Seven Fishes Salad), followed by Buccatini Ala Taormina, Bracioli Siciliano and Osso Bucco for main courses with a side of mussels, and cappuccino and Cannoli for dessert. Italian comfort food in the extreme. Before dinner, Tom and Connie tried to sneak a taste of a few items, only to be hustled out of the kitchen by Mrs. DeFelice. Dinner was early, all the dishes seeming to come off the stove or out of the oven at the same time, so everything was set on the table and the family just tucked in, ate slowly, and relaxed. No one was left to tend to the kitchen while others ate, so the whole family was together for the entire event. Iced tea was the order of the day until the Limoncello came out during dessert. There would be leftovers for days; the only issue is, like the old saying goes, "the problem with Italian food is three days later you're hungry again."

Tom and Connie fared okay when they brought dirty dishes to the kitchen sink, but when Tom tried to start the washing he was again hustled out of the kitchen by the formidable Mrs. DeFelice. People have their territory, and although some can visit, the kitchen belongs to Connie's mother-in-law; to be more specific, his former mother-in-law. His wife Jenny, Theresa's younger sister, was killed a few years earlier in a car accident on Fort Gannon, North Carolina. After struggling with her loss so deeply people swore it would be the end of him, he was almost completely healed when Angelina appeared, and everyone seems to think Jenny had something to do with it. When they saw each other on the beach over a month ago, it was as if they had known each other all their lives, and in fact, she was a couple years behind Jenny in the same high school. Ever since, she's accompanied Mrs. DeFelice and Theresa to morning Catholic mass, and when her own family went back to Philadelphia, Mrs. D. had one of the spare bedrooms ready for her to spend the rest of the summer with them.

Near ten p.m., Curran scurried into the downstairs utility room. Hearing the noise, Theresa descended the L-shaped hardwood steps to the bottom part of the house that holds a small garage in front, laundry room in-between, and the combination utility room and downstairs bathroom in back.

"What are you doing?" she asked.

Curran sets down a cooler he just cleaned and dries his hands on a towel.

"Getting ready to fish tomorrow."

"How far out did you say you are you going?"

"About thirty miles."

"Do you have to go out that far?" she asked, always worried about him. He smiled lovingly at her.

"We'll be okay; we'll try to bring home some tuna for seared ahi."

Early the next morning, Baba's boat passed under the steel drawbridge span of the inlet bridge heading toward the ocean.

Overhead, car tires crossed from the concrete road surface onto the steel grate drawbridge span and back onto the concrete with a deep, 'baa-baa' sounding hum. Just before reaching it, a sizeable chunk of the concrete, two-lane, single-leaf bascule span bridge built in 1940, and continuously maintained, band-aided, and subjected to the ravages of seashore weather for seventy-plus years, fell off the bridge. It hit the water only fifty feet in front of the boat.

"That's not good," Caraballo stated flatly.

"Yeah, as far as omens go, it's not good," Perez replied as he pulled his St. Christopher medal from inside his t-shirt and kissed it.

"Well, the bridge's overall appraisal is 'structurally deficient," Curran reported.

"Never trust a bridge on the National Register of Historic Places," Caraballo said as Perez pushed the throttle forward and the diesel engine noise increased.

As the boat emerges from the shadow of the bridge, Curran's mobile phone rings.

"Yes ma'am," he politely answered, knowing it was Theresa.

"Tommy, where are you?"

"Heading out the inlet. What's up?"

"I'm looking at the water, and straight out about a mile there's a speckled area about the size of a football field. It looks weird," Theresa said, an air of concern in her voice.

"What do you mean speckled?"

"The water's really blue today, but that spot's sort-of grey and silvery, spotted, like maybe its dead fish or something."

"We'll take a look, okay?"

"Okay. Be careful."

"We will. Bye," Curran said reassuringly.

Ten minutes later, they arrived at the spot. The first thing they noticed was is the stink. It was a field of dead menhaden twice as large as Theresa described. The tide and onshore breeze were taking it straight to the beach.

"If this was the Gulf of Mexico, I might blame this on red tide," Curran said, gazing over the mass of dead fish. "This is something else," he added.

"I've seen the netters dump dead fish overboard and drop fish when they transfer them from the net boats to processing boats, but never this many," Caraballo replied.

"Drive through them," Curran directed.

"What for?"

"Remember I told you I was getting into doing research?"

"Yeah."

"Well, this is research."

Perez turned to facing forward and starts motoring toward the center of the mass of fish. As they move though the dead pool, slimy foam stuck to the sides of the boat above the waterline; brown foam rolled in the boat's wake. Curran scanned one side, Caraballo the other. They didn't see any indication of a cause for the mass of dead fish.

"I've seen enough," Curran announced. "Let's go," he said to Perez. The boat turned southwest.

About two hours later, the boat approached the North Cape Reef area. About three miles away the men could see the salvage boat. Off to their left, further out to sea was an unusual sight. A government salvage boat about two-hundred and fifty feet long, like the kind that searched for JFK

Junior when he went down in an airplane off the coast of Long Island. Big, grey, with cranes and winches and all sorts of apparatus, but this one was different. It had a high articulating boom and hose that looked out of place.

"Dude, you know what that looks like?" Caraballo shouted above the din of the big single diesel engine.

"No, what?"

"It's a concrete boom pump," Caraballo exclaimed.

"Are you sure?"

"I'm Italian; we know all about concrete, my friend."

"He's right," Perez interjected. "I worked concrete in Miami for a couple years; lots of high lifts."

Curran and Caraballo stood puzzled by Perez' proclamation.

"When did you do that?" both men said to Perez in stereo. They look at each other, smiling like a couple goofs.

"A few years before I joined the army."

"And here I was thinking I knew all your secrets Oscar," Curran declared. He looks back out toward the distant boat.

"What would they be doing with a concrete truck out here?"

"Other than chunkin'it over the side to make a reef; pumping concrete with it," Caraballo said, stating the obvious.

"It was rhetorical question there, Paisan."

"I know, but they're not pouring a basketball court out here, so they gotta be covering-up something."

"Vessel bearing one-four zero state your intention, over," booms a voice over the boat's VHF radio. Perez looks at his compass, noting he's showing 3-5-0 degrees bearing from the original salvage boat.

"That's us," he announced, standing behind the wheel.

"Military types," Caraballo said to Curran. "State your intention?"

Both men know the caller would have just talked normally, or said 'sécurité,' a French term used before giving important safety information over the radio, and no one ever says 'over' on a marine radio.

Curran slide closer to Perez pulled the radio handset from the clip near the overhead radio and pressed the side button. "This is the lobster vessel Bugsy, going to get my traps," he said into the microphone.

"Bugsy, you are entering a restricted area. Turn away immediately," the voice on the radio directed.

"He's not a very nice man, is he?" Caraballo replied glibly.

"Now that makes me curious," Curran replied. "I'm still outside minimum safe distance, sir. What is your vessel identification please?" Curran said over the radio. They were still over a mile away.

Silence on the radio. The three men continue to motor in the general direction of the first salvage vessel. They noticed a small black object moving quickly across the water in front of them. It was streaking toward them. Perez grabbed the binoculars from the shelf next to the helm.

"Black RHIB, military type, two or three guys on board," he said.

"That'll be the one," Curran said as he smiled at Caraballo.

"Time to get ready" he replied.

"Mark the boat's position on the radar, slow-down, but don't veer off," Curran directed.

Smoothly, Curran and Caraballo opened the small cabin door in the middle of the forward bulkhead and slipped inside as Perez stayed on course.

Down in the cabin, Curran and Caraballo unzipped a black gym bag they stashed earlier in the middle of the cabin, then sat on either side of the v-shaped bunks and laced on their combat boots. Curran went with his tan Belleville's while Caraballo went old-school black leather issue.

"What are you thinking?" Caraballo said in anticipation, his breath getting long and deep.

"I hate bullies, man," Curran growled.

"Are you feeling froggy right now, Tom?"

"Fuckin-ay right, pal," Curran responded. "We could wait for a provocative act," he said as he finished tying his boot. "But fuck that," he added, looking into Caraballo's eyes as he nodded in the affirmative.

"I like the sound of *that*," Caraballo exclaimed.

Curran stood and poked his head out the cabin door. Out on deck, his head appeared next to Perez' left leg. "Oscar, let me know what they're packing, and then tell me when they're about to bounce off the side." He knew that any good attempt at running someone off means they would come alongside and bounce the side of the rubber boat against the hull of the lobster boat. Like a big elephant seal defending its territory; it must slam into its challenger in order to assert its dominance.

"You ready for this?" he asked Caraballo, a deadly serious look on his face.

"You're talking loco my friend, and I like it," Caraballo said exuberantly with a huge smile, his face practically glowing.

Curran reached into his gym bag and pulled out a pair of leather tactical gloves, his favorites, the ones with the plastic guards over the knuckles. He slid them on and then held out a big hand for a low-five from Caraballo.

"Sidearms in flap holsters," Perez announced from the helm. "Two guys dressed in black fatigues, wearing tactical vests with all sorts of bullshit on them," he added. Down in the cabin, Curran just nods in the affirmative.

The black RHIB raced up to the lobster boat; two men stood menacingly behind the center console as two big black outboards effortlessly shoved it forward. They raced toward the stern quarter of Baba's boat, and then cut a hard left, coming up alongside. The driver chopped the throttles and the rubber starboard quarter started sliding toward the side of Baba's boat.

"Now!" Perez shouted.

Curran and Caraballo burst from the cabin, staying low, Curran in the lead. He acquired his target as he ran to the middle of the cockpit, turned, jumped onto the gunwale and launched himself like a professional wrestler off the top rope, flying toward the RHIB's driver! Right behind him, Caraballo identified his own target and launched himself off the boat as gracefully as an Acapulco cliff diver at the man behind the driver; a devilishly mischievous light shone from his eyes as he growled through clenched teeth.

Curran sailed into the driver, aiming a vicious forearm directly at the man's face. The speed of the shocking attack caught the black-helmeted man flat-footed. At the last possible second, he grimaced as turned his head slightly, bracing for impact. Curran's forearm smashed into his face with a sickening thud, sending his head snapping back unnaturally. Curran's other forearm impacted the man's tactical vest. The inertia of Curran's body at impact sent the two men crashing sideways onto the port side deck. The inflated rubber side of the boat absorbed much of the landing. On Curran's trip past the back of the console, his right knee hit the side of the throttles, breaking them clean-off the fiberglass console. To add insult to injury, the red kill switch coil attached to the vest of the driver popped off the console-mounted engine kill button and whipped the man in the face like a giant rubber band. The twin black engines go silent.

The second man in the black boat was not only shocked by Curran's assault on the other guy, Curran had unintentionally managed to hide Caraballo's advance across the deck of Baba's boat. By the time the man spotted the Italian fireball it was too late. Caraballo's mighty jump from the boat caught him by complete surprise. Shocked by the sight of Caraballo's massive chest hurling at him, the man went all "deer-in-the-headlights." He stood flat-footed and stiff-legged in horror. Problem was, the impressive leap sent Caraballo sailing a bit further than intended. His upper torso impacted the other man's chest and helmeted head with such force, the recoil pitched the man backward out of the boat. Suddenly stopped by the impact, Caraballo crashed down on the top of the black fiberglass chair affixed to the deck in tandem behind the pilot seat. The shock-absorbing seat caught Caraballo just right, knocking the wind out of him. On hands and knees, gasping for air, Caraballo collected himself for a moment in the space between the engines and the offending deck chair.

Engine off, boat adrift, the only sounds aboard were Caraballo gasping for air, water lapping against the rubber hull sides, and the hard, packing sounds of Curran giving the pilot a serious ass-kicking. His tactical gloves proved their worth as he delivered multiple blows to the face of the helpless man. Curran hopped-up, reared back a knee and delivered it to the man's beet-red mug. He readied another. Caraballo saw the impending punishment. A chill ran up his back.

"Tom!" Caraballo barked.

Instantly, Curran stopped his attack. He looked back at the man Caraballo sent over the side hanging onto a rope attached to the rubber hull ring near the port stern. Blood streamed from the man's nose and mouth.

With a stiff-arm to the vest, Curran pressed the man in front of him backward onto the inflated rubber ring.

"Why such an aggressive response, dude?" he said. The beaten man sat with his chest heaving, face stinging, breath coming in short bursts. Bewildered from the beating, he wasn't tracking. Curran decided to make things easier for him.

"Why did you come to scare us off? What are you doing over there?" he said slowly. Again, nothing. Curran noticed Caraballo lifted the other guy into the boat like landing a big fish, hauling him up over the side and releasing him. The man landed in an undignified heap onto the deck in front of the engines.

Curran grabs the man under him by the collar. He suddenly realized the man wasn't wearing a life jacket. It was body armor. That made Curran angry.

"Did you do this to the guy driving *that* lobster boat last week?" Curran barked. No response. A bolt of anger shot through Curran. He punched the man in the chest while holding the collar of the body armor. "Huh?" he shouted. "Do you know he died?" Curran added, pushing his fist hard into the man's chest. He grimaced in pain but didn't answer again. The man in front of Curran seemed disoriented. His eyes rolled around in their orbits like a couple pinballs. Curran knew the guy wasn't going to answer him. Curran turned and made eye contact with Caraballo. "This guy clammed up," he said matter-of-factly.

"Oh yeah?" Caraballo replied, one knee pressing down on the side of the man curled into the fetal position beneath him. "What are you guys doing down there, hero?" he said calmly to the man.

No answer. "No?" he added. With his right hand, Caraballo pulled the bottom of the man's tactical vest up toward his armpit, and with his left, delivered a sharp punch to the man's liver. "How about now, shithead?" he growled. The man coiled like a shrimp, his face contorting from the blow, but he said nothing. Frustrated, Caraballo delivered another pile-driver punch. "How about now, asshole?"

"Training," the man grunted through clenched teeth.

"Training?" Caraballo said skeptically. "What sort of training sends out goons like you to run people off?" Caraballo decided to skip another punch. He got an answer and knew another well-placed hit could cause serious damage.

"Is that your story too?" Curran said to the man in front of him. He received no reply. Curran decided fun time was over. "Shake it up, bro," he directed, the expression telling Caraballo to get ready to go. Curran looked around for Perez and finds the boat only fifty feet away. Perez was thinking. After the guys jumped off the boat he came around and used the boat to block the view of anyone on the salvage boat. Curran waved for him to come over. The burst of diesel smoke from the short stack indicated Perez understood and was on the way. "Well boys, next time, maybe you'll be a bit less aggressive," he said to the black fatigue-clad men as he stood. Then he bent his legs and put his knees on the chest of the man under him, letting him feel Currans weight. "Telling people to turn away without an explanation just makes people more curious. I guess you're not doing brain surgery on that thing, dumbass."

The sudden sound of a diesel engine powering into reverse alerted Curran and Caraballo that Perez was coming up alongside. Caraballo stood, turned away from the man beneath him, and grabbed the side of Baba's boat just as it contacted the rubber RHIB. He threw a leg over the gunwale, straddling both boats. He looked over to Curran, kneeling against the boat's driver. Suddenly, Curran reached behind himself, lifting the back of his black t-shirt.

"Oh shit," Caraballo blurted.

With one hand, Curran grabbed the handle of the Marine Corps fighting knife he had in the sheath tucked into the waistband of his black surf shorts. With a thumb to release the snap around the handle he pulled it from the scabbard before holding it out in front of the man under him. The man's eyes locked onto it. He didn't move. Frozen in fear.

"Tom, what are you doing?" Caraballo shouted with arms akimbo, perplexed as to what he should do in response.

"Let's see if you can answer this," Curran said softly, the knife blade menacingly-close to the other man's face. With a flick of the wrist, he spun the knife in his hand blade-down. Curran stretched his upper body as his powerful left arm raised the knife high over the helpless man's head.

A frightening jolt of dread raced through Caraballo. Hairs stood on his arms. Memories of combat raced through his head. Was this payback for Baba? Is it Curran's wrath? Suddenly, with his back to Caraballo, Curran plunges the knife down!

"Tom!"

Back on board the RHIB, Curran gazed at the fighting knife, the five-inch (it's been sharpened a few times) blade buried in the rubber hull ring up to the hilt. Next to it, the immobilized man feels his bowel contents start to mix with the water soaking his fatigue pants.

"The guy you killed on this boat was a friend of mine," Curran said quietly in the man's ear. "You better not come ashore."

Curran stood and yanked the knife out of the hole he made. As he rose, he gave Caraballo the view of where the knife found its mark. A rush of relief flushed through him.

"They say these things can float without the inflated part. I guess we'll see," Curran said, rather happily. He returned the knife to the scabbard with one hand, turned, crossed the boat, stepped up on the mushy rubber ring, onto the top of the lobster boat's gunwale, and hopped onto the deck. "Let's rock and roll," he said to Perez, followed by turning and giving Caraballo a "low-five," slapping hands at handshake level.

"I thought they said you couldn't puncture one of those things?" Caraballo asked.

"They never counted on how sharp my knife is, or how hard I did it."

"Did Perez sharpen it last night?"

"Yep. It's amazing those two never tried to pull their weapons."

A wide-eyed grin came to Caraballo. He reached into the pocket of his sage green cargo shorts.

"You mean like this one?" he said, pulling out a black polymer Glock 22 .40 caliber pistol, the weapon once held by the man he sent into the drink. Seeing the weapon, Curran suddenly beamed the same smile as Caraballo. He straightened his back, standing a little taller. He lifted his shirt, exposing a weapon tucked into the front of his shorts.

"No. Like this one," he countered, touching the handle of another Glock 22.

Chapter 5

Rain fell softly throughout the day on Sea Island, the sky at the
Jersey Shore a white blanket across the heavens dotted with darker
spots of heavier rain clouds. The rain stirred the ocean air, adding
the aromas of salt marsh and dune grass as it crossed the island.
Curran stood on the beach in his black surf shorts, black t-shirt, and
black baseball cap, staring out at the ocean. Rain dripped off the bill
of his cap and soaked his shirt as he remembered the last time he
saw Baba.

Robert "Baba" O'Reilly stepped from his old, white Ford
custom van, zipped the back of his plain black wetsuit, grabbed his
old single-fin ten-foot Gordon & Smith longboard and padded
barefoot slowly across the boardwalk, down the ramp to the beach,
and over the soft sand to the water's edge. He stretched his lean,
6'2" frame easily, attached the surfboard's leash to his right ankle,
and walked into the water. He cupped his hand in the surf and threw
some water on his short, brown, sun-streaked hair, rubbing it as he
thought of the long brown streaky curls he had before he joined the
army. He hopped onto his board and started paddling. Baba left any
thought of his current plight right there, like all other surfers do. He
wrapped himself in the connection with the ocean, the waves he
rode, and the serenity of the calm sea out past the breakers. He was
free.

Baba was always independent, but others called him a rebel. He wasn't the sort that rebelled against people, against his parent's demands, or against what society considers "the way things ought to be." He wasn't a rebel. He just didn't think life meant school followed by job followed by wife and kids followed by getting fat, losing your hair, spending your time making sure the lawn was better than the neighbors, missing out on life followed by insisting your kids do as you did. He found his own way, chased more waves then women or dollars, and that meant keeping life simple, following those things that filled his life with joy, connected him to nature, and let him be a burden on no one. People called him lazy. A bum. His father understood. His father knew that just because he didn't want to be a fisherman like his dada, that didn't mean he didn't love his father. Baba also had a strange drive to never be a burden on anyone else. He showed no political views nor offered opinions he thought might upset others.

Baba's friends understood. As they married, took on mortgages, car payments, multiple jobs to feed the mortgages and car payments, and had kids, Baba didn't do that. One day the ridicule and misunderstanding from others and the "look at the size of my house" boasting he heard from others became "boy, are you lucky you don't have this mortgage hanging around your neck." He saw some people overjoyed by children, while others felt trapped and burdened by them. It was really the accumulation of "normal," insane society's worries that Baba was able to avoid. He was his own man; he did his own thing. He wanted to keep life simple and honest. As Shakespeare said, "to thine own self be true, and it must follow, as the night the day, thou canst not then be false to any man." Baba wanted to take life as it came, not force it or conform to someone else's idea of what life is, or what it should look like. He wasn't into Tao or anything. He was just being Baba. People who knew him well understood; most everyone else did not.

Take for example his best childhood friend "Big" Jim Donnelly. Jim was beanpole thin and arrow straight, and a pretty decent surfer. Baba surfed through high school while Jim, at the insistence of his rather "corporate" father, played football and golf. His white shoe wearing, "Death of a Salesman full-of-shit Willy Loman-style father used to berate his son's desire to play baseball by saying "what are you going to do when you have clients? Take them out for a baseball catch?" Then along came college, where Jim became "Big Jim," where he found he had two loves…big breasted women with big hair…and beer from the fraternity house keg. The collegiate atmosphere and distance from his parents let Jim spread his wings. For once, he got the chance to figure out who he was, and he enjoyed himself immensely.

Immediately after barely squeaking through school, he decided (again influenced by conformist parents) that his life would take the "fast track" if he went right to work in Atlantic City, taking a job as a craps dealer in a boardwalk casino. He hit the gym daily trying keep the beer weight off, but it didn't really work. Then he met a girl with big breasts and big hair, and since the sex was good, and his mother was pressuring him to marry her (as the "logical next step" in their definition of life), he married her. Three years later, society thought he had everything; house, two cars, a boat, and a loving wife that was talking about kids. Truth of the matter was, he had a huge mortgage, two car loans, a boat he couldn't afford to use, a whiny wife packing on the pounds, a job he hated that made him come home every day smelling like an ashtray, and no time or money for kids, nor the energy to even try and make one. Then one day, after having quit the gym and realizing he gained fifty pounds, Big Jim found a note from his wife on the bed next to the latest clump of hair he lost telling him she found someone else, that he didn't love her, and that she left him. His parents said he lived his life for his wife, and this was only a "minor setback." They were only thinking of how their son's breakup made them look. Reality was, he lived his life conforming to his parent's idiotic idea of how life was supposed to go. You know, the same one *they* tried at and failed, and had resisted as one from *their* parents. Jim ended up with a wife that took half of all their assets, left him with all the liabilities, and told everyone in town it was his lack of attention that "drove" her into the bed of an unemployed clam digger (instead of her lack of loyalty and enormous insecurity courtesy of her own parents who told her she was fat from the day she was born).

While society expected Big Jim to embrace his misery, Jim did the Irish thing; he got drunk. Then he used the golf clubs he spent way too much money on and never used to destroy everything in the house, and then, as he put it, he "burned that bitch to the ground." He spent three days in the Cape May County jail, and when he got out (after all, who jails someone that burns down their own house and doesn't file an insurance claim), Jim went back to find his house, cars, boat, and supposedly "normal life" were all gone. While taking a walk down the beach with a loaded gun in his pocket, Big Jim intent on taking one final look at town before ending it all, he ran into Baba coming out of the water after surfing. Baba knew about Jim's situation, but didn't mention it. Only after noticing the gun sticking out of the front pocket of Jim's green hooded college sweatshirt did he say something. He told Jim that his life was a "do-over." He told Jim that most people never get the chance to start over again, to try things again armed with the knowledge they learned along the way. He said, "people always say if they knew then what they know now…well, you know." He showed Jim that he had the chance at a fresh start; that Jim should rejoice instead of despair.

Two days later, Jim started training for the job he always wanted as an emergency medical technician, and today he's a paramedic in Atlantic City. He loves it. He rents a cottage on the bay in Margate, has a kind-hearted girlfriend that understands him (that he thinks the world revolves around), and together they have a son he adores. Oh, and he's once again beanpole thin and arrow straight, and surfs at least twice a week. He believes he owes his life to Baba.

Baba says all he did was show Jim he was free. This was Baba, true to himself, unable to be false to any man.

And then something interesting, or unfortunate, happened to him; September 11, 2001. It was after seeing all the devastation in New York, and all the volunteers from around the area that dropped what they were doing, hopped in their ambulances, fire trucks and civilian cars to travel to a place where they didn't know anyone, yet were compelled to help. Their compulsion was caused by a feeling of brotherhood, compassion, patriotism, or whatever emotions drive people to help their fellow man. Baba started wondering why he was thinking only of himself. Then he figured if he served in some way, he could justify his desire for freedom. He thought if he defended the freedom he so enjoyed, maybe he would somehow deserve it. That's when he made a mistake. Baba joined the army.

Baba figured a couple years serving in some support role, most likely stateside or on some large support base overseas would fit the bill. What he didn't realize when he rushed headlong to the recruiter, was everybody enlisting at that point for a short stint, who was fit, of sound mind, and male, was headed straight into the infantry, and straight to combat units headed for Afghanistan. He didn't expect to find himself in the First Brigade, 101st Airborne Division, at a place called Forward Operating Base Fenty in the mountains of Nangarhar province in northeastern Afghanistan. He didn't expect daily foot patrols looking to make friends with the locals, and dead men of the enemy. He didn't expect living in the ground under constant threat of enemy mortar fire, of friends being killed, of the locals being friendly during the day, and the enemy at night. He expected none of this, but he served, and served well, earning the Silver Star Medal for valor under fire. He charged down a hill under enemy fire to grab a wounded comrade in a forward observation post, killed three enemy that were trying to drag the wounded man away, and ran back up that hill with the wounded man over his shoulder. Baba took everything that came with that tour without complaint, and when the day came to leave, he left, having given it all he could give.

What Baba couldn't handle was the reversal of normal expectations in the combat zone. Normally, soldiers go off to war with the knowledge that this is an activity that could lead to their untimely demise. Normally, people at home sit safely entrenched in their normal lives while worrying if their loved ones off at war will come home in one-piece or come home in a shiny steel casket with an American flag draped over it. It never occurs to soldiers when they go off to war that people still die at home. That's what happened to one Robert O'Reilly. While serving in the Afghan badlands, he received word his father had died during a storm while out on his commercial long-line fishing boat. He was told the boat went down, taking the crew with it. Baba figured it was he that should have died, that everyone at home was safely doing what they normally do. That event really put the zap on his head.

Before dinner, Curran arrived at the home of Grace O'Reilly. He was bothered by something he couldn't put his finger on. He pulled into the circular driveway and stopped behind a big black Cadillac. A small, skinny blue-haired old woman in a blue dress, with white shoes that matched her string of oversized pearls was being helped into the back of the car. The man helping her was tall and broad, his features suggested a heritage reaching back to somewhere in the South Pacific. She glanced at Curran but gave no expression before getting in the car. Grace had been watching the woman leave and turned and greeted Curran.

Curran greeted Grace with a hug before handing her one of the two cups of coffee he stopped at the offshore Wawa and retrieved. By "offshore," it meant off the island in local terminology. They went in the house and sat in the same seats in the kitchen to talk as they did three days earlier. They engaged in some idle chit-chat for about fifteen minutes until Curran brought the conversation around to his intended topic. He didn't want to speak about his trip out on Baba's boat and his encounter with the goons dressed in black.

"You know, with all the talk about recent events, we never spoke about Mr. O'Reilly," Curran said, referring to Baba's father. Grace sat for a moment, flipping mental pages, thinking of which item of conversation would come out first.

"You know, he's buried right next to Frankie Farantino," She said.

"Buried?" Curran responded, astonished by her words. "I thought he died at sea?"

"No, he was airlifted off the boat before it went down."

"And then the other guys went down? Casey Steagal, Stan Chivers and Patsy Bonanno?"

"No, Patsy went to work on a dredge. Stan's son Jerry was on the boat."

Curran was puzzled. "So, as the boat was going down, or after it went down, Mr. O'Reilly was the only one to get airlifted?" he asked, using a finger to articulate his words.

"They said he was the worst off, so he went first?"

"Who is *they*?"

"The people from the hospital. I talked to them at the wake."

"The people at the hospital? Not the Coast Guard or the State Police?"

"No."

"And how did they know that?"

"I don't know."

"And the boat went down?"

"Yeah."

"And that doesn't bother you? The captain of the boat was the *only* one that made it to shore?" Curran asked, watching Grace's face for a reaction. He didn't get one. "Why did the boat go down?"

"They don't know," Grace said flatly.

"What do you mean?"

"They didn't know," she said in a slightly different tone.

"You don't know if it was weather related, a boat problem, and accident, or what?"

"It doesn't matter, Tommy," Grace said somberly. She pushes a plastic bowl filled with miniature chocolates closer to Curran and retrieves a piece for herself. She slowly unwraps it as she stares at the chocolate. "He's gone; what does it matter?"

Curran paused. "Trust me, it matters," he said. The two sat in silence for a moment.

By the various looks on Grace's face, Curran could see a mad rush of emotions coursed through her mind.

"He should have never joined the army. I should have never let him go away. It's my fault," Grace declared.

"Would he have been on the boat that night?" Curran asked. He knew the answer would be no.

"It doesn't matter."

Curran leaned in, trying to get eye-to-eye with Grace as she sat staring at her coffee cup set between her chest and her folded arms on the checkered tablecloth.

"Gracie, trust me, it matters," Curran said, placing a hand on her shoulder. "What happened to your husband wasn't your fault or your sons. Having to deal with it by yourself just made it worse."

"He tried to get in touch with you once he got to his unit, but there was no way to find you," Grace said in a voice sounding both distant, and distracted. It was like someone trying to remember and explain a daydream.

"Well, Special Operations had me pretty busy for a while," Curran said dismissively. He wasn't really working for the Special Forces at the time. The story of Baba's father's death is bothering him. "Why was Baba working on the lobster boat?"

"He thought he had to support me since his father was gone."

"Did he say that to you?"

"Yes, he did."

"And did he?" Curran asked, referring to needing to support his mother.

"No, the insurance company paid me,"

"That money won't last forever. You're not even old enough for Social Security?" Curran said. He knew Baba's father was connected and floated the comment to see if he got a reaction. After sitting for a moment, Grace smiled at him, seeming to snap out of her daze.

"I'll be fine, Tommy," she said, grabbing Curran by the forearm. "How about you?"

"Oh, I'm good," he smiled back.

"Good," Curran replied. Then he heard something in his head; when he unconsciously knows he needs to wrap things up, sometimes the musical score for intermission "Entr'acte" for the Phantom of the Opera starts playing.

"So next week then; Baba, in Arlington," Curran said, looking into Grace's eyes.

"Yes," Gracie said in an exhale.

"Don't worry about getting down there. I'll take care of it," he directed.

"I think I already have that handled," Grace said. Curran thought it had to do with the old woman and the Cadillac.

"Okay. Well, I'm sure we'll speak before then.

Chapter 6

Curran got back to the house as the rain stopped and the sun broke through the clouds to the west. Off to the east, the sky remained black and unsettled. A rainbow cast itself in front of the darkness. People started slowly making their way back toward the beach. Time for afternoon strolls across the sand made crusty by the rains. Curran walked up the front steps, turned and rounded the front deck to the ocean side. There, he found Caraballo and Perez sipping beers and watching the storm retreat to sea. As he faced them, he noticed Mrs. DeFelice, Theresa, and Angelina inside preparing dinner.

"How'd we make out?" he said to Perez.

"No troubles," Perez replied.

"Is it like I thought?"

"Pretty much."

"All right," Caraballo interjected. "Stop talking in freaking code and tell me what's going on."

"Not until I get a beer," Curran taunted.

"Yeah Chief, where are your manners?" joked Perez.

Caraballo reached into the small cooler he had on the deck next to his chair and retrieved a bottle. He opened it and handed it to Curran. "You can have any beer you want, as long as it's a Corona," he droned mockingly, using a line from one of the "Fast & Furious" movies.

"I was thinking about the fishing tournament."

"You're always thinking about fishing," Caraballo interjected.

"Yeah, I know. I was thinking about all the boats. We saw the Titan running out with the rest for the pre-tournament shakedown. Then we saw it on the first day of the tournament tied-up to the salvage boat at the reef."

"So?"

"So, I asked Oscar to do some checking. What did you find?"

"The homeland security track has them going way out to sea both days in an area north of where all the other tournament boats went. Tournament records show they were not only the last boat to arrive back at the marina both days, but they recorded no catch."

"Proctor's a shitty fisherman anyway," Curran said.

"Dude couldn't catch the clap in a women's prison with a fistful of pardons," Caraballo interjected. It drew the required fist-bump from Curran.

"Tournament records also show two boats went out on the second day, but never came in. One boat was tracked by satellite to Ocean City, Maryland. The other returned to a marina in Atlantic City.

"That's weird," Caraballo said.

"Anybody think it was weird, you were asking about a fishing tournament?" Curran asked Perez.

"Some NSA guys think you have fishing addiction issues."

"Good. As long as that's all they think it is."

"What are you thinking?" Caraballo asked.

"We could go old school and find our way on that salvage boat, or we could look into the Titan Chemical Company," Curran said as a grin came across his face.

"Or?"

"Or we could just go fishing."

Caraballo turned his hands over palms up. A crease appeared between his bushy eyebrows. "How does that solve anything?" he said.

"It's not just about the fishing. Relax. I have a plan."

"What about me, boss," Perez said. "Given the chance, I stay off boats."

"Do you think Ma's going to let you get too far away now that you're here?" Curran reminded Perez.

"Teacher's pet. Teacher's pet," Caraballo joked, slapping Perez lightly on the shoulder.

That next day was a good day for Curran and Caraballo. After taking everyone to breakfast, they rented two old wooden john boats with nine horsepower motors and took Theresa and Angelina crabbing. They could have used Curran's boat, but the best crab spots in the bay behind the island are in shallow water and the twelve-foot square bow rowboats sit closer to the water. Besides, it's fun, doing it old school with hand lines and chunks of menhaden and dip nets, and two boats turn it into a "couples" event.

Perez spent the day with Mrs. DeFelice, who over the years has come to think of Oscar as "one of her kids." After sausage and peppers for early lunch, they went to the farmer's market, shopped for wine, and then Perez took her car for maintenance, doing a task she refers to as "man's work."

In mid-afternoon, it was crabs and spaghetti at the house. Everyone tucked in and picked crab meat and ate spaghetti in red crab sauce for what seemed like three hours. Mrs. DeFelice also cooked some Jersey corn on the cob, sliced some big red Jersey tomatoes, and baked two loaves of garlic bread. Comfort food; Caraballo even managed to say the broccoli rabe could wait for another day. Somehow Perez had never had blue crabs in red sauce and declared it one of his favorite meals.

A glorious summer afternoon at the South Jersey seashore eased toward sunset with the grace of a ballet dancer moving across the stage, smoothly, effortlessly. A normal change in the mid-afternoon breeze turned the balmy beach day into comfortable t-shirt weather. The green-headed horseflies and biting black flies disappeared, the sun turned the dial down slightly, and the beach walkers returned as sunbathers packed it in for the day. Some people refer to that time as "the call to cocktail hour," beer-thirty," time to shuck the corn before dinner and for the day-trippers and camp- grounders, time to beat the traffic off the island.

As is tradition in sport fishing tournaments, especially the big ones, a sunset pre-tournament party kicks-off the event. At the second round of the South Jersey Marlin and Sailfish Open, teams gathered at the pre-tournament party, typically themed the "Buffett Beach Party," to "celebrate the event," which is a colloquialism for eating food that comes as part of the ridiculously expensive entry fee while you check out the competition. It's held this time at the expansive Gold Coast Marina and Fishing Center in nearby Stone Harbor, New Jersey, an upscale seashore town nestled between the barrier island towns of Avalon and Wildwood south of Sea Island.

The marina sits on the bay side of Stone Harbor near the center of town, conveniently located to the south of the main drawbridge that spans the Atlantic Intracoastal Waterway before running about two miles across the marsh connecting Stone Harbor to the mainland. The marina is shaped like a giant rectangle with the long sides running north and south. Five piers built inside of it connect to the island on the east side, and project into the basin to the west. Along the west side, the bay and Intracoastal channel are separated from the marina by means of a stout breakwater made of giant granite boulders topped with cement. A seventy-five-foot gap at the northern end allows boats to enter and exit the marina, and the tide to flow in and out without producing too big of a current around the docked boats.

Boats between thirty and forty feet occupy the two most southern piers, each one backed into their slips. At the end of each pier, capping off the tips like a giant "T" are two yachts of about sixty feet. Boats between forty and fifty feet occupy half of the middle pier, some cruisers, but mostly fishing boats. The other half of the pier is reserved for "transients," meaning temporary, not for the homeless. At the end of that pier is a yacht of about seventy feet. The last two piers are the serious ones, the ones they call "Sportfish Alley." Sitting fifteen to a side with sterns facing the pier, the muscular, gleaming, purpose-built sportfishing machines tug restlessly at their lines, seemingly anxious to get out of the marina and chase their prey the way a race horse reacts to the confines of the starting gate, wanting nothing else but to bust out and run. Almost all the boats have high stainless steel 'tuna" towers mounted over the tops used to spot schools of fish or flocks of birds over fish from great distances. With their high bows, large stern fishing cockpits and massive horsepower, these boats are meant to do three things; find big fish quickly no matter the weather or distance, catch them. and return as fast as possible. You can smell the money in the air; smells like fiberglass, diesel fuel, and coconut sunscreen.

At the southern end of the marina is a big parking lot separated from the bay by an artificial beach about the size of a singles tennis court, the beach ending at the breakwater. In the parking lot is a huge white tent, open on the west side, with table and chairs set near a bar and substantial buffet. Between the tent and the beach is an array of high-end patio tables and chairs, and some high tables and chairs like you would find in a bar, the entire area surrounded by palm trees in giant pots brought in for the occasion and artificial rocks with outdoor stereo speakers hidden in inside them.

A little after seven in the evening, Curran and Caraballo and their girlfriends Theresa and Angelina arrived at the marina. They strolled down "Sportfish Alley," admiring the boats. Normally, they would have read the name of each boat and see if it made a connection to the owner's personality, or at least had a bit of creativity. With the full moon, the tide was so low they would have to lean way out over the edge of the pier to see the names on the back of the boats, so they skipped that part of the ritual. Besides, how many boats named "The Office, "Wet Dream," or "Daddy's Toy" do you need to see. The foursome left the pier and moved around the marina to the party area. As they approached the tent, they began to hear music. A crowd was already forming, sitting outside in the afternoon sun having cocktails, beers, drinks, or whatever you call them. Nearby, a guitar player sang off-key Jimmy Buffett tunes. Most of the crowd was spread across the property with some enjoying the afternoon breeze while finding shade under the stubby potted palms.

Theresa made sure she and Curran's clothes were complimentary. Curran traded his usual black t-shirt for a black polo to match his khaki shorts, and Theresa wore a black V-neck sleeveless peasant dress. Both had matching leather sandals. They enjoyed the mild afternoon, the easy breeze, and the casual attitude of the beach party. Nearby, Caraballo sported a light green t-shirt with a helicopter company logo on the pocket and sage green cargo shorts, while Angelina wore a coral color sundress and a wide-brimmed straw hat. They didn't really match and didn't really care.

"You see him?" Theresa asks.

"He's not here," Curran said casually. referring to a former Special Forces officer-turned defense contractor named Daniel "Deke" Draper, the owner of the boat that Curran and Caraballo are on for the tournament.

"Yo Tom!" shouted a man over near the bar. Curran turned and recognized an old friend standing near the bar inside the tent, holding a beer over his head as if offering it to Tom. It was Pete Rogers, a local contractor (it seems like every local is a contractor) and old surfing buddy. Next to him, Janine, his rather tall and skinny yet oddly buxom girlfriend of the last ten-million years stood wearing a strapless white terry cloth baby-doll dress over a bikini. Underneath, her obviously aftermarket and oversized breasts struggled against their restraints.

"Hey Pete," Tom said, smiling while holding up a hand in greeting.

"I got a cold one for you."

"I knew you would!" Curran answered. He looked at Theresa for her reaction.

"I would enjoy a beer," she said.

Pete and Janine didn't really fit in with the sport fishing millionaires, but they always seem to find the party. The fact that Pete built the marina owner's beach house and gave his no-account son a job for a few summers made him a welcome edition at any Gold Coast soiree.

Curran noticed Connie and Angelia were headed toward the breakwater. He and Theresa followed Pete and Janine over to the circle of chairs at the edge of the artificial beach. Fifteen minutes later, Caraballo and Angelina joined them. There was no table, and it's wasn't really necessary. Curran sat with his back to the palms with a view of the entire area. To his right, facing the beach, Pete leaned back on the edge of his stool, shirtless, his abdominal muscles quite impressive for a man around forty-four. He was still in shape enough to wear the same no-elastic surfing shorts the kids wear with nothing hanging over the edge. Elastic waistbands; the mark of the aging. Janine sat on the other side of him. To Curran's left, Theresa had a classic pilsner beer glass in hand. Connie and Angelina completed the circle. The group was somewhere between friendly chit-chat and "catching-up."

Pete seemed to be practicing his burping for volume. There was no indication why Pete seemed intent on intoxication other than "that's what Pete does," or that he thinks he can still drink like he did when he was in his twenties. Nevertheless, it's not for Curran and Caraballo or anyone for that matter (besides Janine) to tell him what to do. Truth be told, Janine was probably a better drinker.

They caught up on what's happened since they did this same ritual last summer at a place called the Carousel bar, a little spot on the boardwalk in Sea Island. It was the same sort of familiar thing, hearing the kids are taking sailing lessons, played soccer, got straight A's, mastered differential calculus, found Jimmy Hoffa, and discovered the cure for cancer. You know…the normal parental bullshit all parents say to convince themselves their kids are little geniuses.

Problem was, Pete and Janine's two offspring were a little different. Little genius number one, thirteen, had a mouth dirtier than a South Philly hooker but blamed it on Tourette's syndrome, "disappeared" all the family pets better than Vinnie the Chin, spat in his little brother's food when the parents weren't looking, and kept a broken glass collection in a box under his bed. Little Einstein number two, the eleven year-old, discovered forgery; he used the home copy machine to put his mother's signature on a letter telling his middle school he was moving, wrote a check for $3000 cash and used some of the money to buy a $1000 hooker off Craigslist. The prostitute in question turned out to be a Puerto Rican man in drag who showed-up at the door on Christmas Eve in a leather bustier and fishnets under a fake fur. Almost simultaneously, Janine and Pete discovered their "rainy-day" fund was dry, their oldest might have a slight "anger issue," their youngest kid hadn't been to school in two months and was a blossoming felon with deviant sexual proclivities. So much for the proud parents; worse still is Pete and Janine think nobody knew.

"You hear about Baba?" Pete asked.

"Yeah, I heard," Tom said softly.

"It's screwed-up what happened to him."

"What did you hear?"

"I heard he fell on the boat and had internal injuries he didn't know about."

"Yep," Curran quipped, trying to minimize the conversation about Baba.

"Sort of the opposite of how people think life is supposed to go."

"Yeah. He shouldn't have been on the boat anyway."

"The whole thing him a bit over the edge," Pete said. Curran just nodded.

"What happened?" Theresa whispered to Curran. He had tried to keep the Baba story from Theresa, but now found it unavoidable.

"He enlisted in the army after 9/11, went through some dangerous stuff in Afghanistan, and came home to find his father and his father's crew died in a fishing accident a few months earlier."

"Oh my God, that's horrible," Theresa replied, her voice velvety smooth. It's how she speaks after hearing disturbing news.

"Yeah, you think people at home are supposed to find out their loved ones gone off to war are dead, not the other way around."

"Well, no more war for you," she said, rubbing his knee.

"Hell no, I won't go," he joked, drawing a smile from Theresa. He leaned over and they gave each other a simultaneous peck on the cheek. He looked back at Pete and could tell the look. It was the "I know you guys are Special Forces, but I won't ask about it." Tom gave him a nod and turned to see Caraballo do the same. Then he noticed Caraballo get an angry look on his face as he looked around.

"Connie, what's wrong?" Curran asked.

"Do you see this bullshit?" Caraballo replied.

"What?"

"Everybody below like the age of thirty-five is on their damned phone," Caraballo exclaimed. Everyone looked around. Caraballo was right, if they weren't speaking on the phone, they were staring at them, texting on them, or plugged into them with headphones listening to music.

"Who the hell are they all talking to?" Caraballo asked in a voice one active higher than usual. "Here they are at a damned expensive tournament party and they're completely oblivious to it. They might as well not even be here," he growled frustratedly. We found Caraballo's biggest pet peeve. The chit chat among the group resumes.

A little bit later, Curran got worried about Theresa. She's not a bar hopper and he started to think the "hanging in the bar fun-meter" might be on full. Then he noticed her mouthing the words to the song being played by the guitarist, while tapping her thigh to the music. Curran decided things were okay for the short time he planned to stay.

Suddenly the guitar dude started playing the Zac Brown song "Toes," and it drew an instant reaction. As if on cue, Tom and Theresa got up, moved to a spot in front of the band and start to dance. It was sort of a combination of Salsa and Carolina Shag. Tom held the side of her waist like holding a beer. No need for the full-on hand on the lower back. There would be no sort of "dirty dancing" here. It was G-rated, innocent and free, and it drew smiles from nearby partiers who joined in. Then something amazing happened. Curran looked over and saw Caraballo dancing with Angelina! Tree-trunk legged, cantaloupe-calved Caraballo, dancing with his fair maiden! This was a man Curran had to practically drag kicking and screaming into a jam-packed mob of people dancing on a beachside deck in Jamaica, with almost a platoon-sized group of women all calling for him. Then again, he looked like he was really relaxed and enjoying himself, so Curran turned his attention back to Theresa, the woman smiling at him like a teenager having fun.

After some twirling and swaying, and a bunch of other couples joining-in on the dancing, the song ended, accompanied by cheers from most of the bar patrons. A few men shook Curran's hand while their girlfriends or wives hugged Theresa or give her a peck on the cheek. It seemed they got the party started and people appreciated it. The guitar player went into another beach music-style country song by Zac Brown and Jimmy Buffett, and the dancing continued. Everybody had fun.

After a while, the foursome got politely escorted to the bar inside the tent for a round of champagne courtesy of the appreciative tournament organizer. Several fishing teams were gathered there, pressed into tight four and five-man groups, sizing up the competition. In this type of activity, there's as much male bravado, posturing, and head games as in a professional wrestling match, poker game, or inside the penitentiary. If it wasn't for the amount of money being spent, the two-hundred thousand dollar first prize, or the other business being done during a gathering of such wealthy people, it would be humorous to see chubby, sunburned men in their short pants, boat shoes, and $10,000 watches talking trash, trying to "game" each other.

Across the room, in a dark spot near the side of the tent, a dark, fat man around sixty with artificially colored short black hair, a barrel-shaped stomach stretching a yellow Ex-Officio fishing shirt and a big cigar jammed between two thick fingers sat watching Curran, his bulging cheeks quivering as he flexed his jaw muscles. His name was G. Blanton Proctor, current CEO and principal owner of the Titan Chemical Company of South Jersey. He owns a very nice fifty-two-foot Viking Convertible docked nearby. Next to him were two of his crew, one a short, very tan man from the Philippines, and the other a ghostly-pale man with a thin, angular face, a pointy, pinched nose, and salt-and-pepper hair typical of someone you might see from Russia or Ukraine.

The brand name on Proctor's shirt was ironic. The Webster definition of 'ex-officio' is "a member of a body (a board, committee, council, etc.) who is part of it by virtue of holding another office." Sounds like small-town politics. In G. Blanton Proctor's case, he was on the zoning board in the small mainland town where he lived when Ken Williams, the owner of the Gold Coast Marina wanted to build a condominium community near a local river leading to the Delaware Bay. It just so happened; G. Blanton Proctor was also the supervisor (in name only) of the construction licensing department. It was said that after a ton of red tape, followed by an under-the-table receipt of a lifetime marina membership including a prime dock location and appointment to the board of trustees, Mr. Williams got the permits and zoning variances to build his condos. The Proctor-style "favor" did nothing to foster any sort of friendship or even mild mutual amity between the two men. G. Blanton Proctor will say Ken Williams is "a great guy, and a good friend." Mr. Williams once said the term that best describes the "chemical company guy" is "bloviating dickhead."

Proctor leaned back in his chair and took a log drag of his cigar.

"Those two are part of Deke Draper's crew," he said. His crew simply nodded. "I've seen the taller one (referring to Curran) around. He's like a god-damned fish magnet," Proctor blurted disgustedly. "He was a dock rat as a kid, always working on fishing boats during the summer."

"Where does he come from?" asked the white crew member.

He was an orphan from Philadelphia; lived in their summer house on Sea Island during the summer. Then he turned into some sort of Airborne Ranger Special Forces guy," Proctor added with an air of derision.

"What did you say his name was?"

"Curran."

"That could be a problem,"

"Which part? The fish magnet or the orphan?" Proctor asked, perplexed.

"The Special Forces."

"Don't tell me you know him."

"No," the crewman said, watching Curran from across the room. "But I know of him."

Chapter 7

Close to sundown, after the requisite commentary from the emcee and tournament director, introduction of the teams and some admin details, Curran and the others moved from the bar inside the tent and returned to their chairs. There they were met by another round of beers from Pete. Strings of beer can-sized lights strung around the area were illuminated, and some Christmas lights added a bit of cheesy, yet festive charm. The group sipped their beers while Pete was in the process of again belching for volume, his stomach tightening, Adam's apple moving rhythmically as his jaw thrusted forward, chin toward the sky.

In a startling response, Janine gave her best belch in reply. Off-putting to most people, Pete and Janine seemed two peas in the same ill-mannered pod. Theresa recoiled a bit. Curran thought that this scene seemed to repeat itself each year, minus the dancing, and the local people here seemed to be happy with their lives. He didn't know if the locals really were happy with their lot in life, or just good at faking it, but he hoped it was the former. Curran realized he was pleased to have this Jersey Shore in-the-summer rhythm in his own life.

Curran excused himself and went to the rest room. As he was returning, he noticed a couple he didn't know standing in front of Janine, with the female closer to Pete. They were talking about the gym, both people visibly quite the gym rats. The woman wore a bright blue, backless Spandex dress over an obviously wet bikini, the outline of which showed through her dress as darker bikini-shaped spots. The fact they were standing in the middle of a conversation seemed lost on them.

Swallowing hard, Pete appeared to be reloading his belching apparatus.

"Here we go again," Theresa whispered to Curran. Caraballo and Angelina, unsure if Pete's maneuver indicated another belch or a more significant production, sat transfixed on his next move.

Pete pulled back his shoulders, stiffened his spine, and produced a thunderous belch, far louder and longer than the last. Oddly, it startled the woman in front of him. She clutched her forearms to her chest and turned her back to him. Suddenly, at the end of the award-winning vocal discharge, a rising sound emanated from Pete's gullet like filling a bottle with water. All eyes moved to him, including some from others nearby in sudden anticipation, just in time to see Pete projectile vomit his internal beer supply directly onto the bare lower back of the spandex-clad vixen before him. An audible "ooh" reverberated through the crowd, followed by a roar of laughter; someone yelled "Yahtzee!" The guttural dirge flowed down the loose back of the woman's dress and into the crack of her ass as the rest hit the pavement. If he was once belching for volume, he was then apparently belching for distance

"We have a winner, ladies and gentlemen," joked Caraballo, smiling like a mule eating peanut butter.

The transgression levied on the woman in front of Pete drew an instant response. The boyfriend cocked his right elbow back and delivered a short right cross directly to the point of Pete's chin. The impact jolted Pete's head backward, and his upper body followed. He landed unconscious on the back of his bar stool. It was that button again. You know, the term "right on the button?" The button hidden somewhere on a person's jaw that when struck, turned out the lights.

Suddenly, Janine slapped the man across the face. Call it maternal instinct, protecting her man, or sheer insanity, it was a good slap. The man started to pull his arm back to deliver the same sort of blow to Janine. Tom sprang forward and extended an arm into the path of the oncoming fist. He caught the man's arm by the crux of the elbow just in the nick of time, then put his body in front of the angry man, catching him eye-to-eye.

"Dude; stop," he quietly directed.

The muscle-headed guy looked at Curran with rage. Misplaced rage but rage nonetheless; Curran just stopped him from punching a girl, and for that the guy deserved to get pounded, but Curran wasn't in the mood, this wasn't the place, and he didn't want to do it in front of Theresa. However, the knuckle-dragging Philistine before him seemed intent on violence. Curran stepped back to get some distance between them, but before he could get set to attack, a pair of huge arms bear-hugged the other guy from behind. Caraballo lifted the guy off his feet as if he were a twenty-pound turkey, turned around, and walked the guy toward the beach. All the while, his girlfriend stood frozen like a statue, too afraid to move in order to avoid any more vomit from flowing down the inside of her dress. Luckily, Theresa had her wits about her. She slid off her bar stool and took the girl by the elbow.

"Honey, there's an outdoor shower right over there," she said. Then she led the helpless woman through the crowd to an outdoor shower closer to the docks.

Janine turned to Pete, who was still unconscious and making a snoring sound. She found the noise unsettling. "Is that normal, Tommy?" she asked.

"Yep; sure is. Take some of the ice from your glass and rub it on his forehead; he'll wake up."

Janine followed Curran's suggestion; in about thirty seconds, Pete woke-up, looked around, belches, and then looked down at his right arm. For a moment, people thought maybe he had problem with it. Much to everyone's surprise, Pete was only checking for his beer. Even more surprising, he never dropped it, so he took a sip.

Caraballo stepped up to Curran, this time without bear-hugging anyone. Curran noticed the missing man and peered off into the diminishing light toward the beach.

"What happened to dude?"

"He started struggling so I choked him out. Left him on the sand," Caraballo said casually, pointing through toward the beach. In the distance, the men could what appeared to be a passed-out drunk laying on the beach. In another direction, they saw the man's girlfriend still showering, with Theresa and Angelina standing nearby.

"What happened?" Pete asked groggily.

"Dude, how many periods of unconsciousness have you experienced in your lifetime?" Caraballo inquires, kicking into his physician's assistant/Special Forces medic mode. "Taking that easy of a tap to the kisser and going out like a light concerns me."

"It was a good punch," Pete said, feeling his manhood threatened.

"I thought you couldn't remember?" Janine asked.

"Uh, I need another beer," Pete replied, changing the subject.

"Ice cream?" Curran said to Caraballo, really changing the subject.

"Definitely. A root beer snow cone would be tremendous."

"Tremendous you say!" Curran said approvingly, a new light in his eyes as he turned to see if he could make eye contact with Theresa. Their eyes met and he thrusted an arm in the air, making a circular motion with one extended finger. It was the "rally" signal, used when you want your patrol or other formation to gather around. Theresa and Angelina immediately broke contact with the woman they were assisting and moved toward the guys. Moments later, they said goodbye to Pete and Janine right as the bouncers told Pete it was time to go home which Curran also thought was nostalgic. The foursome headed to the ice cream parlor (but not before Connie tells

Janine to make sure Pete sees a doctor). Two minutes after leaving the bar, the girls are laughing about the whole affair.

"You know what?" Curran said to Theresa. "The ice cream place we're going to has good cinnamon buns."

"Like Cinnabon!" she asked excitedly, her eyes wide with anticipation.

"Yep, just like Cinnabon. In fact, they are Cinnabon," quipped Curran, smiling. Walking next to each other, Theresa wrapped her arms around Curran's left arm.

"Then I know what I'm getting," Theresa said.

"I knew you'd say that."

"Did Deke ever call you?

"Yep. He said he got held-up with work, but he'd see us at 4:00 a.m. day after tomorrow."

"Good thing they always hold the pre-party two days beforehand," declared Caraballo.

"Yeah, some of those people were getting pretty snockered," Angelina added, wrapping her arms around Caraballo's neck as they walked to the ice cream parlor.

"No way Pete's going to be hung over tomorrow," Curran predicted.

"What do you mean?" Theresa asked.

"All the beer he drank went down the crack of that girl's butt," Angelina interjected, smiling as the breeze flips up the brim of her straw hat and her straight brown hair swings in front of her face.

She moved her hair with one hooked finger, tucking it behind her right shoulder.

"Well, the only fear we have tonight is Connie's reaction if they ran out of cappuccino," Curran jested.

"You got that right," Caraballo responded.

Early the next morning, Curran walked into Caraballo's room shortly after 3:00 a.m.

"The killer awoke before dawn. He put his boots on," Curran said as he stirred his friend awake, borrowing a line from Jim Morrison. It was the first thing that came to him as he got up a few minutes earlier, a line from the 1967 song "The End." Curran wondered if the killer reference was about him. Caraballo wondered the same about himself. Curran thought it odd the song was in his head. He couldn't remember the last time he heard it.

They arrived at the marina at 4:00 a.m. to find their friend Dennis "Deke" Draper standing on the flybridge of his fifty-five-foot Jarrett Bay Carolina-style sports-fisherman, talking to his captain. He was ready to go; huge diesel engines warmed up, everything on board, one mate stood in the dark on the bow ready to handle the lines, and one in cockpit waited to cast off the stern lines. Everybody wore matching white long-sleeve t-shirts with a picture of the boat emblazoned on the back under the words "Comedor de Serpiente," the name of the boat, Spanish for "Snake Eater." Under the picture were the words "Fishing Team." The logo was repeated on the front pocket of each shirt.

Approaching the boat, the guys noticed the small baitfish in the area under the stern of the boat illuminated by blue underwater lights.

"Fellas!" Deke shouted from atop the boat. He scurried down the ladder while facing backward toward the dock, hopped onto the deck, jogged across the cockpit and stepped up onto the stern gunwale. The tide was almost high, and his head was about level with Curran and Caraballo's. With beaming eyes, he extended a hand to Curran. "My lucky charms!" he exclaimed. "Hey Kid-O," he said to Curran."

"Deke," Curran said, reaching out to shake his hand.

"Connie," Deke replied, extending a hand to Caraballo.

"Double D. How you doing?" Caraballo said, repeating the process.

"Come on aboard," Deke directed, hopping off the stern rail. He turned and made a gesture like waiting to catch a football. Gently, Curran swung his bag out over the stern and dropped it into Deke's waiting arms. Deke set it on the seat of the big fish fighting chair mounted in the center of the cockpit and turned to catch Caraballo's bag.

The two made their way onto the boat as Deke dashed into the cabin, returning with two folded shirts.

"You would think Mr. Williams would put in a floating dock running down the sides of the pier," Curran said to Deke as Caraballo retrieved a thermos from his bag.

"He's thinking about it. Here boys," Deke said, handing each of them a t-shirt. "Team gear for the tournament."

"Cool," Caraballo declared.

Standing under the light from the flybridge over the cabin door, Deke smiled broadly; two deep dimples marking each cheek as the light accentuated skin the texture of one-hundred grit sandpaper. With steel-grey hair cropped short and a fit physique, Deke looked like an older version of mild-mannered Clark Kent, only bigger in every way, and not so mild. Deke was one of Curran's old commanders from the teams. He came into serious money after he retired. His family owned the patents to the guidance systems used on most unmanned aerial vehicles. He is what they call a "quiet professional," for sure, choosing to keep tales of his exploits to himself. That's a good thing. So does Curran. Good thing too. Telling details of some past missions could scare the living shit out of most people. There's a connection between the three men only other warriors can understand, and his fanatical approach to fishing was almost a match to Curran's. Deke has, however, been prone to hellraising and he has a special place in his heart for Alex Fillippi, a member of Curran's team and notorious hell-raiser in his own right. Deke's a gregarious, joke-telling, boisterous character that people call a man's man, and although somewhat secretive, inside there is a heart of gold. He's the kind of guy that will throw a party, be the life of the party, and sometimes, toss everyone out of a party.

"Where's Big Al?" Deke asked.

"Vacation in California with his girlfriend," Caraballo reported.

"Did he take a woman home to meet his parents?" Deke asked, astonished.

"Possibly."

"Don't tell me he's getting tamed by a broad?"

"Nothing will ever tame that guy. It's like smoothing the fur on a lion; it calms it down, but doesn't do much else," Caraballo said as he poured coffee from a green metal thermos into the handy combination cap/cup.

"I hear ya."

"Coffee?"

"Negative. I want to catch a couple hours sleep on the way out."

"That doesn't mean you can't have coffee. Tom?" Caraballo said, offering some to Curran.

"Right on."

"Good man."

This boat is an absolute beast; Deke spared no expense taking an older boat and transforming it into the fishing machine of his dreams. First, he took out anything that added too much weight or could be replaced with something lighter; walking into the cabin is an experience in teak wood, TV screens, and light-colored leather seating. Next, he replaced the rear cabin bulkhead, shoving it forward two feet, then adding the molded-in tackle lockers and bait freezers built into the new boats. He added a cockpit refrigerator, replaced the cockpit sole, replaced the fuel tanks, re-wired the entire boat, stripped the hull to the bare wood and laid-in carbon-kevlar, repainted the hull and topsides, re-plumbed the air conditioning system and replaced the headliner, replaced the tuna tower, and finally, he yanked out the old twin 950 horsepower engines and replaced them with a pair of twin diesels with twin turbochargers pumping out 2400 horsepower each. It took some serious engineering, hull strengthening, and a giant shoehorn, but Deke admitted he could have bought a smaller boat, and he could have bought a new one, but he wanted a boat that had "enough ass to get you home if the weather got snotty, and the speed to blow the doors off anything else out there, no matter the weather."

The rest of the fleet, save one boat, left the dock at 3:00 a.m. Comedor de Serpiente departed at 4:10 a.m., passed the rest of the fleet about half-way out, and got to the area known as the "Fingers," at exactly 6:15 a.m. The Fingers is a deep-water drop-off marking the start of the Baltimore Canyon. That far out and you meet the gulf stream, the color of the water changes from a blue green to a deep iridescent blue, and the temperature rises about eight degrees.

Along the way, Deke slept on the day bed in the saloon, while Caraballo went down below and took one of the bunks in the port stateroom. Curran was too excited to sleep so he spent the trip on the bridge taking turns with the captain driving the boat. He considered it great fun, and the captain thought it a welcome relief, even dozing off for a while on the lounge seat in front of the flybridge steering station.

They got fishing even before the sun came over the horizon, taking advantage of getting there first to start their plan to troll the length of the canyon. The plan paid off. The first sailfish came shortly after sunrise, and once it was released, the next one hit. The action went on like that until just before 10:00 a.m., when the tide and breeze stopped almost at the same time. Towing a six-lure spread, they changed three squid imitations for jet-heads. To a layman, a jet-head lure would resemble a polished metal water saver shower head trailing six, seven, or ten-inch long pieces of red, black, green, or silver string licorice tied to the back of it, with a set of fake eyeballs stuck to it near the head. The jigs leave a trail of bubbles underwater that resembles a smoke trail which seems to attract fish to follow it and see where it leads. After that, they dropped in a big string of teasers, towing it about fifty feet behind the boat. This sort of rig would make someone think of a bunch of wire coat-hangers tied to strings, each one with three small plastic fish trailing behind it, swimming next to each other by way of six-inch pieces of fishing line tied to the hanger. Overall, it resembles a school of bait swimming for a place to hide under the boat. Sometimes you can tell the big billfish are around when they strike the teaser, slashing at them with the sword-like bills.

They reached the extreme eastern limit of the underwater canyon, roughly 120 miles from land, shortly after 12:00 p.m. and turned around. Heading back west, another boat appeared. They're not trolling, but running at speed, the boat's outriggers in the raised/stored position. The coral color hull and fat black letters bearing the boat's name near the bow are a dead giveaway…Titan…G. Blanton Proctor's boat.

"That auto-pilot running jackass," blurted Deke from his spot in the companion chair next to the captain on the flybridge. Curran climbed the bridge ladder, reaching the top right as the two boats passed each other.

"Where's he going?" Curran asked contemptuously.

"What's wrong with this picture?"

Curran studied the other boat for a moment as it cruised away. "There's nobody on deck or behind the wheel," he proclaimed.

"Exactly."

"There's nothing to catch past here, unless he's going to stop and follow behind us."

The men on the Snake Eater watched their lines and the Titan as it continued to run, eventually going over the horizon and out of sight.

"He was the last one to leave the marina," Deke reported. "Not sure what he was waiting for."

"And then he runs right out past everybody on autopilot? Does he do that often?"

"First time I've seen it."

"Does he ever win any tournaments?"

"No. I've never even seen him bring any fish in. Those two mates of his are a long-lining shark-finning bait hanger and I think other one's a diesel mechanic."

"Well, they seem to have somewhere to go," Curran replied.

Just after 1:00 p.m., with the days amazing tally twelve sailfish, four Wahoo, one blue marlin, one yellow fin tuna, and with the afternoon breeze starting to blow, the guys tied everything down and got roaring back to civilization. They reached the fuel dock at exactly 3:15 p.m., stopping there to give the boat a long drink well ahead of the other boats.

"You still have time to take Theresa for that evening cruise she wanted," Caraballo reminded Curran.

Curran smiles at him. "Yeah, and we prepped everything for tomorrow on the way in."

The following morning, Curran and Caraballo arrive at the boat at 0400, and the same scene from the day before repeats itself, including the day's new fishing shirts. Only this morning, Deke's anal-retentive attention to detail and his gleaming boat's upkeep has the two mates in the engine room with Simple Green, brushes, towels, and sponges making sure the room and the bilge were spotless.

After offering to help, Curran and Caraballo sat in the cockpit on top of the bait prep station under the flybridge overhang, drinking coffee and relaxing. Deke was too busy supervising in the engine room to join them.

All was quiet on the docks. Then, a lone figure appeared, walking from the land side of the pier carrying two Wawa shopping bags and a cup of coffee. As he approached, walking in and out of the lighted areas of the pier, his head and eyes constantly scanned around him. Slightly hidden in shadow under the flybridge overhang, Curran and Caraballo sipped their own coffee and chatted about Curran's prior evening cruise with Theresa and Caraballo's trip to the Ocean City boardwalk with his girlfriend.

The man walking down the dock reached a spot about ten feet from the boat, heard a low voice, noticed the legs of Curran and Caraballo sticking out into the light in the boat's cockpit behind the cabin bulkhead and stopped in his tracks. He couldn't see Curran or Caraballo's faces. He immediately resumed walking, trying to not bring attention to himself. He averted his eyes and slightly turned his head away as he passed.

"Why does that guy look familiar?" Curran asked.

"Because we've seen him before, but I'm just not placing it," Caraballo replied suspiciously.

The second day played out to be a repeat of the first. The team was clearly in first place, far ahead of the others in the fish tally. Once again, as the boat trolled back toward the west, the Titan passed them, heading farther out to sea. Once over the horizon, curiosity got the better of Deke.

"Pull-em in!" he shouted down from the flybridge. On command, the two mates and the guys brought in all the lines as the captain pressed the buttons on two big wire winches mounted in spaces under the fiberglass flybridge top, which pulled in the outriggers to their stored positions. Once in, the captain pushed the throttles forward, spun the big boat around, and the chase was on! The boat roared toward the point on the horizon where they last saw G. Blanton Proctor's boat. Curran and Caraballo climbed the ladder to the bridge.

"What's up?" Curran asked.

"I gotta find out what Captain A-Hole is up to," Deke shouted above the noise of the wind and the engines.

In no time, Proctor's boat came into view. It was sitting stationary in the water, only they were not alone. Right next to them was a big, black commercial fishing boat, and alongside the Titan was a small skiff. A man in the skiff was throwing what appeared to be a black box to one of the mates who stood in the cockpit of the Titan.

As the Comedor de Serpiente' approached the area, the skiff started moving back to the commercial boat with two nefarious looking characters aboard. Deke circled the three boats at speed.

"Titan, Titan, this is the Snake Eater. Whatcha doing there, captain?" Deke jibed over the radio. No answer. Instead, the Titan made a tight turn back toward the west and the captain hit the throttles, putting the big boat up on plane. "Go right up alongside," Deke commanded his own captain.

They sped right over to within twenty feet of the Titan, then slowed to match the other boat's speed. On the Titan, the Filipino mate was in the cockpit, staring over at the other boat, while G. Blanton Proctor and his captain were on the bridge, sitting in their helm chairs and staring straight ahead, acting as if the other boat wasn't there.

"Hey proctology, you gonna do any fishing today?" Deke said over the radio. No answer. That put a scornful look on Deke's sandpaper face. "That dude didn't get back to the dock until after ten last night," he shouted to Curran and Caraballo. "The weird thing was, I think he came in with more people than he went out with. The one white guy mate put them in a car and drove off right after they reached the fuel dock."

"That is weird," Caraballo replied. Curran reached into the side pocket of his surfing shorts and retrieved a small notebook with an even smaller pen attached to it. He wrote something inside and stuffed it back in his pocket.

"What's that?" Caraballo asked.

"The registration number on that commercial boat. Did you notice it didn't have a name?"

"No."

"Yeah, no name, and the guys on the skiff were purposely turning their faces from us."

"Considering our backgrounds, are we just jaded, or did we run into something weird?" Deke asked. No one answers but the look on each man's face says, "I don't know." Even the captain is puzzled by recent events.

Right then, the cabin door to the Titan opened, and the white guy mate stepped out on deck. He looked over and recognized the other boat. In an instant, he made eye contact with the men on the Snake Eater's bridge, a startled look came over his face, and he quickly turned and went back inside the cabin, shutting the door behind him.

"That was definitely weird. Most people wave to you, not get scared-off by you," Deke added.

"I swear I know that guy," Caraballo declared.

"Let's go in," Deke commanded. With that, the captain pushed the throttles up to cruising speed and the big boat ran away from the Titan, headed for the barn. On the way in, the Comedor de Serpiente' ran close to the Cape May Reef area so they could get a look at the situation there. Close to the reef, they noticed a sportfishing boat trolling for fish.

"Is that boat in the tournament?" Curran asked Deke.

"No. That's Miss Margaret. The owner stopped doing tournaments and sticks to day charters."

As they approached the reef, they passed the salvage boat that was once anchored there, now steaming south away from the area. The big boat with the concrete boom was gone.

Meanwhile, closer to the Cape May Reef, the Miss Margaret rolled slowly in the gentle mid-day swell as they trolled for whatever might bite. Moving easily in the calm seas, the men on board sat sleepily watching their lines as the captain on the flybridge concentrated on driving the boat in a perfectly straight line. Fishermen often say trolling is hours of boredom occasionally interrupted by minutes of panicked excitement.

Suddenly, the port outrigger recoiled as the clip at the end released the line it held. The line whipped back toward the stern, went tight, and the thick fishing rod it was attached to bent and shuddered violently. The mate standing near the port side gazed up to the top of the rigger, only to catch the gleaming sun straight in his eyes. He pulled his sunglasses down from their spot on his forehead as he silently cursed himself for being stupid. There were three men in the cockpit. Facing back toward the stern, one was in the fishing chair in the middle of the deck, one stood behind that man, and another was to his right, closer to the stern.

"Fish on!" yelled the mate standing behind the fishing chair.

"No shit," grunted the fat fisherman in the chair. "That's sort of obvious," he added disgustedly. Sperry boat-shoe clad feet on the footrest, buttons on his sweat-soaked powder blue fishing shirt straining under the pressure of thirty years of beer and hot dogs, he was busy winding-in the line on another broom-handle thick fishing rod. Mounted on the rod was an enormous, shiny golden fishing reel holding about a thousand yards of fluorescent neon-green monofilament line. The reel had clips attached to points on either side of the spool, with short lengths of braided rope leading to similar points on either side of the bucket-style fishing belt around the chunky fisherman's waist. The green color line was supposedly invisible to fish under water, the manufacturer claiming it increased the chances of a fish biting, but it might just be clever marketing.

The pull on the line that came off the outrigger dropped to nearly nothing. No bend on the fat man's fishing rod. He reeled-in something light on the line, something that felt dead and still.

"Shark probably got it," one mate commented.

"Yeah, probably reeling in a head," said another.

The doubled section of line close to the hook comes over the transom, and the mates went into action.

"Stop reeling" barked the mate behind the man in the chair as he moved around the chair to the stern. He peered into the water as he used a gloved hand to grab the doubled line. Hand-over-hand, he started to pull it in.

"Is it just the bait?" asked the captain from up on the flybridge, body facing the stern as he held the controls of the big Hatteras sportfishing boat behind his back.

"Nope; not sure what it is," the mate replied as he faced the water. He bent further over the teak-covered transom, reached out for the line, grabbed it, and then stood-up, pulling the end of the line from the water. He swung the line over the stern in one fluid motion and plopped a cantaloupe-sized glob of blue-green algae-looking sludge onto the deck.

"What the hell is that?" asked the captain.

"I don't know,"

The angler in the chair looked down at the blob on deck, thought about how it resembled his blue metal-flake bowling ball, and then remembered the other line still in the water, bending under the weight of a fish.

"Grab this rod," he directed. "Let's get that other fish," he added as he unclipped the reel and pulled the rod butt out of the gimbal between his legs. The other mate nearby snatched the rod and moved it to a rod holder attached to the ladder leading to the flybridge.

Meanwhile, the mate that pulled in the line with the big blob on it moved to the port-side, grabbed the rod bending in the rod holder next to him, yanked it out under the pressure of the fish on the line, and walked it to the fishing chair. He jammed the rod butt into the gimbal at the front of the seat between the fat angler's legs, and held the rod as the fisherman clipped in. The fisherman leaned back, taking the weight of the load on the rod with both arms and harness, and the mate slowly released it. The mate returned to his place at the back of the fighting chair, deciding to leave the big blue-green ball of goo on the deck until they reel-in the other fish.

The fight with the big fish ensued, the fisherman pulling the rod toward him taking the weight of the fish, followed by easing the rod toward the stern and reeling as fast as he can. In, out, pump and retrieve. Beneath his sunglasses, the fisherman's eyes watered, tears streamed down his face. He looked like he was sweating, but it was something else.

"Frank, get one of those water bottles," he directed the mate standing to his left. "My eyes are burning." The mate was distracted by a strange burning sensation on the back of his own neck. Frank!" he barked.

On the deck next to him, the strange blob had swelled in the sun from cantaloupe to honeydew. An air bubble appeared at the top of the rubbery mass. It swelled to baseball-size and popped with a snapping noise. The glob made a hiss as it shrank slightly. Suddenly, the mate behind the fighting chair started convulsing, his shoulders jerking toward his ears. The other mate didn't convulse but fell over like a cut tree onto the deck, arms down, his face smashing violently.

The fisherman in the chair spasmed violently; thighs jolted; his back hit the backrest so hard he broke one of the horizontal teak slats. With the rod clipped to the bucket-style fishing belt around him, his motion pulls the rod butt from the stainless-steel gimbal mounted to the front of the chair. Then came the point where physics are a bitch; with the enormous pressure of the fish pulling the line on one end, and the sudden release of the hold of the rod butt on the other, the point where the lines clip to the reel acted as a fulcrum. The rod butt swung-in and blasted the man in the crotch like a baseball bat to the nay-nays. Seen on the big screen, movie theater crowds would have yelled a collective "ooh!" The man had no such capacity; instead, he made a gargling sound as white foam poured from his mouth. To add insult to injury, the line parted at the rod tip and the fish was lost. The man went unconscious and slumped in the chair.

On the flybridge, the captain's first instinct was to pull the transmission throttles into neutral; probably his first mistake. From above he saw the mate behind the fighting chair double-over and fall on the deck in a heap. "John!" he yelled. "John!" He wasn't yelling at anyone on deck. He was yelling for his son. The kid' had been inside the cabin for the last few minutes microwaving hot dogs. The captain stamped on the deck of the flybridge, trying to get his son's attention. "John!" he roared; probably his second mistake.

The cabin door opened, and his son appeared between the cabin door and the fighting chair, immediately behind the mate on the deck. Shocked and perplexed by the scene before him, he turned his head skyward toward his father. Suddenly, his eyes and throat burned. A chill ripped through him. He dropped the glass bottle of chocolate Yoo-Hoo he was holding. Goosebumps stood on his arms as the chill turns to a burn. With a panicked expression, he looked up to his father for an answer. "Whuh," is all he was able to mutter before convulsing so violently he lost control of his bladder before falling backward over the body of the mate to the deck.

Paternal instinct kicked-in, good sense and self-preservation shared a ride into the ozone layer, and the captain plunged down the flybridge ladder; probably his third mistake. The drying, bulging blob on the deck popped another exhalation as the captain reached the deck. He turned to move toward his son as a sickening wave of odorless, noxious, toxic air hit him. His reaction is sudden and distinct; he staggered, gripped both hands to his throat in the classic "I'm choking" posture, his legs spasmed, the boat rolled, he lost his balance, the backs of his thighs impacted the port gunwale and he fell backward over the side. His feet flipped up toward the sky in what could be described as "ass over tea kettle," and he disappeared into the deep blue.

The boat lay dead-in-the-water; four men lay dead in the cockpit. Eerily, the song "Who Wants to Live Forever," by the 1980's band Queen played over the boat's stereo system. Ironically, a fish hits the line still in the water.

Chapter 8

"It's good to be the king," Deke says as he hoisted an ice-cold beer to his lips. The crowd was gathering at the big tent for the evening awards presentation and tournament party. Much more elaborate than two nights ago, uniformed waiters moved amongst the crowd as hostesses in gold spandex pencil dresses made sure all were having fun. The band was an improved version from the last one, pulled straight from their national tour to play the tournament's wrap-up celebration.

"I had my two lucky charms with me, and we spanked the rest of the teams," Deke reported, as he sat next to his two mates and across the table from Curran and Caraballo.

"Ah, I just tweaked a few lines and changed a few lures," Curran said dismissively.

"I think it's the school of bait painted on the bottom of the boat," Caraballo added.

"Look what we found," said a female voice from about fifteen feet away. The guys turned to see Theresa and Angelina walking toward them, with a sturdy, dark, obviously Latino man between them.

"Oscar!" Caraballo shouted. Smiling, he and Curran stand up. Both men take turns greeting all three.

"We had to pry him away from Mom. You know how she loves him," Theresa said.

"Yeah, but they told me there were shrimp and Coronas here," Perez happily replied.

"Piles of them," Curran answered.

"Hey snake eater," Deke said to Perez.

"Evening Sir," Perez answered politely, smiling and shaking hands.

"Come on, let's go get some *skrimps*," Caraballo said with a twang as he ushered Perez and Angelina toward the seafood buffet.

"So how did you guys do?" Theresa asked the rest of the group.

"How do you think, my dear!" Deke said confidently. "I had the fish whisperer on board," he added as he pointed with his beer can hand toward Curran.

"It's almost freaky, isn't it?" she said coyly. "One day, the fish will just swim up and surrender. He'll tag them and let them go as gently as can be," she added, eyes beaming at Curran.

"You know what, Tommy?" Deke asked. Curran just moved his head back and forth in the negative. "I get it," he added, pausing a moment. When I see the two of you, I get it. By yourself, you're still a whole man, but when she's with you, you're half the piece of the puzzle. She's the other half; I've never seen it as obvious as it is with the two of you."

Curran smiled almost bashfully as tears brimmed in Theresa's eyes.

"God, I love you guys!" Deke blurted loudly. He sprang from his chair and held his hands up in front of him. He surged with love and wrapped his arms around both Curran and Theresa. He kissed each on top of their head like they were his children. If love and admiration can stream from a person's eyes, Deke did it. Smiling, they all sat back down.

"So how did you guys really do?" Theresa asked after the embrace, wiping tears from her cheek.

"Eighteen sailfish, eight blues, three whites, five wahoo, and one yellowfin tuna," Deke gushed.

"Oh, my goodness!"

"And the fish whisperer here performed his magic act over and over out there!" Deke said, as he reached over and slapped Curran on the knee.

"What do you mean?"

"I've seen a sailfish jump close enough to the boat where we thought it would come in the cockpit, but I've never seen one jump, and someone reach out and grab it by the bill in mid-air. I've definitely never seen one almost jump into someone's arms and sit as calmly as the family pet."

"That happened out there?"

"Three times! As calmly as could be, we took the hooks out and let them go as easy as pie."

"He has that effect on all sorts of creatures," Theresa said lovingly as she looked into Curran's eyes. The five at the table relaxed and talked until the others returned with a veritable mountain of u-peel'em shrimp and new Corona beers.

"After hauling in all those fish, I think I need a massage," Deke said, stretching an arm across his chest.

"Chief can't do massages," Perez interjected, referring to Caraballo.

"Easy," Caraballo advised.

"Why not?" Deke asked.

"Last time he got a massage he got so relaxed he farted on the massage chica."

"Yep, somewhere in Indonesia."

"True story. First and last time he got a massage," Curran added.

"I consider it positive feedback. Like training validation," Caraballo said.

"You could have just tipped her," Perez jibed.

"She got tipped all right. Fillippi was there, remember?" Caraballo answered.

"So, you get that big crystal trophy over there," Theresa interjected, changing the subject.

"Yeah, and the 200K will cover the expenses nicely."

"Did you report the Chinese boat and the fish kills yet?" Curran asked Deke.

"Done."

"What happened?" asked Theresa.

"About fifty miles out we came across a Chinese dragger hauling in a huge net."

"That close!"

"Yeah, they're supposed to stay at least two-hundred miles out."

"What about the fish?"

"About thirty or forty miles out, we saw a couple schools of dead fish floating on the surface. Looked like bluefish."

"That stinks. I love bluefish, you know, with stewed tomatoes on top."

"Yeah, me too," Deke said. "We used to catch them, put them in tin foil, add some stewed tomatoes, roll it all up and put it on the engine manifold for twenty minutes. Excellent."

"What do you think caused the fish to die?"

Could have been red tide, but it's rare up here," Curran answered, referring to the red algae blooms in the summer in the Gulf of Mexico that suck the oxygen out of the water. "I didn't smell anything, but the air burned in my throat and my eyes stung like being close to a red tide."

The group sat for a while and enjoyed the activity around them and the lighthearted banter among fishing buddies. During a lull in the action when Curran went to get some clams, shrimp and beers for the table, Theresa skillfully asked Deke about his ex-wife and two young children. It seemed the wife ran back to her rich father in Texas and into the arms of a man her mother had all picked out for her. According to Deke, her father's attitude was his daughter was too good for some G.I. that was never around very much. Later, when Deke's fortune surpassed her father's and the ex-wife came sniffing back around, did he really understand the content of her character. So, in his words, he "sued the living piss out of her," but still did not get custody of the kids because of the notorious and historic sexual bias the court has in custody matters. Theresa understood about the separation, but not about the slight against a military man. To her, no man is finer than one who answered a call to service, has the courage to face combat and has the commitment and ability to lead and defend others.

After a bit of dancing with the girls like two days earlier, with Perez joining in courtesy of a bit of blonde female eye candy from the event organizer's staff, the group relaxed at their table talking about Caraballo's dancing style and the bad hairstyles on the band members. Curran and Deke noticed the Titan slip up to the fuel dock across the marina under cover of darkness.

"Look, look, look," Deke said hurriedly to Curran as he gestured for him to follow. They rose from their chairs and moved to a spot near the water's edge in the shadow of the tent. Caraballo and Perez joined them. "See, they're hustling people up the dock toward the north parking lot," Deke added.

"Are those suitcases?" Caraballo asked. After a few minutes watching the activity, they returned to their chairs. Curran retrieved another huge plate of clams and shrimp while Caraballo got more beers, and the group acted naturally, enjoying the seafood and conversation while watching the Titan eventually move to its dock with the sound of the diesels rumbling in the distance.

Minutes later, Curran watched as G. Blanton Proctor and his three mates arrived at the tent, purposely searched for space at a table in the back and sat down, scanning the crowd. Sitting on the other side of Theresa from Curran, Perez gave him a look and a wave to slide his chair back for a private word. Caraballo noticed the activity and moved from his chair on the other side of Curran, keeping moving low, not standing fully upright. Curran moved back and the three put their heads together.

"Sir. That guy that just came in with the fat guy in the yellow shirt," he said softly. "I know him."

"Which one?"

"The pale gringo with the Filipino-looking guy."

"Go on."

"Remember about ten years ago in Bosnia, the Serb that ran that prison slaughterhouse outside Celebici? His name was Radomir Kuvarac. They say he personally killed something like ten-thousand men."

"I remember that now," Caraballo said in a whisper. "Yeah, they say he and his men raped the wives in front of them before putting bullets in their heads."

"That's the guy," Perez quietly declared.

"Are you sure?" Curran asked.

"Positive."

"I remember we wanted to go after him but weren't allowed," added Caraballo.

Slowly, Curran turned to see if he could get a look at the guy. He set his eyes on him Kuvarac, sitting at his table like a statue, not drinking a beer or having any chow, but being completely still, looking their way. Curran and Kuvarac's eyes met. An aggressive, almost predatory feeling washed through Curran. He held his gaze as Kuvarac averted his eyes. He turned his attention back to the guys.

"He looks like he knows we recognized him."

"Do we tell Deke?" Caraballo asked. Curran paused.

"Later. We'll make an excuse to go back to the boat and tell him there."

"Ever feel naked without a weapon?" Perez asked facetiously.

"Yeah," Curran and Caraballo said in stereo.

An announcer broke the casual atmosphere, saying it was time for the awards presentations. After running through all the other teams and giving out the other prizes, the winner was announced.

"And the winner of the seventh annual South Jersey Marlin and Sailfish Open sponsored by Gold Coast Marina and Fishing Center is Comedor de Serpiente', team Snake Eater. Boat owner, team captain and three-time winner Deke Draper!" the man said enthusiastically. "Come on up here Deke!"

Deke stood triumphantly and moved to the podium area to accept his prize. First, a check for $200,000 dollars, followed by a gleaming crystal trophy with a crystal marlin sculpture set on top.

"How did you do it again this year, Deke? Say a few words."

Deke took the microphone.

"Thanks a lot. This year's tournament was great. You guys always put on a first-class operation, and I hope to be able to do it again next year."

"So, what's your secret to success?"

"Oh boy, here it comes. He's gonna out us in front of everybody," fretted Caraballo.

"A great boat, a great team, and getting there first," Deke said. He raised a beer "Here's to the team!" he added.

The crowd raised their drinks and repeated "to the team!"

"I told you that guy was a goddamned fish magnet," Proctor mumbled to his crew.

"Thanks everybody." Deke concluded. "See you for the wahoo open!"

"That was close," Caraballo said quietly to Curran.

"Nah, leave it to another spook to square us away," Curran replied. Tell you what; they probably have my last name, but if they have yours too, they might figure us out."

"Good thing I registered as Constantine Beru." It's the name Caraballo used in Panama a few months earlier.

"Good thinking. In the meantime, we have to keep an eye on that guy."

"Do we take that guy here and now?"

"No. What do we know so far besides he's an asshole? We gotta find out what he's doing here and why he's with Proctor."

"Let's just roll him up and beat it out of him," Caraballo suggested.

"Why don't we tell that cop over there who he is?" asked Perez.

It was as if time was speeding up and Curran was trying to slow it down. He could feel his heart rate increasing and he changed his breathing to slow and deep to compensate.

"No. We can't exploit this from an aggressor's perspective. We have the girls here, we're in too public of a place, we're unarmed, and we'd out ourselves in the process."

"We're going to lose that guy now that he knows we recognize him," asserted Caraballo.

"Probably, but Proctor's not going anywhere."

G. Blanton Proctor seemed overly upset regarding the fishing tournament. In his mind, it wasn't his losing as much as it was others winning. By all accounts, no one saw him spend any particular time actually fishing, but ego being what it is, he was still pissed-off about seeing others get prizes and recognition he felt was his to receive. He sat at the table drinking much heavier than necessary, ranting on and on about the "fish magnet" Draper let on his boat, and the way Deke ran his boat out and around the Titan just to taunt him with the Snake Eater's superior speed. His mates looked at Proctor like he went insane. The Filipino mate commented that he was "talking out his ass." Kuvarac told Proctor to keep his voice down, that he was attracting unwanted attention.

At that point, other fishing boat owners smelled blood in the water and circled like sharks. They taunted him for his lack of fishing prowess and apparent irritation at somehow not being the victor. One said that in order to catch a fish he had to actually put baits in the water, while another said he looked lost out at the canyon. A charter captain said Proctor was obviously looking for the Grand Canyon instead of the Baltimore Canyon. He said to Proctor "were you riding around looking for rocks sticking out of the water" and offered to put a buoy out there with the instructions "start fishing here" written on it. Proctor got an offer of fishing lessons, advice to hire a better captain, a recommendation to stop fishing altogether, a suggestion of paying a voodoo priestess to do an exorcism of his "bad mojo," and the promise of a copy of "big game fishing for dummies." He even received a critique of his twenty-dollar cigar; one boat owner said it smelled like he was smoking a day-old dog turd. Not his best moment at a post tournament party.

Deke came walking back to the table holding the crystal winner's trophy at eye-level. Along the way he was congratulated by other tournament participants as one would celebrate a returning Roman warrior just entering the gates of the city. Well, sort of; people patted him on the shoulder. Things fell from the sky. A beverage became airborne and landed across his shirt. Someone yelled "fuck you Draper, I got it next year." He reached the table and the guys filled him in on the situation.

"Well, shit, you want to do a quick extraction, we can use the boat," was his reply.

"He'll take off as soon as he gets the chance. No way he'll even go back down the dock," Curran countered. "All we'll do is create a scene we won't be able to explain. No. I want to cap this jackass but now's not the time."

"Tom's right," Caraballo reluctantly admitted. "What happens when people see us wrestling that guy onto the boat? We can't involve the local authorities."

Chapter 9

The next day, G. Blanton Proctor sat at his oversized oak desk in his surprisingly dated office at the Titan Chemical company. The office was housed in an old wooden building just inside the main gate of the chemical plant outside Millville, a blue-collar town in the heart of South Jersey. Behind the office sat rows of unpainted, rusty metal buildings, rusty white chemical tanks, and rusted silver pipes running throughout the property like the intestines of a mechanized animal spewing a noxious funk the aroma of which can best be described as the combination of that horrible smell that comes from a paper mill and cherry-scented ass.

Proctor was overly dressed, sitting in front of the 1970's brown paneled walls. An ornate sort of fellow, wore a dark blue thousand-dollar suit, a light blue shirt with white French collar and cuffs and links adorned with little Marlins, the ensemble finished off with seven-hundred-dollar cordovan wing tip shoes. A cigar burned in a pewter ashtray under a small Tiffany desk lamp with green stained glass in the shade. Behind him on the wall was a six-foot sailfish, mounted horizontally with the sail standing erect in all its glory. He bought the fish replica in a novelty store in Madeira Beach, Florida.

The phone rang: it was an old multi-line unit, tan with vinyl inset wood grain and a built-in intercom.

"Proctor," he said into the handset. He listened for a moment. "Why didn't you call me on the intercom?" Another momentary pause. "Oh," he said. The voice on the other end reminded him the intercom hadn't worked in years. "Send him in."

His office door opened, and a man walked in wearing cheap grey slacks, a faded polo-style shirt, a worn and ill-fitting blue blazer, and what appeared to be old black hiking boots.

"Mr. Proctor," he said.

"What have you got," Proctor asked, not one for small talk or social graces.

"Not much."

"What do you mean, not much?" Proctor said disgustedly.

"Name, birthday, raised by the orphanage in Philly, high school, military school, no living relatives, and that's about it."

"What do you mean, that's it?"

"His driver's license says 1 Gannon Drive, Fort Gannon, North Carolina, but that address is post headquarters. He drives a pristine dark blue OJ-style Ford Bronco registered to the same address. He has no listed residence, no insurance company, bank account, mortgage, or next-of-kin. All he has is a 1994 25' Mako center console boat and a trailer both registered in North Carolina."

"Well don't you find that a bit odd?" Proctor said frustratedly.

"Yes, I do."

"What about his military service?"

"There's no record."

"How can that be?"

"He must do something they want kept a secret."

A long pause ensued. The man stood, staring at his notes, waiting for Proctor to respond.

"What else?"

"The house on Sea Island is owned by a widow named DeFelice, from Philadelphia. Her husband died some years ago after owning a men's tailor shop in the city."

"What about his friend, the one on the boat?"

"His name is Caraballo. Parents died in a car accident. His wife was a DeFelice who died in another car accident on Fort Gannon a few years ago. One child; lives with the mother-in-law. His driver's license, vehicle registration address, and all his other information is exactly like Curran's."

"Do you have the house address in Philadelphia?"

"Yes."

"Finally! You have something we can work with," Proctor said sarcastically.

"Well, not quite."

"What do you mean?

"The DeFelice-side of the family is mostly cops. A nephew is connected to some Philadelphia leg-breakers, and the neighborhood is all close-knit Italians that have lived there for a couple generations."

"Shit." Proctor blurted.

"Well what are they doing today?"

"They went fishing this morning,"

"Well, find me something I can use."

Chapter 10

The next morning, Curran woke Caraballo with the same "the killer awoke before dawn," line, figuring it worked the last time. Perez was already up and ready. A short while later, they rode over to the bay side of town to a friend's house where Curran's boat was docked, loaded their gear, check the boat's systems, warmed up the engines, and got underway. As the sky started to lighten in the east, they traveled south from their dock, through the canals and down the channel toward the inlet.

"The killers were out before dawn; they put their coffee on," Caraballo said proudly as he poured coffee from his thermos for the three of them. Curran stood behind the boat's center console, as he steered for the inlet bridge.

"Those tanks are secure?" he asked Caraballo about four scuba tanks in forward racks they brought for the trip.

"Yep."

"Jackets," Curran said as they rounded the bayside beach. Looking under the bridge, he could see some whitecaps across the inlet sand bar, meaning the tide was screaming out while the wind was blowing onshore. In Townsend's Inlet, with a shifting sandbar running down the left side and rock jetties on the right, the swell can be short and nasty. This type of sea can cause anyone aboard to pitch rather violently forward and backward as the boat reacts to it. Years ago, Curran learned his lesson the hard way, impacting the steering wheel under his bottom ribs after the boat unexpectedly caught some air while running and came down with a thud. Now he wears his life jacket whenever the seas get rough for padding. Perez pulled two silver-grey flotation vests with white reflective stripes across the front and back from a zippered compartment overhead called a "t-bag" mounted under the boat's T-top. They zipped on the jackets as the boat idled under the center span of the bridge in the middle of the channel.

"Time for the appropriate theme song," Curran said as he thumbed-through his phone's music selections. He picks the song "Voices" from Russ Ballard, a song famously used in a scene from the 80's television show "Miami Vice," when Crockett and Tubbs rode in Crockett's 38 Chris Craft Stinger headed to the Bahamas. He hits Bluetooth sending the song over the boat's stereo speakers.

"Now what I would have chosen, boss," Perez stated as the song started.

Curran smiled and nodded to Perez as he noticed Caraballo's obvious sign of approval (big smile and head nodding). He pushed the throttles forward on his twin Yamaha outboards and they set off due east into the inlet, headed for the cold blue.

They arrived at their destination near the north end of the Cape May reef about an hour later. It was the spot taken from the GPS on Baba's boat indicating where the boat with the concrete boom was anchored. Curran used the structure scanning/side-scanning sonar feature of his GPS/fish-finder to plot areas of interest on the bottom and mark them onto the chart on his GPS unit.

"There's gotta be something down there," Curran said matter-of-factly.

"You think the salvage boats left anything to find?" Caraballo asked.

"It's the convergence of things; a salvage boat with a black RHIB that runs people off, a big salvage vessel with a concrete pumping thing, a chemical company guy's boat tied up to the salvage boat, a known shithead on that guy's boat, and a dead friend that got to close to whatever it was down there."

"Why do you think anything's still down there?"

"Because of the concrete boom. If they could simply remove whatever it is, they wouldn't need it," Curran said.

"Makes sense. So that's what the tanks are for?"

"Yeah. I figure if something really looks interesting, I'll just pop down for a look."

"Why you?" Caraballo asked. Curran started to smile.

"We'll flip for it."

As the men performed a grid-style search of the bottom, Curran saw something odd in the distance. Birds hovered over a spot about a half-mile away but were not diving. Others seemed to be floating on the water beneath them. There were no signs of fish breaking the waters. As a swell rolled past the spot, the guys saw what looks like speckles on the water, like confetti spread across the surface.

"Hang on," Curran said. Curran pushed the throttles to get the boat up on plane, moving the boat slowly toward the area in question.

They reached the spot and are set aghast. In an area the size of a football field, dead fish float motionless. Scattered among them are a dozen or so dead seabirds. Near the center of the mass, a bird caught in the middle of death throes pitifully slaps one extended wing on the water's surface. The hovering seagulls seem to be looking down at the dead ones with an expression like "better you than me."

"What the hell is going on?" blurted Caraballo. Curran remained quiet, slowing the boat, and steering wide to clear the dead pool. "Dude!" Caraballo barks, looking for an answer from Curran.

"Can't tell," he said. "No red tide, no oil spill, no signs of the cause. I don't smell anything so I can't even hazard a guess right now." In the middle of the mass of dead creatures, out of view of Curran but seen by Caraballo, a blue-green blob floats barely above the surface. The men circle the area for a few more minutes.

"It gives you a little sting in the back of your throat," Perez said.

"What are we going to do?" Caraballo asked.

"You still have those urine sample jars in your medic bag?

"Yeah."

"We'll get a little closer, take some pictures, get a water sample, and go back to our bottom search.

A few minutes later, they're motoring straight south toward another spot on the GPS where the wreck of a World War II Liberty ship lay on its side in about 120 feet of water, the ship the victim of a 1940's German torpedo. Ahead, they see a big white Hatteras sportfishing boat trolling for what Curran guesses is either tuna or bluefish.

"Is that the same boat from yesterday?" Curran asked Caraballo, noticing the fat horizontal blue stripe down the side of the boat near the sheer line.

"It definitely could be."

"They're not cutting any water," Curran said over the din of the big outboard motors. Normally, water split by the bow and curling around the stern is visible from far away.

"Maybe they're in neutral."

"I don't see anybody on deck, but maybe our angle sucks."

Curran turned southeast to get a bit closer off the big boat's bow. Seconds later, he cut the throttles.

"What's up?" Caraballo asked.

"Something's wrong."

"How can you tell?"

"I see slack lines blowing in the breeze. Lines are still attached to the outriggers."

Caraballo retrieved the binoculars from the locker underneath the steering wheel.

"Man, you have good eyes," Caraballo said. He could see neon-green fishing line dangling from the riggers loose enough to touch the side of the boat. "Still nobody on deck. Circle around the back."

Almost instinctively, but more likely due to his years of military training, Curran checked the wind direction. Normally, when approaching another boat, coming up from down-sea helps avoid having the swells push one boat into the other. Right now, though, Curran only intends to take a look. They round around the starboard bow and turn toward the stern, being mindful to keep a safe distance. Caraballo moves to the bow of their boat.

"You see the name yet?

"Yeah. Miss Margaret," Caraballo replied. Curran grabbed the handset for the VHF radio.

"Miss Margaret, Miss Margaret, this is the vessel Necessary Evil, over," Curran said into the microphone, trying to hail the boat. No answer; he tried again with no response. "Ears," he directed to Caraballo and Perez as a warning. Both men covered their ears. He gave the other boat a long blast from a compressed air signal horn held high over his head. No response. A moment later he retrieved his .40 caliber Sig Sauer pistol from his little backpack under the center console and set it barrel first in a cup holder molded into the console. He looked over to see Caraballo giving him a puzzled gaze.

"Not sure how close I want to get unarmed," he said. He looked forward and saw Perez tuck his shirt behind the gun he carried inside the waistband of his jeans. Caraballo moved toward the bow.

As the Necessary Evil reached the stern quarter of the Miss Margaret, the boat rolled over a swell. It lifted the boat and gave them a view of the cockpit of Miss Margaret. Caraballo stood bolt-upright and turned to Curran.

"We got people down on the deck!" he shouted.

"You two put your life jackets back on."

"We're leaving?" Caraballo asks incredulously.

"No, but it's stern to the wind, so getting onboard might be tricky" Curran replied as he turned his boat away from the other. "I'll make an approach in toward the stern but put the bow alongside on the left. Oscar, you can step off onto the gunwale," Curran directed. "If I screw it up, padding and flotation helps. The port side cockpit looks like the clearest place to jump on. Just you. Connie, stay on the bow just in case I screw this up."

Caraballo walked back to the center console, grabbed the life jacket Curran held out for him, turned, and threw it on as he returned to the bow. Perez grabbed his life jacket back out of the overhead bag and donned it as Curran expertly maneuvered the boat close to the other. He pulled the throttles gently into neutral. Caraballo steadied himself on the starboard side of the front deck, right knee against the bow rail. Curran slid the throttles into reverse. The two boats came within three feet of each other.

"Go ahead," he said. With that, Perez stepped up onto the bow of the boat lifted a leg over the bow rail and stepped deftly onto the gunwale of the Miss Margaret without hesitation. He hopped down into the waist-deep cockpit, being careful not to land on a man on the deck. Curran backed the boat away without any boat-to-boat contact while keeping his eyes on Caraballo.

Perez stopped immediately; four dead men lay bloating on deck in the mid-morning sun, with a dried or partially dried foamy substance on their faces and oozing from gaping mouths. On the other side of the fighting chair set in the middle of the cockpit, a fat man in a blue shirt lay face-down atop another man in a stained white t-shirt, both next to a young man flat on his back, with a fourth on the near side of the cockpit close to the stern, all four men sunburned and showing signs of bloat.

Perez moved to the cabin door, pulled it open and stepped inside. Next to the door lay the body of a dead man lying in the fetal position, very pale, wearing a blue t-shirt, blue canvas work pants, and black shoes with black soles not meant for boating. White foam is dried on his face and rubbed into the carpet under his face. He's not bloated like those on deck. Perez realizes the boat's engines are still idling, and the air conditioning is on in the cabin. He hopped back outside and shut the door, surveying the macabre scene in the cockpit. One body released some trapped gas with a hiss, causing him to recoil at the foul odor.

"Man!" he growled, pressing the back of his hand against his nose.

The boat rolled to starboard. Laying precariously on the man below, the blue-shirt man rolled off and flopped onto his back on the deck. Next to the man's leg, a shiny blue-green blob the size of baseball reflects the sunlight. Perez has a moment of recollection between the blob on the deck and the thing he saw floating in the mass of dead fish.

On the other boat, Curran and Caraballo see Perez slap his hand to the back of his neck. Back on the Miss Margaret, something stung Perez' skin. His eyes started to burn and his throat became swollen. One eye twitched. His legs began to quiver. Sinuses closed; his pulse started to race; he broke a whole-body sweat. Curran and Caraballo think he's been motionless a bit too long.

"What's the matter?" Caraballo yelled. No response. "Oscar?"

Thoughts raced through Perez' mind. All he knew was everything he felt happened when he came onboard the boat. Suddenly, in three giant steps he went across the deck, leapt up onto the stern gunwale, and launched himself into the air and off the boat. No waiting for Curran to bring the boat back. He hurtled through the air and hit the water in an ungraceful crash like Gump off the shrimp boat.

"Oscar! What the hell?" Caraballo shouted, not knowing Perez to be impetuous and wondering if he's as scared-shitless as he looked.

Curran spun the steering wheel to the right all the way to the lock and bumped the throttles in gear. He gave the boat a jolt of thrust, followed by going into neutral. The boat turned broadside to Perez. Curran reached down and grabs the folded boarding ladder from the rack under the gunwale. Perez swam clumsily toward the boat. "Grab the ladder," he said.

Perez didn't seem to be listening…or swimming very well. "Connie!" barked Curran. Caraballo reached him and the two men leaned over the side and grabbed Perez by the arm. Perez looked pale and had a wide-eyed "thousand-yard stare."

Curran grabbed Perez by the wrist. He put Perez' hand on the boarding ladder, but Perez didn't grab it.

"Oh shit," Curran blurted. In a flash he considered jumping in the water to help (but never put yourself in a position to go from rescuer to victim, especially if the boat gets away), then considered yanking Perez out by the arm openings of the life jacket (but he could slip through and fall out of it), then thought of jumping in and strapping down Perez' arms so he wouldn't slip out (strapping down the arms of a guy bobbing in the water in a life jacket? Are you serious?), then possibly jumping in and fashioning some sort of life jacket crotch strap that went from front to back between Perez' legs (but no time for creativity here, and there he would be, back in the water).

In this flash, adrenaline pumped into Curran and Caraballo, and their course of action was clear. Curran cleared the boarding ladder out of the way, maneuvered Perez' body to put his back to the side of the boat close to the stern.

"Get him under the arm," Curran directed. Both men grabbed Perez under the armpits with two handfuls of T-shirt included. "On three. Ready?"

"Yep."

"Okay. One, two," Curran counted as he pushed Perez down in the water a bit to let buoyancy air their efforts. The life jacket started to push him back up.

"Three," Curran said as the two men heaved their friend skyward in a 220-pound deadlift. They stop and set Perez on the gunwale. Curran wrapped his arms around Perez from behind and with a second effort hauled him the rest of the way aboard. Curran plopped down on his butt still holding Perez to his chest. Caraballo went immediately for the medic bag stored in the bow locker.

Curran pulled himself out from his position wedged between the starboard fish box and the engine with Perez in front/on top of him. Using the arm opening of Perez' vest, he slid his friend up, and then back and leaned him against the same starboard fish box. Curran knelt on the deck and leaned in close.

"Dude, what's wrong?" he said, unzipping the vest.

"At," Perez said in a gasp. "At," he tried to repeat, chest heaving, saltwater dripping in his eyes.

"What?"

Caraballo arrived and knelt next to Curran. Perez tried to inhale deeply as his body continued to tense-up. It seemed every muscle in his body was contracting.

"Atro," Perez growled.

"What?"

"Atro."

"Atropine?" Curran asks, puzzled. Perez nodded with difficulty as the moisture on his face turned from wet, to sweat.

"Atropine?" Caraballo repeated, not believing his ears.

"Atro," Perez repeated, still nodding.

"Atropine," Curran said, nodding in the affirmative.

Caraballo performed patient evaluation in his own head as he opened his medic bag. He removed a clear plastic watertight box, popping it open. Using thumb and forefinger he grabbed an item the size of a highlighter pen with the cap on. He pulled off the cap to reveal a tip that looked like a ball-point pen; an auto injector, spring loaded.

Caraballo thought about "sterilizing the field," or making the injection area sterile, but Perez was wearing jeans. After pausing for ten seconds to evaluate the symptoms Perez was demonstrating, he jammed the tip of the injector hard though Perez' jeans and into his thigh. The spring-loaded needle sinks into Perez' leg. Caraballo holds the injector hard into the thigh until the auto-injector pushes all the medicine into him. After a moment, Perez starts to relax.

"Let's get out of here," Curran recommended before standing and going back behind the wheel. Curran checked around the boat, realized the bow was facing away from the other vessel, and bumped the throttles in gear. He forgot that he turned the engines full over, so he quickly turned the engines back to center using the ball mounted on the steering wheel.

Caraballo put the waterproof box back in the orange medic bag and slid the bag out of the way. He flipped open the padded part of the leaning post behind the steering wheel and grabbed a dry beach towel. He covered Perez' upper body with the towel, and then sat back, watching him. He was doing what medical training taught him; once your patient is out of danger, stable, breathing, conscious, and not demonstrating any other issues requiring immediate attention, monitor the patient and attend to any further issues.

Caraballo thought about current events and he thought about Atropine. Atropine is an antidote. More scientifically, Atropine Sulfate injection is a "parenteral anticholinergic agent and muscarinic antagonist." Basically, fancy language for a drug that calms the nerves and stops an allergic reaction in your body from producing so much mucous it drowns you after exposure to something so irritating it intended to kill you. All Caraballo knew is, he just gave it to Perez after the man jumped off a boat with people aboard whom he can only assume died in a terrible fashion. Good thing Caraballo's medic bag is a medic bag, not just a first aid kit.

A few minutes later and a mile away, Curran pulled the throttles back into neutral.

"Connie, what's going on?" he asked Caraballo.

"He's doing okay. He's going to feel like shit for a couple days, but he'll be fine."

"Do we need a medivac?"

"Not unless you want everybody and their sister to know what's up," Caraballo replied flatly.

"Yeah, you're right about that."

Curran flipped open the cabinet under the steering wheel on the side of the console and retrieved his satellite telephone. He dialed seven numbers, heard a click on the phone and another, slightly different sounding dial tone, and then dialed nine numbers he knew by heart. It was a number only government warrior spooks like Curran know, the one that brings the black helicopters that conspiracy theorists always claim to see, and the government claims don't exist. A casual voice on the phone said, "home plate."

"Umpire, this is Tarpon. I need a rain delay, over," Curran said. It's a phone, so saying "over" seemed silly, but that was the protocol. The baseball references bother Curran. They were amateurish at best, but don't flip the switches on the electronic surveillance done by the company or any other three-letter outfit. Rain delay was the phrase to go next-level secure on the phone.

"Standby, over."

Curran heard some clicking and two short tones on the line. He pressed a button on the phone, and then puts his ear back to the earpiece.

"Tarpon, are you there? Over," the man on the phone said.

"Roger"

"We are secure. What is the problem? Over."

"I have at least four down, possible NBC exposure. Bluefish was exposed, atropine administered.

"Do you need medivac? Over."

"Negative. Notify appropriate parties for presence of possible nerve agent. The vessel 'Miss Margaret,' a fifty-three-foot sportfishing boat, over" Curran reported. "Grid to follow, over." Curran pushed another button on the phone which his position over the phone. "one-mile due south of that point," he added. There is a short pause.

"Are there any other vessels in the area? Over."

"Negative, over."

There was another short pause. Curran heard several clicks on the line.

"Is the vessel Miss Margaret still in the area."

"Roger. Adrift at that location."

"Standby and await response. Umpire out."

"Dumb bastard," Curran thought to himself. Normal procedure is the party that initiates the call is the one that ends the call. "Okay, help is on the way," he says to Caraballo.

Perez seemed to be coming around. His eyes were open, and he appeared to be dealing with something caught in his nose. It's like when you smell something bad and it sticks with you or get some cleaning fumes burning in your nose and it just won't stop. He pinched his nostrils together in a vain attempt to rub-away whatever was in there. His head was uncomfortably propped-up against the side of the boat, his chin almost touching his chest. He closed one nostril at a time and forcefully exhaled, but nothing came out. "You call the Coast Guard?" he asked.

"No. If this went over the radio the news would get it and cause a shit-storm."

"You call Umpire?"

"Yep," Caraballo said as he handed Perez a water bottle.

"What did he say?"

"They're calling the response team on the secure line."

Perez drank some water, trying to collect himself. He hated looking weak.

Curran and Caraballo stayed well away from the other boat, making sure to stay upwind. After providing some padding for Perez' back by way of a couple seat cushions, Caraballo gave him some carbohydrate gel, an energy bar, and some more water. Perez spent considerable time growling-up excess mucous caused by his exposure to the unknown caustic agent, spitting the results into the engine well. No blood; that's a good thing.

Minutes later, as the clear sky let a scorching mid-day sun beat-down on the two men, Caraballo tended to Perez further, giving him some sunblock and a red Phillies baseball cap, placing the hat on Perez' head.

"You hear that?" Curran said.

"What?"

The sound of an approaching aircraft rose above the sound of the idling engines. Curran turned his head skyward to see what's coming. At first, he didn't see anything. Suddenly, behind him from the east, a whirling roar punctuated the air. Curran turned to see an F-16 fighter jet about a quarter mile away in a hard-left turn about three-hundred feet above the water. Not a completely unusual sight. Ever since 9/11, military aircraft fly combat air patrols, or "CAP," over the northeastern seaboard. Curran and Caraballo even know several of the pilots that fly those missions. The fighter made a circle around the area.

"Something doesn't smell right," Caraballo said.

"You're not catching exhaust fumes, are you?"

"I mean that fighter," Caraballo said in a grimace as he squinted into the mid-morning sun.

"What do you mean? It looks like Thunder 3."

"Why would he make a circle? Every time we see one of the guys, they rock their wings and keep on going. This guy's looking at us."

Suddenly, floating about a mile away, the Miss Margaret exploded in an enormous fireball. It sounded like a sonic boom. Curran watched as the fighter jet seemed to emerge from the flames, flying directly at them! The streaming whir of the engine became a blast from the jet as it passed overhead, hit afterburner, and launched itself at a sixty-degree angle skyward.

"Connie hang-on!" Curran barked before turning back to the wheel. "What fresh hell is this?" he said lowly as he shoved the throttles all the way forward and turned northwest. The boat jumped onto a plane and tore out of the area. It's the OODA-loop, "Observe, Orient, Decide, and Act." After seeing the other boat go sky-high, Curran thought the worst, and he beat feet out of there. It was the nautical equivalent of "feet don't fail me now!"

"What happened?" Caraballo yelled over the din of the outboard motors.

"The fighter blew-up Miss Margaret!"

"I told you that plane was weird," Caraballo said adamantly.

Curran knew when pondering the question to fight, or flee, with all things being equal, the decision comes down to a matter of combat necessity. In this case, the "fleeing" was due to the instinct for self-preservation. Fighter jet blows-up big boat nearby…small boat runs away. Too easy, but Curran knew better. He's been around devious, sinister government types for a long time and knew how they operated. The only way to figure out what Perez encountered on the boat was to get people in biohazard protective suits on the boat to look for it. The best way to nullify the situation and blame it on something else was to eliminate the evidence. Curran realized he and Connie were evidence. But they were party to all sorts of covert activities at home and abroad, so no need to eliminate them, right? No time to ponder over it; he had the throttles in a death-grip, jammed balls-to-the-wall, trying to push them farther than full forward, the steel shafts of the throttle handles bent slightly under the pressure. The boat skipped across the tops of the slight chop, engines screaming, salt spray shooting to the sides as they reached nearly 50 miles-per-hour.

He looked behind the boat and saw the burning hulk of the Miss Margaret far behind, black smoke billowing skyward. He didn't see the aircraft. He thought "supersonic airplane with supersonic weapons verses a fiberglass boat that tops out at 50." He then thought about checking high-up behind the boat. Before he could step to the side out from under the T-top to look, Caraballo spotted the aircraft.

"There it is! Forty-five degree angle up, straight behind us," he shrieked, pointing to the sky. For a second, the sight of Perez on his back, bouncing on the deck made Curran think of the Bugs Bunny episode where Bugs is in the house of a giant at the top of a beanstalk and bounced on the floor from the giant's footsteps as the giant approached. He looked where Caraballo was pointing and spotted a small dot in the sky getting bigger by the second.

Curran considered his options; he could veer-off to the left or right forcing the fighter to take an angle shot (delaying the inevitable), wait until it gets close and try to shoot it with a flare, his pistol, or the 12-guage shotgun he has under the console (completely ridiculous), or jump off while the plane is still high and let the pilot destroy an empty boat vice one with two guys on it (most appropriate decision). Then he thinks "what if the guy doesn't shoot? The boat could go full-speed right onto the beach in Avalon, and we'd be bobbing around out here like idiots." He decided to veer to the west and see what happened when the F-16 gets closer.

The plane dove right for them. Curran unconsciously grabbed his waterproof cell phone and shoved it into his pocket. The plane reached the point where Curran thought a missile would fire, but it kept on coming, diving straight for them. Curran turned the wheel hard left as he watched the aircraft. He couldn't help but think how awesome it was. It pulled out of the dive right behind the boat and ripped overhead so low the guys swore they could read the writing on the sidewinders.

"Holy crap!" Caraballo yelled. "I can smell jet fuel!"

"Low enough to suck us into the intake," Curran thought.

The boat turned back to the northwest at top speed. Curran trimmed the engine out a bit, trying to eek every bit of speed out of the aging boat. The aircraft made a flat, high-performance, maximum-G turn to the right about fifty feet over the water, followed by a flat approach right back to the guys. It roared across the bow in front of the boat, and then repeated its earlier turn, this time to the left. It came straight back, but before passing overhead the pilot pulled it into a climb, hit the afterburner and roared into the sky.

"He's chasing us off," Curran said into the wind. As he fought the tears caused by the wind in his eyes, he looked behind the boat to see the F-16 crossing the line of the wake about a mile back, about five-hundred feet up, like severing the connection between Curran's boat and the Miss Margaret. Curran thinks of how occasionally, you see a smaller bird chasing off a hawk, prey chasing off a predator.

"You're right! He's chasing us off!" Caraballo replied from his spot standing behind the leaning post behind Curran.

"Yep, we're thinking alike!" Curran shouted into the wind.

"Well don't slow down, just in case!"

"Yep, we're still thinking alike!"

When the outline of Avalon, New Jersey finally appeared on the horizon, the guys figured no way a fighter jet would blow them out of the water within sight of people trying to get a suntan, little Susie with her pail and shovel digging a sand castle, or the dozen or so recreational boats with fishermen drifting for flounder near the inlet. Curran pulled the throttles back, taking the boat off plane. It settled back into the water moving just faster than idle speed. He moved around the front of the console and grabbed three water bottles from the cooler seat in front, and then returned to the helm. After checking the boat was still on course for the mouth of Townsend's Inlet, he went around the leaning post to the cockpit. He finds Caraballo kneeling over Perez, with Perez in the supine position, using all the cushions he previously had as padding underneath him.

"You look comfy," Curran says as he handed out the water. He rubbed back of his neck; keeping it on a swivel for twenty-five miles searching for a fighter jet while trying to navigate back to safety made it a little stiff.

"I should have thought of this a long time ago. My back is completely adjusted," Perez said. He took a bottle from Curran. "Help me up. It would look pretty weird to have somebody lying flat on the deck when we go back in."

Curran and Caraballo help him up and over to the console cooler seat.

"What's that" Curran said, noticing splashes in the water near the one-mile bell buoy. "This day might not be a total bust after all." He ran the boat up to where he saw the activity and found a school of sea trout being attacked by a marauding group of big bluefish. Curran selected a rod with a small surface lure called a "Top Dog" and hurled it into the school. After catching four blues on just eight casts, and keeping two for dinner, they cruised back to the dock. Perez stayed in his place in front of the console as

Caraballo joined Curran behind the console. To the casual onlooker, it was just three guys coming in from a fishing trip.

Chapter 11

Instead of returning to the house, the three men drove out to the airport. Reaching the end of the road in front of the FBO, they instead turn to the right, punch the code into the keypad for the gate, and when it opens, drive down past a long set of hangars to the end near the airport perimeter fence. They round the hangars to the taxiway side. Curran presses a button on the door opener clipped to his sun visor, and the door to the hangar second from the end starts to rise.

Curran, Caraballo, and Perez pull in and park the Bronco next to the Cessna. They get out and move to a door leading to the hangar next door, the one at the end of the line of hangars. This one contains Curran's boat trailer and 6 large steel storage lockers along with all the gear for aircraft maintenance and a bathroom with stall shower. At the rear of the hangar is a stair leading to the second floor. At the top of the stair is a large living room area, small dining table and kitchen, a small bedroom with bunk beds, and one with a queen bed. Caraballo opens one of the lockers on the ground floor and retrieves a portable oxygen bottle with a mask and tube hanging from the top. He heads back into the hangar with the plane in it to do his pre-flight.

Reagan National Airport is due west from South Jersey, about 110 miles as the crow flies. The team's Cessna landed and taxied to the executive airport fixed-base operation at the southwest corner. There, they found their team ride, a black Chevy Suburban with deeply tinted windows, and drove a few blocks over into Crystal City. They considered dropping in on MacPherson, the boss in his office nearby, but skipped that and brought Perez to the doctor. Curran and Caraballo left him there and went on another errand.

"What the hell!" Caraballo yelled in disgust! "Get off the phone, asshole!" he blared at the windshield. "If we get cut off by one more teenager on the phone, I'm going to freaking kill somebody!" he said to Curran, a clenched fist in the air. The guys drove southeast through Alexandria on the way to the stop they had to make. Now, after being cut-off, they were stuck behind the alleged perpetrator in his old maroon Honda Accord going 15 in a 25-mph zone.

"I got you covered," Curran said calmly. He sped-up and planted the truck's front brush guard firmly in the trunk lid of the offending vehicle, sending the driver's head bouncing back off the headrest. Inappropriate hand gestures came from the driver.

"Oh, so now *he's* pissed?" Caraballo exclaimed.

The two vehicles moved to the shoulder of the road on Jefferson Davis Highway, route 1 near the Braddock street Metro station.

"You can take it from here," Curran said. Caraballo eagerly opened his door and slid out of the truck. "Remember!" Curran blurted, getting Caraballo's attention. "We're only here to correct the behavior, not exact punishment." Caraballo gave him a half-hearted nod to the affirmative.

The driver got out of the car and started moving toward the truck with complete confidence, a good pep in his step; about 5'10", skinny, brown curly unkempt hair, a sweatshirt that said "William and Mary," low-rise denim jeans and skateboard shoes; You know the type ; Mr. Metro-sexual, completely sure of himself and his place in the world, a quasi-humanitarian, pseudo earthy, pretend-environmentalist poser only in it for the chicks, his self-absorption only surpassed by his utter cluelessness and indifference to it.

He stared at the windshield of Curran's truck like he was irritated the driver hadn't yet emerged, and then was surprised to see a hairy tree trunk with huge arms called Caraballo coming around the front of the truck between the vehicles.

"Hey, you guys ran into me," he said, his voice slightly quivering at the sight of the swarthy fireplug coming at him with ill-intent.

"No shit, *Stanley*," Caraballo barks. He calls people he doesn't like 'Stanley.'

"Rear-ending me is your fault!" the driver proclaimed, seemingly pulling the phone far enough from his ear to speak. The two get eye-to-eye.

With an open hand, Caraballo flicked his arm out like a praying mantis, lightly striking the driver on the Adams apple with the soft portion of the crux of his hand between his thumb and index finger. The man blurted out a noise like saying the word "caught." His eyes opened wide, bulging like a fish. He sucked in air that seemed to be far thicker than normal. The strike was a move that doesn't cause permanent damage but definitely gets someone's full attention.

"Jeez, he always does that," Curran said out loud, chuckling to himself inside the truck.

The man placed the hand holding the phone against his throat, instead of his free hand as if the phone would heal his throat or something silly like that.

"Keep your mouth shut," Caraballo said, wagging a finger at the kid. "Cutting us off is your fault, dipshit," he added. The guy presses the phone to his aching throat. "Give me that!" Caraballo growled through clenched teeth, snatching the cell phone out of his hand. "Driving under the speed limit just adds insult to injury."

The kid tries to speak, but only manages a squeaking noise.

"You were concentrating more on this stupid thing than driving a two-ton vehicle," Caraballo said, holding the phone up to the kid's face. He grabbed it with both hands as if holding a harmonica, and with one rapid, violent motion, snapped the device in half.

"Holy shit!" the coed and Curran both said in stereo. It's incredible to think what sort of hand strength it would take to snap a smart phone completely in half. Adrenaline is a wonderful thing.

"It's been proven that drivers on the phone are more dangerous than drunks. We hit you on purpose, and probably saved your life," Caraballo said as the kid stares at his broken phone. "We even saved you from a brain tumor in your pointy little head," he said as he dug a finger into the kid's forehead. He grabbed the guy by the hand and slapped the destroyed phone into it. "Now you drive safely. Have a nice day."

Caraballo turned and walked back around the front of the truck to the passenger side. He left the astonished college kid standing flat-footed next to his car, gently cradling his broken phone like holding a baby bird. Caraballo hopped back into the truck. Curran checked his mirrors for traffic and pulled out. Caraballo leaned out the window.

"Jackass!" he shouted raucously as he passed the other guy, a shit-eating grin on his face! He started to laugh.

"Feel better?" Curran asked.

"Fuckin-ay right, dude!" Caraballo said, eyes beaming. "Maybe we should just do that the rest of the day!"

"It's a good idea. We'll have no shortage of shitheads, but we have something a bit more pressing at the moment.

The skies opened up in the mid-afternoon in Arlington, Virginia as the northeastern storm front pushed its way from the Appalachians to the sea. In a quiet, tree-lined subdivision of red brick and white siding post World War II duplexes not unlike the neighborhood where the team has the safe house, a mid-size tan sedan pulled into the driveway of a house at the end of the cul-de-sac. Leaving the car running, a man, mid-fifties, dressed in grey slacks, black shoes, white oxford shirt with sleeves rolled to the elbows and a dull maroon tie slid out of the car carrying a black leather briefcase. He walked down to the curb and retrieved the day's mail from the rusted white mailbox, holding the briefcase over his head to block the rain. Ignoring the black suburban parked in front of his house, returned to the car. He slapped the briefcase on the roof, opened it, tossed in the mail, closed it, and pulled it off the roof. He hopped back in the car with the wet briefcase on his lap. The garage door started to rise. The man shut the car door and pulled forward, watching the jerky movement of the door as it lifted clear of the car. He guided the vehicle inside the two-car space, the other slot piled full of various items collected over years of suburban life, things deemed too valuable to throw away, or considered necessary at some point in a typical year, relegated to cardboard boxes the rest of the time.

He stopped the vehicle with the driver's door perpendicular to the door to the kitchen, turned off the motor and got out, holding the briefcase to his chest. His eyes tried to adjust to the darker space as the garage door closed. Taking a step back, he shut the car door, and turned toward the house. Suddenly, the briefcase is pushed tight to his chest. He lurched backward, his middle back pressed against the upper car door and roof. Two powerful arms hold the briefcase to him. He started to struggle, but the case and the car acted like a vise, immobilizing him. The air in his lungs started to squeeze from him. His eyes opened wide; panic ensued.

"Hello Umpire," an unknown voice said calmly. The man snapped his head to the left in the direction of the sound. His eyes opened even wider. "Surprised to see us?" Curran said, stepping out of the darkness.

"What?" the bewildered man replied.

Caraballo changed position, placing one foot on the back of the small wooden step to the kitchen behind him for better leverage. His powerful legs flexed as he pressed forward, increasing the pressure of the briefcase against the man's chest. After a moment, the pop-pop sound of the man's spine adjusting was heard by all three men. The man's face turned red.

"You know why we're here, right?" Curran asked.

"What are you talking about?" the man replied breathlessly, chest restricted.

"Come on, dude!" Caraballo growled. "We called you for help and almost got a missile up the ass!" he added, punctuating the word 'missile' with a jolt to the briefcase. The man looked at Caraballo and then back to Curran.

"What are you talking about? I relayed the situation and that was that," the man said incredulously.

Curran stood thinking about the situation.

"That's all you did?"

"Yes. I swear!"

"Don't swear. Are you lying to save your ass?"

"No," the man said, panicked panting restricted by the briefcase held tightly to his chest. "You called and I relayed the information to the naval hazmat team. That was it."

Curran considered the situation for another moment.

"Let him up," he directed.

Caraballo gave him a perplexed look, almost one of disappointment, and then complied. He stood and held the briefcase out for the man to grab. Umpire smoothed the front of his button-down shirt, fixed his necktie, and stuffed the bottom of the shirt back inside his pants.

"I dialed the number in the correct way. You came on, I told you the issue, and you responded. Was the line secure? Yes or no?" Curran asked, a vein protruding down the left side of his powerful neck.

"It was; I heard a couple stray clicks on the line, but that's not unusual."

"I heard them too."

"If you heard them, it's possible the line was breached," the exasperated man says. "When was the last time you called the fill number?" The 'fill' number is a secret number at the National Security Agency you had to dial every few months in order to get the latest communications security 'COMSEC' algorithms to be automatically loaded in the phone.

"Last month," Curran replied.

"Well, that covers level one. Still using Falcon on an Iridium sat phone?"

"Yes."

"We've heard rumors of a couple programs that can bypass the Falcon encryption. Nothing definitive, but we're starting to hear things."

"Who's trying to break the codes?"

"We are," the man said ironically, the "we" referring to the U.S. government.

"That freaking figures," Caraballo blurted disgustedly.

"But how did they react so fast to where we were?" Curran asked.

"All sat phones are locator chipped."

"But I turned off the locator."

"Unless you take it completely out, they can still access it. Besides, I gave the coordinates to the Navy. Jesus Christ, I'm just a commo specialist," the man exclaimed, apparently fearing for his life.

A strange silence ensued as Curran paused to contemplate the man's words. The man tried to relax while thinking he might be toast, and Caraballo wondered how much pressure it would have taken with that briefcase if he pushed it harder and harder until he cracked the man's ribs. The man's eyes moved rapidly from Curran to Caraballo and back again. Finally, the silence is broken.

"We're not going to hurt you," Curran softly declared.

The tension in the garage broke like the bursting sound of a tractor trailer's air brakes. An interesting metaphor considering the man broke wind immediately following Curran's declaration; embarrassing, but not as much as the wet spot on his pants caused by involuntary urination sometime after Caraballo jammed him against the car.

"Maybe you can explain this to me a bit further," the man said tentatively. He received no response. "You boys want some coffee?" he asked in a surprisingly friendly yet flustered tone. "I grind my own."

"Hell yeah," Caraballo replied eagerly.

"Good," the man said. Eyeing the door, he raised his left hand to place it on Curran's right shoulder.

"Don't touch me," Curran directed. The man stopped, dropped his arm, and then nervously straightened his tie with one hand as he turned for the door.

"You're going to explain this to me, right?"

Curran thinks about how much he wants this man to hear.

"Depends on how good your coffee is."

Curran didn't expect for the doctor to want to keep Perez for a few hours. He was never one to complain about an injury or illness. He reminded Curran of Caraballo. Once as a young man he sent a framing nail clean through his foot with a pneumatic nail gun while he and Curran were helping an old family friend replace the deck on his rotted old bayside bungalow. Without so much as a whimper he calmly asked if he could borrow a hammer, hoping to pry his foot off the deck without any further drama. When told one was only five or six feet from him, Caraballo reluctantly divulged his plight.

Curran had a couple hours to kill. He figured two things; first, he needed to gather some information. Second, he hadn't been to the Smithsonian in a while. He texted 8888888 to a number on his cell phone. He and Caraballo hopped on the blue line Metro train at Reagan National Station and got off at the Smithsonian Station. They walked out into the mid-afternoon haze and heat on the National Mall and made a beeline for the Air & Space Museum. For sheer airplane buffs, Air & Space is not quite as awesome as the National Museum of the Air Force in Dayton, Ohio, but it's still awesome, especially for the space-related exhibits.

He made a circuit through the museum, starting with the Wright Flyer, going through the World Wars, Space Travel, and eventually, the café. He left Caraballo watching a 25-year-old IMAX movie about the space shuttle, went and got a glass of iced tea and sat at a table in the middle of everybody. It's called hiding in plain sight. The easiest thing to spot is one man out on the lawn, or two men talking at a bookrack or exhibit and trying to look inconspicuous.

Five minutes later, a grey-haired man snaked his way through several nearby tables and sat down with Curran. He wore a dark suit, white shirt, pale blue necktie, a gold ring on his finger with a Masonic symbol in a black field, matching cuff links, gold Rolex that looked real enough. Two minutes later, they were nothing but two men having coffee and iced tea amongst a crowd of others. He's a man Curran contacts when Curran smells corrupt government types doing something sinister. Only Curran contacts him. No one else on the team reaches behind the black curtain of government spooks in Washington. Well, usually no one else, but no one does it as well. Curran knows people like this and uses them to his advantage. Some call them the "Deep State." They have numerous things in common; they're all dirty, have secrets, want to remain anonymous, and have their hands plunged deeply into the bowels of the system, gripped firmly on the innards. They all tell you they're simply playing the game, or doing things designed for the greater good. That's bullshit.

This guy is connected. Curran knows his name but isn't one-hundred percent sure it's the real one. He once thought about verifying his identity. No, the value of the information he gets is greater than the need to identify him. Besides, the process of doing that could end their arrangement. Curran doesn't trust him. Why should he? It's like trusting a rattlesnake won't bite you.

The two men have a bit of idle chit-chat, and then the mystery man moved into the real conversation.

"I heard you caught some fish in that tournament," the man said to Curran, a twinkle in his eye.

"Deke likes to talk about fishing, doesn't he?"

"He surely does."

"Yeah, we did really well. It's was fun, you should have come along."

"That's a nice thing to say."

"What else did he tell you?"

"That you found Radomir Kuvarac in South Jersey."

"We did."

"Talk about the turd in the punchbowl," the man quipped disgustedly.

"Yep, like swordfish in the Sahara."

"Definitely a strange place to find that guy."

"For sure, but the area is getting more and more popular with Eastern Europeans."

The two men sip their drinks and watch the other patrons for a couple minutes. Normally a destination for tour groups, the café is less crowded on the weekend than during the week.

"Do you always wear a suit to the museum," Curran asked.

"I have an appointment this afternoon."

The men paused as a waitress brought Curran a steak and cheese Panini sandwich and the man a cheeseburger. Curran knows not to ask anything else about the man's business.

"Thanks Joanie," Curran said as the plaid mini skirt-clad grad school student set the food on the table. It's no surprise he knew people in the museum, or anywhere else for that matter.

"You should have zapped him ten years ago," the man stated before taking a bite.

"We never got the sanction."

"People were too scared to make the tough decisions."

"After we figure-out what's going on, we'll punch that ticket?"

"*After* you figure out what he's doing," the man reiterated the past tense.

"There's something else," Curran says with an air of dread.

The man motions for Curran to wait a moment. He goes over to the counter and refills his coffee, and then returns to the table. "Go on," he said.

Curran proceeded to tell the man about what could be called the "Miss Margaret incident." The man showed no discernable reaction one way or the other.

"You need to look into your history. This nation's done some extremely ignorant things regarding chemical weapons," he said.

"Can you be more specific?"

"Some of the most tragic decisions regarding chemical weapons were made by people that are still alive today."

"If we start looking into it, how far can I take it?"

"MacPherson would tell you to hand it to the EPA."

"Actually, he said Department of Natural Resources," Curran replied. "So how far can I take it?"

"Only up to the beltway before we talk further."

"What if I connect the incident with the response?"

"*Only* up to the beltway before we talk further," the man reiterated as he gazed into Curran's eyes. Curran nodded in the affirmative.

The two men continued eating their sandwiches.

"So, how's Mr. MacPherson doing?" the man asked. Curran knew that was the end of their conversation regarding the two issues at hand.

"He's doing well; I won't tell him you said hello," Curran says ironically, smiling.

Chapter 12

Curran and Caraballo collected Perez from the doctor, went back to the airport, flew back to South Jersey, and arrived back in Sea island shortly before 6 pm. Curran turned the Bronco onto 52nd street, and right away noticed something strange. In the distance, he saw Theresa, Mrs. DeFelice, and Angelina standing on the front porch in front of the front door, all three facing the same direction. They were clearly watching the street waiting for them. Theresa had her forearms clutched to her chest, elbows at her sides, hands separated in little fists.

"Something's wrong" Curran said.

"How can you tell?" Caraballo asked.

"Look at Theresa."

Caraballo noticed her posture.

"Yep, she does that."

Curran swung the truck into the parking spot to the right of the front steps next to the protruding front porch. He slid out, looked up and made instant eye contact with Theresa.

"What's wrong?" he asked.

"Someone's been in the house!" she said, pulling her windblown black hair back from in front of her face. Curran could see her trembling.

Without another word, he turned back to the truck, reached in the pocket behind the seat and retrieved his weapon. He tucked it into the front of his black surf shorts and pulled his black t-shirt over it. He turned, rounded the bottom of the steps, climbed smoothly up, glided past the women, and entered the house. He paused at the inner entrance to the downstairs room, waiting for Caraballo to come up behind him. In his peripheral vision he saw Caraballo approach, and can tell he was holding his own weapon with both hands pointed down.

Without a word they moved together, Curran concentrated on right and up toward the stairs, while Caraballo concentrated on down and left toward the downstairs rooms. They've done this sort of thing before in war zones and jungle villages, but never in their own house. They swept the entire house and returned to the front porch where Perez was watching over them, having found no one inside. Curran tucked his weapon in the rear waistband of his shorts, while Caraballo held his straight down by his right thigh, index finger along the side of the gun.

"There's nobody in there, but the bedrooms are all messed up," Curran reported. Theresa and Mrs. DeFelice stared at Curran, obviously shaken. Angelina faced the boardwalk, watching a group of people walking by. "Tell me what happened," Curran added.

"We went out to the farmer's market and Shop Rite in Somers Point, and when we got back, I was carrying groceries inside when Mom came out panic-stricken," Theresa explained nervously, arms still tight, palms overlapped flat to her chest under her neck. Curran reached out with his right arm for Theresa. He pulled her to him and reached his left arm out for Mrs. DeFelice, pulling her in next to Theresa.

"It's alright," he said calmly. "It's safe."

Caraballo moved around the group slightly blocking the door and over next to Angelina.

"Are you okay?" he asked softly, touching her gently on the shoulder, noticing a tear on her cheek. At first, she nodded without speaking as she wiped a tear off her tanned face.

"I'm fine. I just don't like seeing people get scared," she said in a tiny voice. She flashed Caraballo a quick, forced smile.

"Put that away, Connie," he hears Theresa say, the right side of her face resting on Curran's shoulder. Caraballo looks at her, and then down at the gun in his hand. He takes a quick look around as he shoves the weapon into the pocket of his baggy cargo shorts.

"Sorry," he said sheepishly. "I know they make you nervous."

Curran let go of the two women he was hugging. "Come on, let's go inside and see if anything's missing."

They went inside and scanned the overall house before going to the upstairs bedrooms. The third floor was comprised of three suites, each with their own bathroom, dressing room, walk-in closet, sitting area, and bedroom with cathedral ceiling and sliding glass doors that open to the oceanfront deck. The doors were heavy, hurricane rated triple insulated monsters that have multiple locks and a drop bar intended to make absolutely sure storm winds won't open them. They were all locked and the drop bars still in place. No one came in or out that way. The women found all the dresser drawers pulled out and dumped on the floor, with the empty drawers thrown on the bed in a pile. Curran returned the empty drawers to their rightful places, and Theresa and Mrs. DeFelice began the task of re-folding everything and stacking the items on their beds.

Curran paced the hallway on the west side between the rooms, making sure Theresa and Mrs. DeFelice knew he was still there by slowly whistling a tune. The Ballad of the Green Beret's; what else? He thought if this was just somebody looking for money, they looked in the usual places, but if this was some chicken shit attempt at intimidation, upsetting the family will only lead to his taking retribution on those that perpetrated the act.

After a short while, Theresa and her mother emerged from opposite ends of the long hallway, both carrying laundry baskets.

"Anything missing?" he asked.

"No," Theresa reported. Curran looked at Mrs. DeFelice.

"Me neither," she said.

"No jewelry, money, or laptops taken?"

"No," they said in stereo. "I had my laptop with me. Mom hasn't used her in weeks so it's in the safe."

Theresa stopped, looked at Curran and made a motion as if tucking his hair behind his ear. Of course, his hair is cut above his ear, so it's just something she does. She was unconsciously trying to feel normal after her space was violated. She looked at her mother.

"I have to buy new underwear," she said.

"Me too."

Curran noticed both baskets were full of women's undergarments. Theresa noticed his puzzled expression.

"I don't want to wear anything some stranger might have touched."

"Mine are just old," Mrs. DeFelice added. Curran smiled.

"So, your room gets ransacked, and you're self-conscious about having old underwear?" he said.

"Yep! And if I catch who did this, I'll make them eat a few pair. Dirty ones," she said defiantly. What a tenacious little woman. Then again, Curran was a bit uncomfortable talking about her underwear.

"Awesome," he said. He looks at Theresa. "Victoria's Secret here we come!" he said gleefully, playfully shoving two fists into the air.

"You're not going," she said bluntly. Curran dropped his arms and started a big, closed-mouth smile. His connection to Theresa showed in his eyes.

"Your truck's in my way," Mrs. DeFelice said. "We have girl shopping to do."

Without further delay, Curran shuffled the girls out of the house and into the big, black family Cadillac. Caraballo had a close word with Angelina before she joined the others, and the ladies set off to shop and clear their heads. The guys watched the car drive off before speaking.

"Oscar, why don't you go crash for a while. It looks like the medicine is kicking your ass."

"Roger that," Perez replied before trudging off to the guest room. Caraballo looked back at Curran.

"You're not going to dig it," he said.

"Dig what?"

"Dude, your stuff is totally fucked-up," Caraballo reported, an incredulous look on his face.

Curran marched straight inside and made a beeline across the room to the kitchen, turned a quick right-handed one-hundred-eighty and descended the L-shaped steps to the downstairs.

"What the hell," he blurted. In front of him was his small lure and sight fishing tackle box, looking like someone pulled it out to the middle of the floor and smashed it with an anvil. A few feet away, a toolbox normally kept in a nearby closet was pulled out from it. A short sledgehammer sat on top of the open box. Scanning the room, Curran found the sledgehammer's next victims. In the vertical rod racks attached to the wall, all the reels had been smashed off the rods, the reel seats torn completely off from a hard blow on the top. Five broken spinning reels sat in a pile on the floor. On the horizontal rod racks nearby, each reel was struck by the hammer on the side, crushing the cranking mechanism and bending the reel handles.

"Dude, what sort of man screws with another man's fishing gear?" Curran rhetorically asked.

"Considering it's *your* gear, it's a man with a death wish," Caraballo stated as he gazed at the dented reels on the wall. Curran stood, hands on hips, and told himself that getting mad would not change what is already done.

"This is personal, Connie," Curran proclaimed. His raised eyebrows showed his bewilderment.

"Sure is."

"No, I don't mean it upsets me personally, which it does," Curran said as he used his hands for added emphasis. "Tossing some drawers upstairs is random; smashing all my fishing gear is something directed right at me."

Caraballo contemplated Curran's words for a moment.

"So, either they were trying to send you a message, or they were sloppy in their activities."

"Both," Curran said. He stood pensively for nearly a minute. "Well, let's see what else is wrong," he added before turning and bounding back up the steps. He crossed through the dining room and turned left around the bottom of the stairs leading to the next floor, to the hallway leading to his and Caraballo's rooms. On this floor, there were two bedrooms on either side of a shared bathroom. His room was on the left and looked untouched. The bed was crisply made, the clothes in the drawers and closet appeared undisturbed.

His normal fishing sunglasses were on the top of his head, but the backup pair sat crushed and in pieces on the dresser.

"Damn it! I just got those,' He realized he didn't leave the mirrored sliding closet door open. It was pushed to the right, exposing the small hotel safe screwed to the closet floor. He knelt in front of it, entered a five-digit code and the safe door popped open. He looked through the contents and found everything there. He closed the safe and stood back up. When he slid the once hidden closet door closed, he noticed something written on the glass.

"Fuckface," he said, the word written in what appeared to be lipstick on the glass. "Looks like we're dealing with a brain surgeon," he added gruffly. "Did you get one?"

The two men left the room and walked past the bathroom into Caraballo's room, where the closet was open. Caraballo slid one mirrored closet door to the left to expose the other. A bright red word appeared.

"Dipshit," he said. He stood contemplating the last few minute's activities. He heard unique music playing outside and scanned through the nearby windows. "Ice cream man," he announced. Almost automatically, Curran and Caraballo walked silently out of the bedroom, down the steps, through the foyer near the dining room, across the inside porch, and out the front door. They walked down the front steps and moved across the sidewalk.

"Fuckface and Dipshit," Curran muttered.

"Fuckface and Dipshit getting some freaking ice cream!" Caraballo said boisterously.

"Oh yeah." Curran stuck out his right hand and Caraballo slapped it triumphantly

A little after 10pm, fire flickered from the ocean blue glass fire pit set inside a black circular table on the oceanside deck. The flames illuminated the faces of Curran, Caraballo, and Perez as they sat out on the front deck enjoying the cool air and the sounds of the ocean. They watched people walking by on the boardwalk between the house and the beach, thinking about where each group might be headed.

"You know what?" Curran asked, breaking the comfortable silence. "Between 1944 to 1970, the Army dumped thousands of tons of chemical weapons into the ocean all up and down the coast, including Alaska and California."

"Oh yeah?" Caraballo replied. Perez simply turned his attention to Curran.

"Yeah man. Tragic, short-sighted, idiotic, ignorant stuff only doable by the government and their misplaced benevolence, staggering greed, and incredible stupidity.

"I'm going to need another beer for this," Caraballo said. He went inside and retrieved three beers and a sweatshirt for Perez. "Here you go," he said, handing Perez the garment. "I see you shivering over here." He sat down. "Okay Tom."

Curran sat forward with his forearms on his thighs. He leaned-in to keep the conversation private. Think of this; mustard gas, nerve agents, phosgene, arsenic trichloride, white phosphorus, hydrogen cyanide, cyanogen chloride, and a nasty little chemical agent called Lewisite, all dumped out there," he said as he pointed toward the ocean.

"All that stuff?" Perez asked. "Right out there?"

"Well, not all of it," Curran replied as he leaned over on one cheek and pulled his little notebook out of his pocket. "I'll tell you about Jersey first," he added as he flipped the notebook open to the appropriate page. "Operation NJ1; In 1967, the Army began filling old Liberty-class ships with mustard and nerve gas ordnance and scuttling them off New Jersey in deep water.

"Scuttling?" asked Perez.

"Sinking. Most, but not all of the nerve gas was encased in concrete. They were called CHASE operations…, "Curran said making air quotes. "…for 'Cut Holes And Sink' Em,' was dubbed CHASE 8.

"First one named number eight? Sounds like the government," Caraballo jibed.

"June 15, 1967, the S.S. Cpl. Eric G. Gibson was sent to the bottom packed with 4,577 1-ton containers of mustard agent and 7,380 rockets filled with VX," Caraballo and Perez' eyes got real big. They knew VX was the deadliest of all nerve gases. "The Army said ship loaded at Colts Neck Naval Pier in Earle, N.J., and sunk in

7,200 feet of water off Atlantic City. Three years later, the wreck was tested environmentally, with no contamination detected.'"

"1967," Perez said. Curran nodded in the affirmative.

"An entire ship full of stuff," Caraballo said. "*Most* of it encased in concrete."

"Yes."

"That word 'most' bothers me. Has it been tested since 1970?"

"Not that I can tell."

"A time bomb sitting there for forty-five years."

"That's not all. It gets better," Curran said facetiously.

"Or worse," declared Perez.

"Operation NJ2. June 19, 1968, the S.S. Mormactern loaded at Colts Neck with 38 1-ton containers of liquid nerve agent.

"Barrels?"

"Sounds like it. Additional cargo included 1,460 concrete vaults of M55 rockets filled with nerve gas and 120 drums of arsenic and cyanide. Ship was sunk in 6,390 feet of water. The wreck was photographed on the ocean floor and sampled in 1972. No agent was detected in the water."

"Has *that* one been tested in the last forty-five years?" Caraballo asked.

"Not that I can tell. Operation NJ3," Curran continued, pausing to check his notes. "The next ship full of chemical weapons material they sank off New Jersey exploded on the way to the bottom," Curran reported. His words made Caraballo and Perez sit forward in their chairs. "Aug. 7, 1968, the S.S. Richardson was sunk with its hold filled with 3,500 one-ton containers of mustard agent mixed with water and an unknown quantity of conventional, high explosive ordnance. Army officials believe water pressure set off one piece, triggering a chain reaction."

"Sounds like bullshit," Caraballo determined.

"Yep. The Army went back in 69 and again in 1972 and couldn't find anything. No ship, no nothing. Not even a trace. Ironically, they found no water contamination."

All three men wag their heads side to side in the negative.

"What idiot decided to mix chemical weapons and high explosives?" growled Caraballo.

"How do you misplace an entire ship?" Perez asked rhetorically.   "Do you think they even tested the water?"

"No, I don't. I think the army was more worried about Vietnam in 69. I also read that in 1945, seven shiploads of munitions were thrown into the water off the Maryland/Virginia coast."

"Not inside sunken ships?"

"No, just dumped at sea. Some of these were Willy Pete cluster bombs, fifty-five thousand gallons of arsenic trichloride, and 23,000 chemical smoke rounds. I read the Coast Guard even helped with the dumping."

"It just keeps getting worse," Caraballo declared.

"Yeah it does. I read that between 1957 and 1962 they dumped almost 600 tons of an 'unknown' type of radioactive waste along with about a hundred tons of mustard gas and something called Lewisite."

"What's Lewisite?" Perez asks.

"The dew of death," Caraballo replied. "That's what they used to call it. It was added to mustard gas to help it penetrate protective suits, but it was nasty enough to do its own dirty work. They said when you smelled geraniums, it was your ass."

"Remember the story a few years ago about the guy that uncovered a mustard gas round in his yard in Delaware," Curran asked Caraballo. "It came as part of a delivery of crushed clamshells for his driveway. Apparently, the clam dredge dug up the shells in about 130 feet of water, about twenty miles off the coast of New Jersey."

"I remember that," Caraballo reported. "Nobody seemed to be particularly concerned about it."

"You think someone would wonder why that chem round was out there 20 miles off the coast. Only two ways to end up there, dumped by accident, or dumped on purpose."

"But Tom, those rounds were mustard. What we found wasn't mustard," asserted Caraballo.

"You're right," he agreed.

"How do you know?" asked Perez.

"Because mustard blisters you on the outside, and as we can see…" Caraballo said, elbow on the fire pit table, using an open hand to point to Perez, "…there are no marks on that pretty face of yours."

"Remember all the dead dolphins that washed up in North Jersey back in the 80's?" Curran asked.

"Yeah, hundreds of them."

"They all had wounds that looked like burns."

"They said it was a virus that made the wounds look that way, but no one admitted it was from chemical weapons!" Caraballo said frustratedly. Like any child of the 70's, he had a warm spot in his heart for Flipper.

"No one's going to do that."

"I know, see a thousand soldiers die on TV and people say, 'oh well, that sucks, is American Idol on,' but one innocent little dolphin washes up and people go freaking nuts," Caraballo said derisively. "So, is it possible the burn marks on the crabs and lobsters off North Jersey could be from chemical agents and not from the trash dumping New York does?" he added.

"It's possible. Do you know of any natural phenomenon short of the plague or even Ebola that could make almost eight-hundred dolphins wash up at once, all demonstrating the same pathology?" Curran questioned assertively, appealing to Caraballo's medical training.

"No. Most mass marine mammal deaths happen over a longer period of time or are much smaller in nature."

"And in your opinion," Curran calmly continued as if questioning Caraballo on the witness stand "Could we assume what we saw as a blue-green blob in the water and Perez saw on the Miss Margaret was some sort of nerve agent that somehow came up from the cold, deep blue?"

"In the absence of further information, yes."

"And if it washed up on the beach, say right here in crowded summer Sea Island, how many people would it drop before it was over?"

"Depending on the wind direction and how much came ashore, it's hard to predict. A grapefruit-sized piece might only take a platoon-size chunk of people, but washed-up all along the beach, a lot of it, who knows?" With his extensive military medical training, Caraballo considers the scenario. "It depends on the agent. If its mustard; mustard gas is a colorless, odorless liquid at room temperature that causes extreme blistering," Caraballo said calmly, almost like giving a briefing. "The name stems from its color and smell in its impure state. It's not related to the condiment mustard in any way. It's commonly referred to as a gas because the military designed it for use as an aerosol. Even slight exposure leads to deep, agonizing blisters that appear within four to 24 hours of contact. If it gets into the eyes, they swell shut, and blindness can result. If inhaled at high doses, the respiratory system bleeds internally, and death is likely. Exposure to more than 50 percent of the body's skin is usually fatal. It also causes cancer. But it's heavier than seawater, so if let out of a container, it would sink and roll around on the ocean floor with the prevailing current, and it only lasts about five years in seawater in a concentrated gel so not much chance for a mass casualty scenario.

"Mustard was some nasty stuff. I hear a bunch of stories about the troops in World War 1," commented Perez. "But I know there are others that are worse."

"True," Caraballo continued. "Phosgene was used during World War I, and then stored for years. It's a highly toxic gas that has no color but smells vaguely like moldy hay. It's sneaky too; exposure doesn't result in symptoms until 24 to 72 hours later. Skin contact won't kill you; it *must* be inhaled. The gas combines with water in the respiratory tract to form hydrochloric acid

"Acid in the lungs."

"Yep. The acid dissolves lung membranes. Fluid fills the lungs, and death comes from a combination of shock, blood loss and respiratory failure."

"Blood loss?" blurted Perez, horrified.

"Ever see the horror movies where the people vomit up blood and collapse on the ground?" asked Curran.

"Yep."

"Just like that."

"A Dios mio," Perez muttered.

"Then there's phosgene. It dissolves slowly in seawater, eventually converting to its chlorine base and dissipating. The issue is, it's not certain how long that takes, and if it's been stored in a container, it has a habit of becoming more toxic over time. Then there's white phosphorous. It's a colorless, waxy solid with a garlic-like odor. It reacts rapidly on contact with air, bursting into a flame that's difficult to put out. In contact with skin, it will smolder if covered, and when re-exposed to air will burst back into flames. The only way to stop it is to cut off the skin it's attached to. I've talked to doctors who said they cut open patients on the operating table that were hit by a white phosphorous bomb, and they burst into flames."

"Jeez, Louise," quipped Curran. "Good thing we never got any on us in the desert.

Caraballo went on.

"Breathing it in small doses can cause coughing or irritation of the throat. Eating or drinking it in even small amounts can cause stomach cramps, vomiting, drowsiness, and death. It's heavier than water, so it sinks to the bottom.

The Nazi's used hydrogen cyanide in their concentration camps under the infamous brand name 'Zyklon B.' It's either colorless or pale blue and has a faint almond-like odor. It's easily dispersed in the air and readily absorbed through skin contact or inhalation. At the cellular level, it cuts the body's ability to take in oxygen. In high doses the effects are quick and final; people gasp for breath, go into seizures, the cardiovascular system collapses followed by coma and death within minutes. The gas is flammable and potentially explosive. It's lighter than air, so if it was released in the sea, it would bubble to the surface. Dumped into the ocean, it would be in gas cylinders, so left unprotected, it would only be a matter of time before they corroded and ruptured."

"Could it form a blue-green blob?" asked Perez.

"Probably not."

"Go on, Curran directed.

"Cyanogen Chloride is a cyanide-based chemical weapon also used during World War I. It killed quickly and dispersed even faster. It was known as a blood agent, circulating quickly through the bloodstream on exposure through either inhalation or skin contact. It's was colorless and said to have a biting, pungent odor you never got the chance to smell because the agony hit you instantly. The skin quickly turned cherry red, seizures followed within 15 to 30 seconds, accompanied by vertigo and vomiting and death was likely in six to eight minutes."

"Well, I saved the best…or worst, for last," Caraballo exclaimed

"Worse than the dew of death?" asked Perez.

"Definitely. Nerve agent is the most-deadly chemical agent. One drop of nerve gas can kill a person within a minute. Death comes through seizure. It's colorless and odorless, and easily spread through the air. It attacks the human nervous system, causing almost-instant spasms before preventing involuntary muscle actions, including the heart pumping. The Germans developed it during World War II, and only a few countries are known to have any of it now."

"Could that make a blue-green blob?" Curran and Perez both said, almost in stereo.

"In its raw state it has the texture of motor oil, so years under the sea, possibly combining with seawater or other chemicals, plus aging and reacting to the cold, it's possible.

"Yeah, and if the government said it wasn't possible, I wouldn't believe them," Curran said

"I've seen the possibility first-hand," Perez added. "It's a cold blue killer.

"Definitely. So, what do you think the concrete boom was doing?

"I have a fairly good idea," Caraballo replied.

The three men sat for a few moments watching the flames flicker among the blue-colored stones of the fire pit.

Eventually Curran broke the silence. "I think we're all asking ourselves the same question," he said pensively, a hand rubbing his chin.

"What's the question?" Caraballo asked.

All eyes turn to Curran, sitting back in his chair, right elbow on the chair's arm, chin held between thumb and forefinger. "How big is this going to get?"

Caraballo and Perez nod in the affirmative.

"I was looking on the chart and the Miss Margaret was probably fishing closer to the Cape May Reef than where we found her, and the same goons that beat-up Baba tried to run us off, so this could be confined to that location.

"But we saw that school of dead fish right off Sea Island that morning, right after Theresa called you.

"Yeah, but that might not be connected. You know what's really scary?" Curran asked Caraballo and Perez.

"No. What?"

"In the reports I read, they said sixty-four *million pounds* of liquid mustard gas and nerve agent *alone* were dumped into the ocean." The vein down the side of Curran's neck began to protrude and match the one on his forehead. "The possible magnitude of this alone makes me think this is an isolated incident."

"How?" Caraballo asked incredulously.

"If this was a huge problem, with the possibility of mass casualties and all sorts of tragedy, there would have been no response at all. What happened to Baba and happened to us proves they knew about it and were in position to do something to keep it quiet."

Caraballo thought for a moment. "I get it," he said.

"Because if this was an impending disaster, the area would be so big there would be no point in trying to defend it all," Perez added.

"Exactly."

"So, the issues are; who are they, what did they do, what do they have to lose, what's Proctor's involvement, and is Radomir Kuvarac involved," Caraballo said, talking with his hands.

"Overall, yes, but first things first," Curran replied, using an index finger to punctuate the words.

"Meaning what?"

"What really happened to Baba's father.

Chapter 13

Perez awoke the following morning and padded around the house looking for signs of life. Unsuccessful, he went out on the deck, carefully managing to simultaneously put on his sunglasses, close the screen door behind him, and not spill any coffee out of the over-filled and undersized cup he was holding, the one with the finger loop too small for him to put his digit through.

He looked out at the boardwalk to find Curran standing, dripping wet, on the ocean side near the wooden steps to the beach, having just returned from a morning session with his stand-up paddleboard. Next to him was Caraballo in green running shorts, and a soaked green t-shirt, just having finished a morning run. Perez' chest still ached from the day before, but the rest and oxygen helped, and the stress level was low. He wondered what was in store for the day.

Minutes later, all three met on the deck for coffee and sticky buns.

"Where's Ma?" Perez asked?

"Went back to Philadelphia for a few days," Curran reported.

"Break-in, right?"

"Yep. I recommended they go back until we update the security status of the house and get ready to bring the kids down the shore at the end of soccer camp.

"Freaking soccer camp," Caraballo muttered under his breath. Curran and Perez heard him and smiled at each other.

"Buck-up there, Francis," Curran jibed as he slapped Caraballo on his muscular arm. "We'll wrap this thing up by the time the kids get back, then take them fishing and crabbing, out on the beach, to the boardwalk and all that."

"Freaking soccer camp," he repeated, watery-eyed, looking at Curran.

"I know you miss him, dude. He'll be back soon," Curran said as he gave Caraballo a light thump on his chest below the collar bone. Caraballo missed his son Terry and wanted him home. Theresa had put all three kids in soccer camp before he even had a chance to object.

"What's next boss?" Perez asked.

"We're going to un-ass the house and stick by the hangar. I want to see if anyone comes sniffing around here again. I need you to do some very specific internet searches in a very targeted way that I'll tell you about when we get there. Then I have to go to see something."

Later, a man walked into the emergency room entrance of the Southern Cape Memorial Hospital down in Cape May Court House, New Jersey off Garden State Parkway Exit Ten. People say if you anyone in New Jersey where they're from thy give you an exit number, not a town. Usually the exits are from the New Jersey

Turnpike or Garden State Parkway. Ask anyone the location of Sea Island, and instead of naming the shore islands that bracket it north and south, they say exit seventeen.

The man walked purposefully into the hospital's emergency room entrance wearing a doctor's white lab coat with black t-shirt underneath, black pants, and black running shoes. He adjusted the 80's style black glasses on his face and crinkled his nose at the strong smell of antiseptic. It was odd to see a doctor walk in off the street to the Emergency Department rather than the main entrance or outpatient clinic, but no one seemed particularly puzzled or even interested. Embroidered on the white lab coat's pocket was the name 'M. Martinelli.' He walked up to the reception counter and peered through the window at a small, pale, seriously fat receptionist who sat drinking an iced Wawa coffee in a 32-ounce plastic cup.

"Hello, I'm hoping you can help me," the doctor said cordially. The woman gave him a blank stare as if an upright wall of drying paint just walked in. The doctor stood still and waited.

The fat woman eventually set the giant plastic cup on the counter between them and uttered a muffled "humpf." She adjusted the strap on her overly tight and tragically non-flattering camisole top, then straightened the nametag affixed to it. Cheri…with an I.

"Can I help you?" she said brusquely, as if bothered by the man.

"Yes, I'm hoping to talk to someone in medical records regarding a patient of mine."

The woman paused, seeming to need a moment to decipher his words.

"Records?" she said impatiently. She reached for her drink but reached too slowly. The doctor snatched the iced coffee from the counter and pulled it to himself. The woman's eyes grew wide with incredulity, her glare transmitted "how dare you" to the doctor.

"That's right, records," the doctor said. He tilted his face down, his lips wrapped around the plastic straw, and he took a long pull of his newly acquired beverage. He stared directly into the woman's eyes as he drank. She breathlessly stared back at him for a moment.

"Take the double doors on your left, down the hallway to the end. Someone there will help you," she said begrudgingly.

The doctor sucked-in hard on the straw. With six big swallows, he emptied the drink, and then slapped the empty plastic cup on the counter.

"Thanks," he said. "That hit the spot."

The doctor turned to the right, moves around the reception area, passes through a set of double doors, and begins walking down the hallway. He still had the taste of coffee in his mouth, and it made him think of a movie he once saw where a man asked for a sip of a big soda and drank the entire thing. He started to chuckle as he walked.

He reached the records section, a window set in front of a room filled with huge floor-to-ceiling file shelves on tracks with what appeared to be bright stainless-steel steering wheels at the end of each one. On the right side of the room, five rows of cabinets sat jammed against each other. From there, spread across the room to the other side were five more rows separated with room enough to walk between them. The shelved bulged to near bursting with multi-colored medical file folders. The antiseptic smell of the emergency department gave way to the aroma of paper files and carpet glue. Behind a counter made from the closed bottom half of a door, a small blonde woman sat turning pages in a file, two fingers on her right hand covered in what appeared to be small condoms. They may be to guard against paper cuts, but it made the doctor smile anyway.

"Can I help you?" the woman said cheerfully.

"Yes ma'am," the smiling doctor replied. "I must say, you seem much friendlier than the woman in E.R."

"Oh, her," the woman scoffed. "She has that attitude because she thinks she's pretty even though she's so fat."

"Probably so; I'm here to see the medical records of a former patient of mine please."

"Patient's name?"

"Robert P. O'Reilly, senior."

Without asking for further information, she stood and walked to the file racks. After moving to the third rack from the right wall, she grabbed the wheel mounted at the end and started turning it counterclockwise. It's slow going, each revolution only moving the cabinet row about three inches. The twenty-foot long row of shelves moves left along with the two next to it. The woman kept cranking away.

"Those must be some kind of gears," the doctor thought to himself. "The Titanic would have come clean around by now."

"That's far enough," she said audibly. She disappeared into the space between the shelves.

"That must be some workout!" he said loudly.

"It's actually quite easy; it just takes a while," she replied, concealed behind the medical files. A moment later she returned empty-handed. "I'm sorry. They aren't there. How long was he a patient of yours?"

"The record should be about eight months old."

"Then it should be here," the woman said abruptly. "Let me look again."

The woman returned to the shelves and searched with quite the sense of alarm. It was clear she took her work seriously. A few minutes later she returned.

"Let me take a look at something," she said as she sat in her chair and rolled it to the left in front of a computer terminal. She hammered away at the keyboard with the ferocity of popping popcorn, but every few seconds were punctuated by short silence and a slight 'hmm,' muttered just loudly enough for Doctor Martinelli to hear. "The file was scanned to electronic record and the paper file destroyed," she announced.

"When?"

"Almost eight months ago," she reluctantly confessed, her face twisted in confusion. She returned to hammering at the keyboard, her activity only punctuated by mouse clicks and single stabs at a function key. "It's not here," she exclaimed, seemingly astonished by her unsuccessful computer search.

"It's not there?"

"No.

"Is it normal to destroy files so soon after the patient was in the hospital?"

"No."

"Where else can I find the record?"

"Copies would normally go to his personal physician." An aura of suspicion rose in the room. "You are his doctor, aren't you?"

"Yes I am. Not the one that saw him when he got the sniffles or stubbed his toe. He saw me for more important matters," the doctor said seriously. "Can't really discuss it."

The woman stood, sizing him up. She knew the law dictated she can't really ask personal medical questions about one Robert P. O'Reilly, senior.

"I recommend checking with his family doctor."

"Copies of his in-patient record would go to his family doctor. Emergency Room records would not. Besides, the patient died here so there should be a death record, morg admittance and disposition of remains. The record should still be here," the doctor proclaimed. Revealing the patient was dead is something she didn't expect.

"Doctor, I don't know what to tell you?" she said. "Hold-on," she blurted, shoving a finger in the air followed by a phone to her ear.

The doctor pauses for a moment, followed by giving her a reassuring smile and slight nod. He can hear she called the morg and asked for any record of Robert P. O'Reilly. A moment later, with a downtrodden facial expression, the woman hung-up the phone and looked up at him.

"Sorry, the morg has no record either," she said in a "see, it's not just me" tone.

"It's okay," he said. "Losing a file would be a problem for you," he added, turning the tables on her. "I won't say anything. Once I leave, I'll forget we ever met."

"Thank you, doctor," she said sheepishly.

Doctor M. Martinelli turned and walked back down the hall, through the double doors to the Emergency Department, and across the emergency room reception area. Noticing the fat woman behind the window, he just couldn't help himself. "Thanks for the coffee!" he said with a wave of his hand and a pointed finger at her. He pressed the button on the automatic exterior doors and walked through them out to the ambulance loading dock. He removed his eyeglasses and replaced them with green-mirrored black wrap-around style sunglasses.

As an ambulance from nearby Stone Harbor pulled into the ambulance area, the doctor walked down the sidewalk, crossed the parking lot, and stopped at the back of a blue OJ-style Ford Bronco. He popped the hatch, lowered the tailgate, removed his white lab coat, folded it, and placed it inside a black leather bag. He raised the tailgate, lowered the hatch, scanned the area around him for a moment, then walked around and climbed in the truck. He started the engine, sat back and relaxed. After a moment, he shifted the trucks transmission into gear and made his way out of the lot. "I gotta get one of those iced coffees," he thought to himself. He pulled out his cell phone and hit speed dial as he drove north up the back road toward the municipal airport.

"Hey, it's me," Curran said. "Want anything from the Wawa?"

Curran returned to the hangar with three iced coffees and handed them to the other guys. He found Caraballo cleaning a large caliber sniper rifle in front of one of the steel cabinets against the wall on the first floor. The doors were open, and a small table was set in front.

"Why are doing that?" Curran said quietly, handing him a coffee. It was odd since Perez was the team sniper.

"I worked on some medical gear first and when I cleaned my Sig Oscar asked me to," Caraballo reported. He was first to sample the brew

"God," he exclaimed as he spat out the coffee, bending forward as if protecting himself from dripping battery acid. "Shit that's awful," he grimaced.

"Coffee snob," Curran jibed, smiling. He sipped his own.

"That'll work," Perez added, setting his cup next to his laptop after sampling it.

"I'll show you what iced coffee should taste like," Caraballo said before bounding up the steps to the kitchen.

Curran turned to Perez.

"What time are you showing?"

"1421 Sir," Perez replied, looking at his black rubberized, oversized watch. It's a game Curran plays with him. On missions, the team all wears the device with its GPS capability, rifle scope and communications wireless telemetry. It's an expensive and very specialized piece of kit. When not on mission, Curran changes either to a fake Rolex he bought in the United Arab Emirates, or a G-Shock he can wear surfing. Perez never changes his watch.

"Status on Fillippi and Mr. King?" Curran asked regarding the two remaining permanent members of the team.

"Flip's in California with the new girlfriend, and Mr. King is in the Caribbean with his wife."

"Yep, count them out. Fillippi's in all new territory with that one and once you get Sharon to one of those all-inclusive resorts, forget it."

"I know what you mean."

"Okay, so did you get anything from your computer searches?"

"I had an interesting hour or so. Yourself?" Perez asked

"Enlightening," Curran said before reaching behind himself, lifting-up his black t-shirt and removing a Marine Corps Fighting Knife still in the sheath. He placed the knife on the top of a workbench nearby and turned back to Perez, noticing the odd look he was getting. Perez watched him intently, as if his comment and the knife have some sort of connection, waiting with what could be best described as 'baited-breath.' "So many modern weapons out there, but I still like the classics," Curran added.

"Did you use that thing today?" Perez asked.

"Only to cut a hoagie. What do you have?'

"Spooks love to drive grey Crown Vics."

"Spooks plural?" asks Curran.

"Yeah, I used a proxy server in the Arlington Virginia library and a terminal ID for a computer there. Using that list you gave me it was only thirty minutes until the first one came in."

"Came in?"

"Yeah, he was looking for someone else." Perez pressed a button on the laptop and the screen divides into the computer on the left, a camera view in the upper right, and a different camera in the lower right. "Now here comes subject number one; pulled right in and walked right in, scanning the room like he's looking for somebody and being far too obvious," Perez narrated, showing a man arriving in his car in the top right of the laptop screen, then walking into the library below.

"Looks like your basic, white bread, nondescript, plain wrapper government knucklehead not unlike MacPherson's new assistant, a white guy keeping his sunglasses on indoors," Curran described.

"He sat down near the periodicals but chose a copy of Vogue off the rack."

"A cherry spook."

"Yeah, but it appears he was looking for his boyfriend. See right here," Perez said, pointing at the screen. "Now here comes the other one," he added, pointing again.

"Same stupid obvious car, but this guy is a bit better. Look at the time lapse." Perez hit fast-forward on the video to show that after parking in the slot closest to the library door, the man sat in the car for over twenty minutes. "Now here he comes."

In the video, the man walked into the library as if he was a patron. Same white bread, nondescript, plain wrapper government shithead type, just a little older, thinner, salt-and-pepper graying hair, with no sunglasses to hide his dull eyes, weak chin, and lackluster expression. H

"He walked to the computerized card catalog and acted like he was searching for a book. He looked around the room as he pretended to wait for the computer to process his request. After that, he walked past the terminal I tagged and over to the far end of the library. There, he took his time in the fiction area. After that he came back, this time acting like he was interested in the numerous pieces of art displayed throughout the library. He actually walked behind the dude sitting in front of the computer I was running. The guy on it didn't know anything; my stuff was running in the background. The spook checked out the screens of my guy and the five others at the circular table where the pay-by-the-minute internet computers are; recognize him?"

"Get me a still shot," Curran directed. Perez scrolled though some video footage and stopped when he had a full headshot of the unknown government man. Perez caught the man trying to use a mirror to disguise his looking around the room. Perez zoomed-in on the mirror image.

"Yeah, I know that guy."

"Who is he."

"A flunky for somebody further up the food chain. Deep-state types. And this guy had the brassies to stand and look at the screen?

Yeah. Check it out. I got his reaction on the webcam," Perez said. On the left size of Perez' laptop is the computer screen in the Arlington Library. On the top right is the webcam. On the computer is a pair of cartoon breasts. The breasts are small at first, then pulsate, followed by growing into enormous 3-dimensional boobs, followed by shrinking down to their original size, this activity repeating itself. As the breasts grew larger, the eyes of the unidentified man grew larger and his head went back as if the breasts in question were coming at him. Curran and Perez chuckled.

"Jackass," Curran muttered. Then what?"

"Look at that shit!" Caraballo interjected. He stood ready to hand Curran and Perez two glasses of his own homebrew iced coffee. "Everybody's on their damn phones!" he added. Curran grabbed the two glasses from him and set one down next to Perez.

"Where's our guy?" Curran asked, redirecting the conversation.

"He's sitting near the periodicals, using a spoofing program on his laptop to figure out what the guy at my computer was looking at."

"Did you throw him any breadcrumbs?"

"Sure did. I looked up a few more of the things you put on the list...and some of it is pretty troubling I might add." After a while I spoofed him back. I read his registry data, but I doubt we'll find a Wyle E. Coyote working in DC.

"WIFI is so unsecure," Caraballo said.

"Then what?" Curran interjected.

"He went right out and sat in his car a while."

"What about you?"

"I searched a few more things unrelated to the issue, and..."

"Searching porn again," joked Caraballo. Perez paused; he's not a porn guy.

"And I hacked into his cell phone's tracking software and put a tag on it.

"He didn't seem too interested in the guy on the computer, did he?" Curran asked.

"No, I think he knew he'd been had when I interrupted the kid on the computer's Fantasy Football session to flash the titties at them."

"I'm glad you did that. Maybe we'll get some action out of this guy now.

"Why did they, whoever they are, even send someone?" Caraballo asked. "There are more surveillance cameras in the DC area than anywhere else in the world, enough surveillance cameras to make that unnecessary. Besides, NSA can monitor all the computers in the country at the same time"

"Accessing cameras normally takes some doing, and computer monitoring won't show you who's on it unless you can activate the internal camera or a camera you know is nearby and you have recognition software. That usually takes a search warrant," Curran said. Or someone skilled like Oscar.

"These people don't care about search warrants," Caraballo replied.

"I know," Curran replied before taking a sip of his Caraballo-brand iced coffee. He smiled. "Now that's some good stuff."

"Told you."

"That'll work," Perez added.

Curran turned to Perez and changed the subject. "What do you have on our boy?" he asked, referring to Radomir Kuvarac.

"The marina firewall is a piece of crap, so I was in right away. We have two solid days of activity."

"What did you get?"

"He's the nervous type, but he seems to be acting like he works on that boat. He's been sleeping on it too," Perez reported, having downloaded the video from the marina and surrounding area.

"Any movement around Avalon or Stone Harbor?"

"Only to the Wawa and back to the boat."

"Any movement off the island?"

"No."

"Visitors?"

"None. The only other guy around him is that Filipino."

"Signals?" Curran asks. This is short for Signals Intelligence, meaning intercepting mobile phone conversations, emails, text messages, radio communications, and talks the subject was having.

"It took me a few minutes to break the rust off my Slavic, but Croatian is easier than the others. He's a Serb but has the dialect of southern Bosnia. He spoke to his mother a couple times, but no other calls."

"Proctor didn't call him?"

"No."

"Positive I.D. on the mother?"

"Roger. It was a Skype video call over the internet. She's had a hard life. You can see it in her face. I only have one issue."

"What is it?"

"She was well dressed, tall and lean, and the room she was in was decorated in Parisian style. There were sounds of car horns and an ambulance outside the window that make me think she was in France."

"So what?" Caraballo says. "Bosnia was a shit-heap when we were there. I would move my mother too."

"Emails?" Curran asks, trying to drive through the briefing.

"None."

"Personal contacts?"

"Negative. He's a pretty solitary guy. He didn't have any casual conversations with anybody around the marina, he doesn't small talk with convenience store clerks or the girls in the marina store or the gas dock. He had nothing delivered, no calls, didn't drive anywhere, and spent most of his time polishing the boat."

"Internet searches?"

"No. He only used the computer to contact his mother."

"He's lying low," Caraballo said.

"Anything out of the ordinary?"

"He washed something in the marina laundry room each day. The same dude went in there while he was in there both times. Looks western-European like Kuvarac. Works for a company called 'Titan Hatcheries.'"

"What's that?"

"The Titan chemical company seems to have a fish hatchery internet says they've been releasing juveniles in South Jersey to counteract the population crash caused by Japanese demand for eels and local overfishing for the others."

"Really?" Curran replied. "I didn't know that."

"Apparently it's been up and running for ten years."

"Far out. Who's the guy?"

"Don't know yet but it could be a contact; I have a facial recognition search in progress, so I'll know more soon."

"Okay, we'll have to stay on him. See if you can get a profile on the owner of the Miss Margaret. We also need to shadow Mr. Proctor. In addition, we need to look into the death of Robert O'Reilly's father and the loss of their boat."

Chapter 14

Later in the afternoon, a slim, white-haired old woman was led into the lobby of the Doubletree Hotel on South Broad and Locust streets in Philadelphia. Her dark, rather enormous bodyguard stayed at the door as she moved toward a red velvet, kidney-shaped settee nearby. Her royal blue dress hung on a bony body weathered by the years, but her regal walk suggested a woman of stature. She wore a necklace of large white pearls shaped like macadamia nuts and carried a small, black patent leather clutch that matched her short black patent leather pumps. She sat and waited, hands crossed, placed on her lap atop her purse.

A short while later, a nondescript black Lincoln town car with deeply tinted windows pulls to the curb out front, the door opened immediately by a waiting bell captain. A rather unimpressive man emerged, grey haired, dressed in a black suit, white shirt, pale blue tie; gold ring on his finger with a Masonic symbol in a black field, matching cuff links, gold Rolex that looked real enough. He moved casually into the expansive lobby, hardly noticing the gargantuan bodyguard standing at the door. He walked directly to the settee where the old woman sat. He sat next to her, about two feet separating them, and retrieved a copy of the USA Today newspaper from the small coffee table in front of him. He opened it to the middle, glanced at the page, casually crossed one leg, and turned the paper to the next page as he scanned the room from behind it.

"We have a situation," he said lowly. The woman didn't reply. "This might turn into something we can't control."

"And the sea gave up her dead and death and hell delivered up the dead that were in them, and they were judged everyone according to their works," the woman said nonchalantly as she stared out the window, her eyes fixed on the traffic outside.

"Revelations 20:13," the man replied.

"We all knew we would eventually pay for what we've done," she said flatly.

"Your family more so than others."

A pause as the woman watched the traffic inside the lobby. She removed a white handkerchief from her purse and dabbed her chin. She returned the cloth to her purse, closes it, and folded her hands back on top.

"What do you intend to do?" she asked.

"Contain what we can. Lay the blame on others where we can't. What else?'

"Bread of deceit is sweet to a man, but afterwards his mouth shall be filled with gravel," she said." Proverbs 20:17.

"Then be careful; done right, none of this will come back to you."

"Be not a witness against thy neighbor without cause, and deceive not with thy lips," she added. Proverbs 24:28.

"It will be handled delicately. Nothing will be publicly declared," he said.

"Have you already started?"

"Yes."

Another pause as the woman contemplated the man's words.

"Let me know when it's over," she said.   Without turning to the man, she rose, smoothed the sides of her dress, and walked to the door. Her bodyguard held it open and she glided through it, following her out. They both turned left down the sidewalk and disappeared, the sight of them blocked by the building. Inside, the man turned another page of the newspaper.

Curran sat back in the oversized reclining chair on the second floor of the hangar, dozing a bit as he thought about current events. He thought about the day a few weeks ago when he and Caraballo dropped in on Baba.

Curran drove over the bridge into Sea Island after flying up for the weekend in Caraballo's Cessna. Summer hadn't started yet and the town was only half-full. At the highest point of the bridge, his vantage point gave him a view across the island to the ocean. He noticed the waves were disorganized and mushy in the afternoon southwesterly breeze. Curran turned right on the first road after the bridge, then another right into the marina area.

"Dude, where are you going?" Caraballo inquired.

"I want to talk to Baba real fast."

"What for?"

"Just to check on him. I told you his old man died at sea while he was in Afghanistan."

"Yeah, you did," Caraballo replied, irritated.

They passed Baba's van parked next to the ramp leading to the dock. Curran pulled in on the other side of it facing the canal bulkhead, right in the middle, at the spot where commercial boats ended, and recreational boats started.

"Time to go play with this goldbrick," Caraballo said derisively as he opened his door and slid out. What one generation calls 'goldbrick,' another might call slacker.

Curran turned off the motor, stepped out of the truck and shut the door. His ears picked-up a strange noise.

"You hear that?" he asked as Caraballo rounded the back of the truck. Curran stood with his left ear tilted toward Baba's van. Caraballo stopped in his tracks. Both men pause.

"No," Caraballo replied.

Suddenly, they hear a muffled scream.

"I heard that," he said.

The scream turned repetitive, a terrified, grinding, agonizing, horror-movie style scream.

"It's coming from the van," Curran declared before moving with a purpose toward the van's right-side door. He cupped his hands against the glass to cut the glare and tried to look inside.

"See anything?" Caraballo asked.

"No."

The screaming turned louder, the burst from a set of lungs more pronounced. Caraballo tried the door handle; locked. The two men moved quickly around the other side to the sliding door. Caraballo tried that door. Also locked. Then, with a mighty heave, he broke the lever-type door handle clean off. Holding the handle in his powerful left hand, he looked at Curran with a disgusted expression like 'stupid weak door handle.'

"Okay Hulk," Curran said mockingly. "Let's try the back."

The two men rounded the back of the van with the screaming still going on inside.

"I got it," Curran said, waving off his friend. He tried the door; locked. He removed his wallet from the side pocket of his black surfing shorts. He looked quizzically at Caraballo, slightly chuckled, still tickled by his choice of fashion, a predominantly yellow and red tie-die tank top with a picture of Bob Marley on it, and the faded sage green shorts he seems to live in. Curran pulled a small metal device from his wallet.

"You always carry your lock picks?" Caraballo asked.

"This one I do," Curran replied, carefully inserting the pick into the van's door. With a coordinated combination of left-hand movement of the lock pick and right hand jiggling the rear door handle, the door popped open. The screams were instantly louder. Curran slid the lock pick back in his wallet and the wallet back into his pocket, and then he and Caraballo opened the back doors as wide as they could go. In front of them on the van's fold-down bed, Baba was flat on his back, head toward the door, screaming at the top of his lungs.

"Dude!" Curran barked, grabbing Baba on the shoulder, and giving him a good shake. Baba's hands jolted vertically as if he was ready to catch a basketball.

"Dude," Curran repeated a bit more easily. Baba started to wake; the screams diminished with each exhalation. Curran leaned into the van in order to let Baba see him without having to arch backward. "Hey man, you okay?" he asked.

"Tommy?" he said, bewildered.

"Yeah. How you doing?"

Baba wiped his face with a hand, rubbed his eyes with both, and sat up. He moved forward and tried to open the sliding door; locked. He tried harder and got the same result. He turned and looked at Curran and Caraballo, his eyes wide open as big as two saucers. He had the look of a cornered animal, trapped, with no way out.

"Come on! Come this way!" Curran directed, using a hand motion to urge Baba toward the back. He had seen that look before, the one shared by soldiers caught in tight spaces, or under fire with no means of escape. "Come on, come out the back," Curran pleaded. It's probably easier for Baba to just hop out one of the front doors, but the back was open, he could see daylight, and he made a dash for it. Baba clambered over the bed, caught his knees in the comforter on top, and lurched head-first out the back doors. Curran and Caraballo caught him by the shoulders, grabbed him under the arms, and guided him out. Baba swung his feet down and put them on the ground. Once on firm footing, Baba stood erect, his chest heaving from a combination of sudden onset claustrophobia and slight embarrassment. Taller than Curran, and much taller than Caraballo, he looked downward sheepishly. Both men steadied Baba with a grip on the upper arm.

"Looks like our friend here has a little PTSD to go with that Silver Star," Curran announced, as he watched Baba for a reaction. He didn't get one. Baba swayed like a lone palm tree in the breeze, his brain busy trying to shut the mental trap that let the demons out while he slept. Post-Traumatic Stress Disorder can take on many forms. For Baba it seems it was in the form of nightmares. Curran understood; for years after being trapped in a pitch-black underground bunker in Iraq, and having to fight his way out, the nightmares came fairly regularly. He looked at Caraballo.

"Silver Star?" Caraballo mouthed silently. He didn't know about it. Curran gave him a nod to the affirmative before he looked around his general vicinity and noticed a flip-down seat about bumper level at the back of the van. The seat was raised in the up position. He flipped it down.

"Hey, sit here, bro," Curran said.

Blindly, Baba let Curran and Caraballo guide him over to the seat.

"Dude, do you sleep with your flip-flops on?" Caraballo inquired. He noticed Baba was wearing his leather sandals. It drew a small grin from the troubled man.

"It's kind of automatic," he said. "I swing my feet down right into them without thinking about it."

"Kind of like you with those green shorts, dude," Curran said. Caraballo nodded.

"Ah, quit bustin' my balls," he replied. His eyes scanned back and forth between the other two men. "What say we run out to the Wawa?" he added.

"Yeah, he could use some pork roll and cheese," Curran declared, referring to the Wawa bagel sandwich. "You probably need more coffee by now, right?"

"For sure, but I brought it. I could dig a soft pretzel though."

"In a minute; let's let him get his legs under him."

"Tom, what song am I thinking of right now?" Caraballo asked.

"Gorillaz, Clint Eastwood," Curran answered.

"How do you do that?" Caraballo blurted, absolutely amazed.

"Too easy, 'I'm useless, but not for long, the future is coming on.' What else would you be thinking right now?"

"I guess it has nothing to do with hearing it on the way over here?"

"Maybe," Curran said coyly. "But definitely nothing to do with that tank top."

Chapter 15

"Feel like taking a late afternoon flight?" Curran asked Caraballo as the two men lounged in the hangar's upstairs living room. It wasn't really a question.

"Always. Where to?"

"I'm curious if the big salvage boat with the concrete boom is still out there, and if there are any more schools of dead fish."

"Let's go," Caraballo said as he made his way past Curran to the steps leading down. "Bring a couple bottles of water," he added as he reached the bottom and turned for the other hangar.

Shortly before dark, the aircraft returned. After the post flight check, the two men pushed the airplane tail-first into the hangar and shut the big hangar door. They crossed back into the hangar on the end and Curran went straight to a map of the area hung on the front of one of the big metal cabinets lining the far wall. Nearby, Perez sat in a green resin busily cleaning weapons, with gun cleaning supplies and Curran's handgun on another chair set in front of him.

"We saw the weird salvage boat," Caraballo reported.

"Strange?"

"Where was it?" asks Perez.

"Almost in the same place as last time. On the Deepwater Reef where we saw the crab boat with the ROV."

"Did you get a look at what they were doing?"

"Looked like pouring concrete," Caraballo said matter-of-factly.

"Secret concrete," Curran said facetiously. "Secret spooky concrete; they had two RHIB's out there this time."

"Did you see the boat with the ROV?"

"No"

"See anything else?"

"No."

"Let me see the photos," Curran directed as he removed the map from the cabinet and set it on the table in the middle of the room. Perez returned to his place behind the laptop.

Caraballo handed him the camera. Curran popped the memory card from it and handed it to Perez, who slid it into the port on the laptop. Curran moved to a spot behind Curran to look at the pictures.

"Most of these are from the other day," Curran reported. The first photo appeared.

"Same boat in almost the same position as the other day," Caraballo said, looking at the picture.

They scrolled through the rest of the pictures, going slowly enough to examine the detail of each one. After twenty minutes, only the aroma of the fresh coffee Caraballo was making distracted him from his task. Curran had Perez save the pictures on a thumb drive and remove the camera's memory card.

"Oscar," I need to borrow your expertise," Curran said, standing up from the computer while holding out a hand as if saying 'your turn' to Perez. "I'd like to know where those fishing boats call home, who *paid* for them to pick-up *dead* fish, what the orders are for that salvage boat, and what happened to the crab boat with the research container on it.

"Is that all," Perez said playfully.

"No. Where did the boat loads of dead fish *go*?" Curran adds.

"Piece of cake, Sir. With a little help from our NSA friends," he added sarcastically as he plugged the thumb-drive into the USB port, "that should take me about fifteen minutes."

Curran walked to the small refrigerator nearby and retrieved a bottle of water. He set it on the nearby workbench and added a small packet of iced tea mix to it. While doing so, he heard Perez easily tapping on the laptop keyboard. Curran stepped to a small computer monitor held inside an open pelican container and switched through all the surveillance video feeds in the area, the airport perimeter, rows of hangars, approach road, parking lot, security gates, etc., stopping to look at the sleepy little airport office, noticing nothing moving except the tall grass near the small building. Perez' activity takes on a staccato canter, and the taps become heavier key strikes.

"Boss, we might be screwed," he said. His fingers worked feverishly over the keys. Curran turns toward him as Caraballo enters from the other hangar having heard his comment. Perez stopped, hammered a number of keys, and continued. "Not only have they shut off our access, but they're banging on the firewall," Perez added. "I'm trying to backtrack and see who's doing it,"

"Turn it off."

"I got it. I got it."

"Do it quickly," Curran directed. The sound of fingers hammering computer keys filled the room.

"One second; almost got it."

"Turn it off." Curran repeated, walking calmly to the table. He touched the laminated map with the tip of one finger.

"Almost! Got it!" Perez declared before simultaneously popping the sim card and battery out of the computer as he disconnected the satellite uplink.

"When we log on, they know it's us, right?" Curran said, not really a question.

"Roger. Nothing we haven't done a hundred times."

"Did you trace it back?"

"Roger.

"Fort Meade?"

"Roger."

"How far did you get?"

"To their firewall, but that's it.

Curran nodded, knowing that's as far as could be expected. They're warriors, not computer hackers. Well, Perez might be, but his outward appearance hides it completely.

"Cutting the connection is a bit suspect but trying to hack into our laptop flat-out bothers me," Curran said. "WE use that system all the time. Why would they come back on us like that?"

"I don't know."

"You know why I said turn it off, right?"

"So they don't get anything we have saved on the hard drive."

"That's right."

"I wiped it clean an hour ago. Saved what we had to our external drive...but I probably should have told you that."

"No. Good man. Sempre pensando, Senior," Curran said.

"Semper Paratus, Sir," Perez replied, smiling.

"Nothing like a government agency born out of failure to screw with you," Caraballo said derisively, referring to the NSA.

During World War II, the U.S. Government created the Signal Security Agency (SSA) with the intent of intercepting and deciphering the communications of the Axis powers. When the war ended, the SSA was re-designated the Army Security Agency under the control of the Pentagon intelligence office. A few years later, after the intelligence bureaucracy had a chance to grow, the Armed Forces Security Agency (AFSA) was formed in the hopes of centralizing all the communications and electronic intelligence activities under one agency…ironically, *except* those of the United States military intelligence units. AFSA proved unable to centralize communications intelligence and failed to coordinate with or link their information with civilian agencies that shared similar interests, namely the US State Department, Central Intelligence Agency, and the FBI. In 1951, President Truman ordered a panel to investigate how AFSA failed to achieve its goals. The results of the investigation led to revamping the way they did things and re-designation as the National Security Agency.

"Well, at least new school proved something's going on," Curran said, using his fingers to make "air quotes" around the term "new school."

"Yep, you don't deny your brother use of your computer unless you don't want him finding out something," Caraballo replied.

"Roger that," Curran and Perez said in stereo.

"Well, we can use Theresa's external hard drive for a few more internet searches…"

"It's clean," Perez commented

"Right," Curran responded. "But other than that, we're doing it old-school."

"Finally!" Caraballo barked, as if anticipating something.

"What?" Curran asked.

"It's way past time we got to kick somebody's ass."

"Well, I have a feeling there won't be any shortage of candidates for that."

"I'm in," Perez adds.

Curran went upstairs and retrieved Theresa's external drive. He came back down with it and put it on the table next to the map. "Now let's see what Theresa was talking about," he muttered softly.

Twenty minutes go by; Caraballo finished cleaning the kitchen, Perez was busy bore-sighting the weapons. Outside, a light rain began to fall, cooling the night air.

Suddenly Curran sat bolt upright in his chair. He grabbed the laptop and moved swiftly around the table, stopping in front of the map. "North, north, north," he said as he traced a finger across the map. "East, east, east," he added as he moved the finger to the right. Then he looked up at Perez and Caraballo. "Right between the shipping lane and the Deepwater Reef," he stated.

"What's up?"

"Theresa said she found something and she's right. Right here where my finger is; Oscar, throw me that grease pencil." Curran marked the spot on the map and stepped back far enough to stand straight. "She found the location reported by the Coast Guard where Mr. O'Reilly's boat sank. It's about thirty miles out, right between the shipping lane and the Deepwater Reef, closer to the east-west channel coming out of Delaware Bay."

"That's interesting," Caraballo acknowledged.

"Why is that?" asked Perez.

"Because the activity we saw the other day and again today was all in the same area. Theresa found out that the official record of the location of the rescue of Baba's father, as reported to the state police, was about a hundred miles northeast, but the location entered on the Coast Guard's official transcript was right there," Curran said, poking a finger on the spot on the map.

"Girl's got skills," Caraballo said.

"For all our military training and technology, it took a woman and a laptop."

"That's not all," Curran added. "Something Baba said makes a bit more sense. He said 'they' said when his father was rescued, that he was the physically worst-off, so he went first. That means the other guys on the boat must have *still* been on it. I say probably already dead. Theresa found out the vessel was then officially reported to the state police as lost with all hands, but the Coast Guard's official transcript had it declared a hazard to navigation."

"That means it was both declared sunk and declared still floating," Caraballo chimed, sort of to confirm in his head what he just heard.

"Correct." Curran tapped a button on the computer. "The weather report said it was a clear night with calm winds and seas two-feet or less. So, the possibility of a weather-related sinking was slim, and if there was a hull failure or something else that would cause it to sink, the Coasties wouldn't have called it a 'hazard to navigation' so it sank some other way. Hazard to Navigation means they couldn't tow it in, so they had to sink it on purpose. Calm seas, no reason for the sinking, conflicting reports. It has me curious."

"Then they open the valves and let it fill with water or shoot holes in it at the waterline."

"Or let the F-16's blast it out of the water."

"What are you thinking?" Caraballo asked.

"I want to go take a look."

The three men slept in the hangar apartment. The next morning, Curran decided to skip the whole "the killer awoke before dawn" thing. Instead, he found Caraballo ready to go, coffee cups in-hand. They arrived at the boat before dawn and got going. The same process applied; everything secured, navigational electronics on, life jackets on, appropriate music added, and hit the throttles. As the boat traveled out the inlet flying over the wakes of some outgoing charter boats, Curran noticed something odd.

"You know, we don't even have one fishing rod on the boat," he barked over the din of the engines.

"That's okay. We won't need them."

"It's bad luck to not have a rod on the boat."

Caraballo thought for a moment as he rocked back and forth with the swells.

"Awe shit."

They guys ride out straight across the Deepwater Reef, spotting the salvage boat the aerial recon they saw the previous day, but nothing else. Caraballo was right; the boom looked like a concrete pump. Oddly, there were no recreational fishing boats to be seen, and the air had a biting quality that made their skin itch.

"Just like a red tide," Caraballo said, already scratching the skin on his neck until its red.

The men reached their target, thirty miles out, right between the shipping lane and the Deepwater Reef, closer to the east-west channel coming out of the Delaware Bay. Curran slowed the boat to idle speed about a quarter mile away.

"Take the wheel," he said. He moved forward to the starboard bow seat, opened the hatch, and removed a large spool of black cable mounted on an orange reel. He transferred it to the stern and then returned to the bow. This time he reached into the port-side hatch and retrieves a black box the size of a small carry-on suitcase. He brings that to the stern, sits on the port bait well and opens the black box.

"What do you have there?" Caraballo asked.

"Our own personal underwater ROV."

"Where'd you get it?"

"Bass Pro." Curran said. He looks up at Caraballo with a grin.

"Do they normally come with a hundred-meter cable?"

"No, I bought that separately."

"What do you need that for?"

"Well, you know how I'm a sport fisherman, not a meat fisherman, right?"

"Yeah."

"Ever wonder why I don't bottom fish the reefs in Florida?"

"Not really."

"It was once we got scuba certified and dove on that reef in the Caymans," Curran said as he connected the long spool of cable to the small spool of cable from inside the black box. "I saw how deep into the corals the fish could go, and how ridiculously hard it was to get a bait to them without snagging your line and either damaging the reef or breaking off your rig. I'd rather chum things up to the surface and catch them on light tackle, but I'm still curious to see what's down there."

"Sounds reasonable."

Curran returned to the helm. He scrolled back in the history of the side-scanning sonar by touching the screen and sliding it from bottom to top, going back in time. When he found the hump on the ocean bottom depicted on the screen, he touched it. The GPS unit made a beep and the cursor appeared on the spot. He touched the menu button and a drop-down list appeared. He touched "go to cursor." Then he changed to the navigation screen and saw his hit route back to the location of the spot on the ground. He steered the boat over the course to the location he intended to search on the ocean bottom. He maneuvered the boat into a position above and beside his target, making a slow turn to port around it. He stared at the side-scan sonar screen. The expression on his face was troubling. Furrowed brow, lips pressed tightly together, eyes slightly squinted. He pushed his sunglasses up, perching them atop his head. Caraballo noticed the lull in the action and his friend's puzzled look.

"What's wrong?"

"If there's a boat down there, this thing would show it in 3D as a boat. You've seen it; it looks just like a picture of whatever's on the bottom."

Caraballo leaned in to take a better look. "Looks like a pyramid."

"A pyramid with a tail."

They circled the area as Curran adjusted the resolution on the sonar hoping for a more precise image. He doesn't get one.

"The current's running north, so we'll stop a bit south, lower the camera and drift over it. The sonar does a great job of depicting the target, but the camera will let us see exactly what it is."

Once they reached the right location, Curran pulled the throttles into neutral, moved to the stern, knelt on the deck, and removed the underwater video camera from the slot in the foam cut-out inside the carrying box. It looked like a five-pound black baseball with a fin on the front and back. He lifted the cover on the small video display stuck in the foam next the place for the camera and unfolded little sun shields from under the cover. Cupping the camera in his hand, he turned it to face Caraballo.

"Smile!" he said as he watched his friends face on the small screen. "Let's see how this thing does."

Curran lowered the camera over the side and let the cable slide through his hand. Then he clicked a button on the side of the plastic spool housing and pressed the palm of his other hand on the edge, controlling the descent of the camera like controlling a flyfishing reel.

"I see that thing on the sonar," Caraballo reported.

"I told you it was sensitive."

"Looks like you're getting close."

"About fifty more feet."

The camera reached the appropriate depth, about one-hundred twenty-feet, about ten feet from the target. Curran gazed into the small video screen. He adjusted to the sun and glare by placing one hand on the side of the sun shield and bending down, connecting the hand shielding the sun to the side of his face. He thought he saw a giant termite mound slowly moving past as the boat drifted with the current. Curran looked up and checked the attitude of the boat. "Bump it into gear," he directed.

Caraballo shifted the engines into forward gear. The thrust stopped the boat in the correct position.

"It looks like they buried whatever was down there."

"Buried?"

"Yeah, take a look," Curran dire. He leaned away from the display but kept his grip on the reel of cable.

Caraballo stepped from the side of the console, knelt, spun the brim of his Phillies baseball hat to the back of his head, cupped both hands on the sides of the video screen and pressed his face into it.

"Does Bass Pro always sell I.R (infrared) underwater cameras?" he said facetiously.

"I got the best one."

"You're right. It looks like a butt-load of concrete poured on whatever's down there." Caraballo pulled his head back and looked directly at Curran. "Which begs the question; what's so special about it they came out here and covered it in cement?"

"Roger. Keep watching. I'm going to tow the camera around a bit."

A few minutes later Caraballo spotted something on the sonar.

"About a hundred meters north there's another small pile on the bottom." The boat eased over to the target.

"I got it," Caraballo said, kneeling on both knees and elbows with both hands on the sides of the video screen, head pressed into it. "Looks like another pile of concrete."

"Okay, I've seen what I need to see. Let's wrap it up."

Curran and Caraballo changed places. Curran retrieved the camera, placed it back in the case, recovered all the rest of the cable and gear and stored the box and the reel back in their original places on the bow. He returned to his spot behind the wheel and they started moving westerly at a fast cruise.

About ten miles closer in, they spotted a small black dot on the horizon coming from the northwest traveling southeast. It appeared to be headed out in the direction of where they just came, but when they get more west of it, the black dot seemed to turn and started following them. Getting larger, it became a small black center console inflatable boat coming closer at a high rate of speed.

"That's the same kind of boat we already dealt with," Caraballo reported.

"Now they're chasing us," Curran replied. He pushes the throttles forward a bit, increasing the boat's speed.

"Yeah, I doubt they'll be so unprepared this time."

The black boat comes within a quarter mile and then seems to slow to match their speed. Two men appear to be aboard; both dressed in black, both wearing black helmets and tactical vests, both seated.

"I wonder if they want their guns back?" Caraballo shouted above the engine noise

"Best to save that for another day." Curran replied.

"Yep. I know it goes against your nature, but best to avoid them this time. We can always go give them a pounding some other time."

The black boat followed them for about five miles before turning to the northeast and breaking off the pursuit. They could have caught the Necessary Evil if they wanted to.

Fifteen miles out, the guys heard a familiar sound. It came on fast and interrupted their peaceful cruise; a sudden roar followed by a whistling whine of a single jet engine. They sense ill-intent. Normally, the homeland security air patrols fly in a team of two aircraft.

The jet roared overhead about fifteen-hundred feet overhead, streaking past going due north until about a mile ahead. Then it made a sudden high-performance turn to the west. It came completely around, dove so low it nearly dipped its raptor-like tail in the water and blasted straight back at the boat. It thundered over and pulled into a forty-five-degree, full afterburner climb.

Both men stiffened behind the console's windscreen. Goosebumps bulged from Caraballo's arms. "I think we saw this before," he said. "Dude, it's Thunder 3!" Caraballo wailed incredulously.

Curran thought *'Thunder 3...he knows who we are."* He would have said it out loud, but instinctively knew it would be superfluous chatter. "It's definitely not good," Curran replied, stating the obvious. He pushed the throttles to their stops as he turned the boat northwest. "There's no Miss Margaret for them to shoot at, so we're the lone duck on the pond," he shouted.

"Yep, I think we're screwed."

"Life jackets," Curran directed. With one hand on the wheel, he flipped open the storage compartment on the leaning post behind him and retrieves their waterproof satellite phone, his .40 caliber Glock, and a small zippered pouch holding his cell phone, wallet and truck keys. He shoved the items into the pockets of his surfer shorts and then grabbed a life jacket.

"Here it comes!" Caraballo yelled. Curran broke into a cold sweat.

The Necessary Evil made a valiant, yet ironic attempt to escape like a rabbit from a bird of prey. After all, the trade name for the F-16 is the Fighting Falcon (although F-16 pilots call them 'vipers'). The boat skipped across the water throwing spray sideways as the bow split the waves. The engines whined at full throttle while Curran once-again pushed them hard enough to feel the throttle handles bending under the pressure. For a moment he thought about the variables.

"If it's just messing with us, don't do anything. If he shoots, jump."

"No need to tell me that!" Caraballo shrieked.

"Yeah, I know. Dumb thing to say."

The boat was rocking and bouncing, engines wailing, wind rushing past their ears and causing tears to flow from their eyes.

"Hold on!" Curran said. He made a sudden turn due west, trying in vain to get away.

It was good timing.

A burst of fire came from the M61 Vulcan six-barreled 20mm cannon like a long burp. Rounds hit the water behind and beside the boat, sending spray in the air in a strafing line Curran turned again, heading due south. The aircraft pulled up and banked a hard right into a long, sweeping turn.

"When the bullets run out, the missiles will come!" Caraballo declared.

"I know," Curran reluctantly replied, seemingly resigned to his fate. He turned back to the west.

Here he comes again!" Caraballo said as he pointed up at a forty-five-degree angle straight behind the boat.

Curran turned the wheel slightly in order to put the boat in a slow arcing turn to the left. "Let's go," he said. Caraballo calmly turned and put his rear end on the left gunwale. He made eye contact with Curran, then looked down, spun his lower legs up over the side and rolled over the gunwale, turning away from the direction of travel as he fell toward the water, face up, arms crossed, chin to his chest. Curran turned from the console and without touching the rail, dove off the boat, lifejacket in-hand. He turns his body in the air to land on his back, feet facing away from the direction of travel, face-up. He tucks his chin to his chest, arms tightly crossed across his torso clutching the life jacket and the satellite phone, feet together. His back impacted the water with a thud at near forty-five miles per hour, skipping across it like a stone on a calm lake. After about thirty feet, his momentum stopped, and he sank into the water. He turned to see the boat sailing away at full speed, and then twisted to see Caraballo bobbing in the water about one-hundred feet away. The water was surprisingly warm, and he was unharmed by the high-speed water entry.

The fighter jet roared past overhead after the boat, going after its prey like a cheetah on a baby gazelle. This time he's didn't take the chance on any target practice. Above, a missile detached from the bottom of the plane, its rocket engine fired, and the deadly device screeched toward Curran's unmanned boat. The missile hit the boat on a downward trajectory onto the deck behind the console. A pressure wave burst from the sides of the boat as the fiery blast blew the center console and small front deck into the air, split the hull down the middle, and shattered nearly everything else. The ripping hull and forward motion caused the superstructure to catch the water. The hull broke; momentum flipped the outboard motors up and over the rest of the burning boat, somersaulting before hitting the water ahead of the burning mass, both engines still attached to a small piece of transom. The whole mass of fiberglass comes to a dead stop.

Not looking at the demise of his boat, the explosion told Curran the missile hit its mark, the Necessary Evil was no more. Curran swam over and grabbed his life preserver before turning to see the remnants of his boat burning. The F-16 hit afterburner and roared nearly straight up into the sky. Curran thought the maneuver was almost like giving him the finger with an airplane. He clipped the satellite phone to a ring on the lifejacket and started to roll his body into the vest when he heard a streaking noise overhead. The fighter jet was diving on them.

"Connie! Look Out!" he shouted before taking a deep breath and disappearing under water. With three powerful thrusts of his arms he managed to get at least ten feet under, as deep and he could to avoid the bullets he knew were coming. Overhead, the fighter slowed to take careful aim. The cannon fired and a long b-u-u-u-r-r-r-r-p-p bellowed from the plane. Curran heard the ripping sound of the rounds hitting the water and their plunge into the deep.

Curran waited until the sound of the aircraft and the bullets subsided, then he popped to the surface. He scanned the area crazily for Caraballo. He saw Caraballo's empty life jacket floating nearby. A rush of fear swarmed over him.

"Connie!" he screamed. After all the operations all over the world, all the firefights, recons, covert ops, special training, skydives, and all the crazy crap they did as kids, it's was the first time he actually thought he lost his best friend. "Connie!" he repeated. "Connie!"

Curran spun around and spotted his own life jacket a short distance away. He swam over and grabbed it, then turned and started a side stroke over to Caraballo's floating life vest. He swims over and grabs his own life jacket, then starts to swim to Caraballo's life jacket. Then, almost miraculously, Caraballo broke the surface about three feet away. Curran was both amazed and relieved.

"Son-of- a-bitch!" Caraballo growled, spitting seawater.

"Dude! Here!" Curran said, pushing Caraballo's life jacket toward him. Caraballo grabbed it and hugged it to his chest for flotation.

"It wasn't enough that asshole shot the boat, he had to come back for us!" Caraballo exclaimed, wiping his wet face with his hand.

"I thought he got you."

"Nah, right before he opened up, I unbuckled my vest, lifted up my arms, and slid right out."

"You always did sink like a rock."

"Fortunately, I still do. You okay?"

"Yeah, I'm good."

Only five minutes later, from the intense heat of the explosive warhead in the missile, the seventy-five gallons of gasoline on board, and the highly flammable nature of fiberglass resin, the destruction of the boat was so complete, the last pieces sank. The fire went out, the smoke cleared, and only various bits of flotsam blown free of the blazing boat by the force of the explosion remained; a scorched scuba tank, a rubber bumper, the cooler, and Caraballo's medic bag. The guys reached the area about ten minutes later and collected the items, linking them together with the length of blue rope attached to the bumper.

Afterward, the two men bobbed in the water among the remnants of their once mighty vessel. Another fifteen minutes passes in silence. No further sign of the fighter jet.

"How ya doin? You all right?" Curran asked. Some South Jersey/South Philly slang made the last part sound like "yah-ite."

"Nah, dude, I'm pretty damn far from all right," Caraballo growls. He spat some ocean water and glared into Curran's eyes. "Somebody has an ass-kicking coming."

"Roger that."

They both thought of Thunder Three, errant fighter jets, and their current situation.

"Dude, when we get back in, we gotta go see that guy," Caraballo said.

"Yeah you do."

"I'm ready to beat the information out of him."

"Me too."

"So, what do we tell the Coasties?"

"I don't know. I don't think we should call them," Curran replied.

"Why not?"

"Last time we called for help it didn't work out so well."

"We say we had a fire and the boat sank," Caraballo offered. "We don't mention a fighter jet attacked us."

"Nope," Curran said, distracted, looking away. "It's only about twenty miles; piece of cake."

"Dude, you're shitting me, right?" Caraballo's voice went up two octaves.

"Yep," Curran said casually as he looked off in the distance. He noticed a buoy nearby. It was a large float with a long shaft holding a metallic radar reflector about six feet above the water's surface. He used the flotation of the cooler to raise himself a bit higher in the water and scanned the 360-degree horizon. "No way," he muttered to himself. In the distance to the north, he saw the pinched bow of a lobster boat headed southeast. "I have an idea," he said.

"You always do."

With the satellite phone, Curran called Pete Rogers, the guy from the fishing tournament party. After a brief exchange, he made another call.

"Hey, is this Jason?" he said into the receiver. Caraballo's facial expression was more than quizzical. "Hey man, it's Tom Curran. How are you doing?" Curran said. "What are you doing today?" he asked. Curran listened a moment as Caraballo stared daggers into him. Curran laughed. "It's funny you say that; you'll actually run into me in about two miles if you turn a little south." There was a slight pause. "I know; Yeah, that was me. The boat sank. We're floating here looking for a ride in." Another slight pause. "Okay, I'll keep the line open and steer you over."

"Jason?" Caraballo asked. "Jason Hadley, the fisherman guy?"

"Yeah. He's right over there, Bro," Curran replied as he pointed to the lobster boat in the distance.

"What did he say that was funny?"

"He said he was out on his boat working; maybe he would *run* into us in the next few days."

The two men start laughing.

"So, we tell Jason it was a ruptured fuel tank that caused a fire," Caraballo says.

"Right."

The two men again sat quietly, bobbing in the water, waiting for their ride to get closer. A short time later, Curran waved as the boat approached.

"I told you it was bad luck to not have a rod in the boat," he said.

Chapter 16

On a traffic circle close to the Atlantic City International Airport in
Pomona, New Jersey sat a rectangular, faded- yellow, aluminum-
sided, nondescript building. It could have been a hardware store,
bakery, or a printing shop, but it wasn't. It was a strip club. A neon
sign stretched across the front of the building above the first-floor
windows, the pink and green letters spelling "The Fence Post
Tavern." Bad attempt at a phallic reference, but at least they tried.
The term "strip" however was a bit of a misnomer. The girls don't
take off their clothes. They worked in lingerie or swimsuits that
basically meant they hung around the place in bikinis. No nudity.
Can't serve alcohol in a club where there was nudity. Weird state
law. The parking lot was around back, with only the side of the
building lit at night.

Curran, Caraballo, and Perez left their black suburban under
a tree at the far end of the lot and approached the back door. Curran
reached it first, grabbed the handle, and paused, noticing words
painted on the steel mesh-encased glass.

"Come In; Have a Drink, Play Some Games, Keep Your
Hands to Yourself," Curran read aloud.

"Good advice," Caraballo replied.

The four men entered and stood near the door, taking in the
scenery. The room was about sixty-feet-long and thirty feet wide.
Running most of the way down the right side was a three-foot high

stage for the dancers, laid out like a reverse 'E' surrounded by padded low-back chairs, with a brass rail mounted around the edge of the stage. Brass stripper poles were mounted at the ends of the protrusions and back near the indented spaces near the mirrored side wall. The configuration allowed at least six girls to use the poles simultaneously. All the upholstery was red vinyl. The walls in the stage area were painted red. The ceiling was red. At the end of the room on the right was the small bar. It was meant to be small. They wanted people sitting around the stage paying double for beers instead of at the bar staring at the bartender, who doubled as a bouncer.

On the left side of the room were areas for playing darts on two dart boards, a shuffleboard table laid parallel to the left wall with a few regular tables for patrons set in front of it, and at the end sat five billiard tables, each one with the traditional stained glass light hung by chains from the ceiling and set to hang about head-high. Next to each billiard table against the left side wall sat a high-top table, each about two feet in diameter, each flanked by a pair of high bar stools. In between the tables were wall-mounted racks of worn pool cues. A triangular piece of chalk about the size of a pineapple was mounted on a small shelf about head-high in the corner of the room.

The guys stepped inside.

"Smells like stale beer and bad perfume," Caraballo said as a thin, dark man appeared. He was your basic lounge-lizard type; a bit old to be in there, button-down polo shirt with the weird big logo and the collar turned up, designer blue jeans, silver-tipped tag of his black leather belt hanging down like an arrow at the disturbing bulge in his pants, cheap brown loafers, cheap watch, cheap silver bracelet poorly hiding his medic-alert tag, all bathed in bad after-shave.

"That's a ten-dollar cover, fellas," he said as he nervously adjusted his shirt collar. "Each," he added, like he had to.

"Dude must think there's a turnip truck parked in the lot," Caraballo whispered to Curran.

The man extended a shaky, peculiarly tanned, liver-spotted hand.

"Johnny Salami," Curran said boisterously to the man with a smile. It wasn't his name. "What do we get for the cover charge?" he asked over the loud music.

"Two beers and two games of your choice."

"Sounds like a deal," Curran replied. He didn't like strip bars. He said having to pay to "look at ass" made him feel dirty.

The men moved from the door across the expansive room toward the pool tables. As they went, one-by-one, the dancers all eyed Perez like he was a tall piece of Latino man candy. They moved to the pool table in the far corner. It was still early so business was light. About ten patrons sat around the stage interspersed by dancers, with only one girl on the stage. She was just skipping around, not yet fully committed to the dollar-generating stripper routine. Two guys played darts with one girl tending to them, and men and women used the two pool tables in the middle.

Taking up a position at the end pool table, Curran racked up the balls as Perez picked out a cue. picked-out cues. Two bikini-clad girls closed-in on them as Caraballo made his way to the bar. Approaching the dated, "looks like art deco-by-accident" bar, the burly biker type behind the bar set his eyes on Caraballo and watched his approach. Caraballo walked up to a space between a couple dressed like they were fresh from the beach and a guy that looked like he lived there and already had too many. The bartender waited until Caraballo put both hands on the bar before speaking.

"Can I get you something?" he said in a tone that sounded like 'what the hell do you want?'

"Can I get a real drink instead of two beers for the cover?"

"What'll it be?"

"Crown, straight."

"Coming right up,"

Caraballo collected his drink and walked across the room to the table against the wall, taking the empty. Curran sat in the other.

"The girl could have brought you that," Curran said, noticing his drink.

"Thought I'd get it myself."

The two sit and relax. The crack of the cue ball smashing into the rack of pool balls on the break shattered the air. Both men looked over to see Perez evaluating the success of his shot.

"You trying to kill them?" Caraballo joked. Perez just smiled. He sat for a moment watching Perez trying to clear the pool table. "What are you having?" he asked Curran.

"Here it comes now," Curran said, noticing a girl in a bikini top, plaid skater skirt and white skateboard sneakers coming his way holding a tray. She reached the table, threw both men a friendly smile and said "here you go" as she sat a small plastic wood-grained coffee thermos and a regular coffee mug on the table. "Thank you dear," Curran said as he handed her a folded $10 bill. He turned and noticed Caraballo looking at him, right elbow on the table holding his glass close to his face, left eyebrow raised. "She got me coffee from the diner next door."

Curran poured his coffee, added some half-and-half from a tiny creamer cup brought by the girl, and stirred. He took a sip, noticing Caraballo was still looking at him. "It really is good coffee. There's something about it. You should try it.

Caraballo looked at the coffee, set his glass down, reached over and picked-up the coffee mug and took a sip. He swallowed, his brow furrowed, and he took another. His brow returned to normal and he set the mug back down in front of Curran. "You're right. There is something about it. It's good."

"Told you."

Curran noticed Perez standing nearby, looking at him with his stick at the position of 'order arms.' Curran eased off his seat. "Time to show this young man a thing or two," he mumbled.

Caraballo looked across the room and noticed the shift change on the stage. Basically, dancers danced for the time it took to play four songs on the stereo, then ran up the steps at the far end of the stage to the second floor where they kept their gear. They danced in bikinis and high heels but returned to the first floor wearing short skirts and sneakers. It's because there were no waitresses. The girls would amber up to the patrons, take their orders, then sit with them until it's their turn to dance, then dance for the men they were with, using the mentality that familiarity will pay off in dollars. The girl that brought Curran his coffee stood on the other side of the pool table talking to Perez as she kept an eye on Curran.

Twenty minutes later, after Curran ran the table on Perez, he broke a new game and was setting up his second shot with his back to the club's front door. The front door opened. He heard the scuffling of footsteps mixed-in with the sound of the Led Zeppelin music coming from the speakers hung high on the walls throughout the room. Suddenly, a sound rang out, reverberating off the room.

"Tommy!" he heard someone bellow above the music! He turned to see a man as big as a bear, brutish, tan, black-haired, wearing black pants and a black polo shirt (small logo, collar down) standing with his arms out at his sides in a stance that says 'come give me a hug.'

"Rock?" Curran said quizzically.

"I'm here my friend!" the man boisterously exclaimed. Curran noticed Perez protectively approached from the other side and stood three feet away.

"It's okay," Curran said. He turned and stepped toward the man. "Rock Zanni, you're a sight for sore eyes," he added, eyes beaming, big smile on his face. Reaching him, the two men embrace like old, dear friends. For Curran, it's like hugging a bear. The hug ends and Rock grabs Curran by the shoulders.

"Damn, dude, it's good to see you. How long has it been, huh?"

"Since Panama."

"Yeah, I see you still hang out with those fellas there," Zanni said, noticing Caraballo and Perez. "You teaching these guys how to play?"

"Just hanging out. What are you doing around here?" Curran said coyly. He knew he would run into Zanni.

"Working for the contractor."

"Great. How's your mom?" Curran asked.

"Doing great! You should come by."

Standing on the other side of the pool table, Perez leans over to Caraballo.

"Leave it to the boss to know somebody everywhere we go."

"He always does," Caraballo replied.

"I mean everywhere; Iraq, Panama, Cuba, Colombia, Bosnia, Somalia, Asscrackistan, freaking everywhere," Perez said rapid-fire, counting on his fingers in front of Caraballo.

"Yep."

"You know, you were supposed to come see me when you got back to Fort Gannon after Panama," Curran said to Zanni.

"I did. They said you were off on something else."

"Yeah, we've been kind of busy," Curran said before turning to Perez and Caraballo. "Connie, you remember Rock."

"Sure do," Caraballo said. He stepped forward and shook Rock's hand combined with the appropriate one-armed bro hug. "Good to see you Rocky," he added.

"Rock, this is Oscar Perez, one of my guys. Oscar, Rock is an Air Force Cargo pilot and an old friend of mine," Curran said as he grabbed Perez on the shoulder. Perez looked Rock Zanni in the eye and shook his hand, smiling.

"You were with these two down in Panama a couple years back," Zanni said.

"You have a good memory," Perez replied.

"You have people coming?" Curran asked Zanni.

"A couple guys from the group. There they are now," Zanni said, noticing a group coming in the back door. "I'll come have a beer with you in a minute."

The 'group' is the 841st Air National Guard fighter group housed in their hangars on the Atlantic City Airport along with

Coast Guard Air Station Atlantic City and the Federal Aviation Administration Technical Center. The Air Guard pilots fly the Homeland Security flights known as CAP around the northeast and have been on active duty since 2001. The call sign for one of those aircraft was Thunder 3.

As Rock Zanni walked away, Caraballo approached Curran. He leaned in close for a private word.

"Any of those fellas our guy?"

"It could be all of them."

"What about your friend?"

"We might have lucked out with him. He's agency now."

"How can you tell?"

"Said he was working for *the contractor*."

"Yep. Spook for sure."

Curran glanced at Perez and noticed him pointing at the pool table, telling him it's still his shot.

Rock Zanni greeted his party and escorted them over to Curran and company. After group exchanged friendly greetings the others took the pool table third from the end. They said it's so they could be closer to the stage. Each man broke out a big cigar and the whole area over their table soon became shrouded in cigar smoke. A couple of them actually enjoyed their cigars while others made a game out of it, purposely blowing their smoke at each other.

"Bunch of jackasses. I'd like to thrash each one of them," Caraballo jibed.

Rock Zanni came back over to Curran and the two caught up on home, family, when Rock retired early from the Air Force during the drawdown, and how he married the girl next door. He grew up about six blocks from Caraballo's parent's house, about ten from Mrs. DeFelice.

About an hour later, Curran told Rock he needed to talk to him. The two men went out and sat in the truck. Curran turned on a portable scanner that detecting listening devices. After getting a green light, he flipped a switch on the scanner to the white noise generator, used to mask listening devices. Rock Zanni sat with a tentative look on his face. This was no ordinary conversation.

"Are you read in?" Curran asked. It's a question about his current security clearance.

"Read into what?"

"Come on Rock, I know you work for a three-letter agency. Which one I don't care."

"Beta clearance with SCI level four," Zanni declared. It's a level way above Top Secret with insane need-to-know restrictions. "Why? What's up?"

"I have a problem I need some help with."

"Okay."

"There was a boat offshore down here last week that held an apparent chemical agent that killed everyone on board. An F-16 came along and blew it out of the water."

"How do you know?"

"We went on board before the missile shot. Connie got a taste of the agent and bailed off it. We got out of there and reported it on the secure line, and then the fighter showed up. We got out of there as fast as we could."

"And?"

"A couple days later we were out looking around and the plane came back and did the same for us."

"What do you mean?" Zanni blurted, slightly alarmed.

"We jumped off the boat right before it took a missile up the ass."

"A fighter blew-up your boat," Zanni said incredulously. Curran didn't detect Zanni was withholding anything or being insincere.

"Yep."

"When?"

"Yesterday.

"No shit?" Zanni said, his voice an octave higher.

"And then it came back around and fired at us in the water."

"They put the guns on you!" Zanni bellowed.

"Yep."

"What were you doing?"

"We were looking into the sinking of an old friend's fishing boat. We found it about thirty-five miles out, sitting on the bottom covered in concrete."

"Concrete?"

"Concrete. There's a salvage boat out there that seems to be going from spot to spot covering up things with concrete."

Zanni sat thinking for a moment. "What's your idea about that?" he asked.

"I think there were chemical weapons from World War II dumped where they weren't supposed to be dumped," Curran says. "Something either busted open their containers, or being sixty or seventy years old, the just broke open on their own. Now some of it's coming up and things are getting bad."

"How bad?"

"Boats are netting-up schools of dead fish. Lobsters are dead in their traps, we've seen blue-green blobs of something floating near the dead fish, in one place making birds flying over sick enough to hit the water and die."

"This doesn't sound good."

Curran decided to sit and wait for Rock to provide some input of his own. He waited patiently. After a few minutes, he pulled a roll of Spree candy out of the armrest. He popped a couple in his mouth and offered them to Rock, who took a couple and gave back the roll. Patience only lasts so long. His question was quite direct.

"Rock, are you hearing this for the first time, or figuring out how much I know?"

Zanni sat for a moment staring straight out the windshield, then turned and looked directly at Curran.

"Brother, it breaks my heart to think you might be wondering if I'm putting one over on you," he said. Curran stayed quiet. "If the order for something like that came from Langley, I would have known about it. Problem is, these pilots sometimes get separate briefings from me, and every time a weapon is released its automatically listed as 'expended in training.'"

"Dude, the weather's going to change in a few days and the wind's going to blow mostly toward the beach for about a week. Anything bad out there could come ashore. If the boats I see are trying to take care of it, I'd like to know. If they're just trying to protect the people that illegally dumped it short of its destination, I'd like to know that too."

"Still a crusader!" Zanni proclaimed. He reached over and slapped Curran on the knee. "Want to know a dirty little secret?"

"Sure."

"Not all the CAP patrol aircraft are flown by Air Force pilots."

Curran felt the hairs go up on his arms. He considered what Zanni just said. "Company pilots?" When referring directly to the CIA, most spooks use the term "company."

"Yep."

"What for?"

"In case a civilian airliner needs to get shot down. The Pentagon doesn't want a military officer to do it, but they won't tell you that."

"How many of these guys do you have over there?"

"The people rotate, but it's always around four or five. They hide-out as contractors, but they're company guys sure as shit. Shifty eyes, dishrag personalities."

"Do they know your status?"

"They think I'm a contractor for the manufacturer on the airlifter side," Zanni said. He sat and thought for a moment. "I know what you're thinking. Whoever can get an F-16 to respond within minutes, faster than the Coast Guard, to a location out at sea and cleanse the area with a missile shot *has* to be both connected, and expecting something like this to happen," he added. He looked at Curran, scanning his expression in the darkness of the truck's interior. "Did the aircraft come from the air guard out here?"

"It looked like Thunder 3."

"Thunder three!" Rock said through clenched teeth. He popped open his door and started to swing his right leg out of the truck. Curran grabbed him by the arm.

"Where are you going?"

"One of the guys in there flies that patrol!"

"Close the door," Curran said calmly, looking into Zanni's eyes in dim light of the illuminated vehicle. Zanni paused, swung his right leg back in and shut the door. The light dims slowly to darkness. Curran can see Zanni's chest heaving. The man was seriously pissed. Any doubt Curran had about his friend's sincerity washes away.

"What were you going to do?"

"I was going to haul him out of there and beat an answer out of him."

"What was going to be the question?"

"Did he shoot at a boat out at sea and was one of them a boat like yours."

"And then what?" Curran said calmly. He offered Rock another candy. The man took it and popped it in his mouth, sucking hard on the sour candy as if he was tormented by thoughts. "If you drug some dude out of the bar and kicked the crap out of him, it would let all the others know you're up to something. It could also land you in jail, and that could blow the whole show."

"You're right. You're right," Zanni repeats.

"Is the guy in there one of the company guys"

"No, he's an air force officer. Smug little shit; call sign Peeper."

"Peeper?"

"They say he was a peeping Tom back in flight school," Zanni said. "No offense," he added sheepishly.

"No issue. They never give calls signs based on something good. I've seen some doozies."

"Yeah, there's a dude over there they call 'Huge.' His last name is Cramp."

"Nice. We have to figure out just wouldn't let the Coast Guard and the Department of Environmental Protection in on this but would respond with a clean-up crew and protect their little secret so violently. Somebody's protecting somebody on this thing."

"You always were the calm one, even growing up."

"Still have my number?"

"Sure do."

"Good, then see what you can find out and call me. We can meet somewhere like we're just old friends hanging out. Maybe get some clam chowder down in Somers Point."

"Tommy," Zanni said seriously. He reached over and grabbed Curran by the collar. "Somebody over there tried to kill you. I'm going to find out who, and why."

"I hope so. Now let's go get a beer."

Chapter 17

Back at the hangar after the strip club, the men entered the downstairs portion of the end hangar with Perez carrying two pizzas. Caraballo walked straight to the old-fashioned 50's era refrigerator with the beer taps mounted in the door. He opened it to see a slim beer keg on one side, with cased of soda on the other, with growler bottles of locally made beer set on top of the soda.

"Damn. You got about five cases of old-fashioned cokes in here!" Caraballo exclaimed.

"Only the best for you my friend," Curran replied. "Oscar; that set of lockers to the right of Mr. Caraballo over there has everything you might need," he added. He had a habit of speaking formally when he was thinking operationally. Perez made a beeline straight for the cabinets with a facial expression like he's about to get a Christmas present.

"Chief," Perez said to Caraballo as he passed him.

"Sarge," Caraballo replied, smiling at Perez. "What's in this beer keg?" Caraballo asked Curran.

"Birch Beer."

"Birch Beer?" Caraballo asked quizzically. "You mean like the Pennsylvania Dutch Birch Beer?"

"Yep," Curran replied in a draw. He was busy with the surveillance cameras.

"What's birch beer?" asked Perez.

"Man, I'll tell you what," Caraballo happily exclaimed. "It's like root beer, only better."

"It's soda?"

"Yeah. It's good. Let's have some. If I know Tommy," Caraballo said as he opened the freezer above the refrigerator. "There we are!" he added as he discovered root beer mugs in the freezer.

Curran turned to a 32-inch flat-screen television on the right-hand wall. He touched the power button on the lower right side and watched it power-up. On the screen he saw the view of the front and back doors to the hangar. He hit a button on the small keyboard in front of the television and changed the camera feed. The TV view changed into four sections, each a video feed from a different surveillance camera. The top left and right were the front (street side) and beach-side of the Sea Island house from a point probably on the power pole in front of the house, and the light pole on the boardwalk. The bottom left was a view of the west side of the house cast in darkness. The camera was mounted somewhere on the second floor of the neighbor's house. The bottom right screen showed a view of the south side of the house. The camera view is high and slightly set back, which indicated the camera was mounted on the roof of the duplex that replaced the parish orphanage's summer home where Curran spent his summers as a kid.

"Damn, I didn't put the trash out," he mumbled. Curran watched the video for a moment, and then reached to a small box resembling a cable TV receiver mounted on the wall. He flipped a switch and the video on the lower right turned to thermal/infra-red. The house came into full view.

"Now that's what I'm talking about!" Perez exclaimed fervently. Opening the double-door locker, he encountered a rack of weapons containing six completely kitted-out M-4's, two combat shotguns, some demo, detonators, a spool of detonating cord, two radio encryption fill devices, night vision goggles, two different night scopes, two AT-4 light antitank rockets, personal coms, and some other secret surprises known but to spooks and special operators. On the floor are green metal ammo boxes with 9mm, 5.56 mm, .40 caliber, .338 Lapua Magnum, and 3" magnum 12-guage rounds, plus 40 mm frag, smoke, and incendiary grenades, and multiple varieties of flares. Hanging on the doors and overhead are climbing ropes, Swiss seats, and bore cleaning cords. No need to store handguns in here; all the guys normally carry or keep them handy. "Man, I can't wait to see what's in the other locker," Perez said. He had yet to see inside the locker between the one he was in and the one at the end near the stairs where he found his sniper rifle and the gun cleaning kits.

Curran set a laptop computer on the top of the workbench next to the television. After firing it up, he logged onto a special web portal and entered an eleven-key encryption. Once cleared onto the portal, he entered a twelve-digit encryption to log onto the channel he used to communicate with MacPherson, the boss. A box popped-up, asking for him to scan his fingerprint. He pressed the third finger of his right hand into the reading device on the laptop. The fingerprint appeared on the screen, blinks green, and disappeared. Another box popped-up asking if he would like "active voice." Curran clicked "no." He waited; he didn't have to wait long.

"I've been waiting for you to contact me," appeared on the screen. On this screen, it's one line at a time so to not keep a record. When Curran started to type, the line from MacPherson disappeared.

"Why?" Curran replied.

"No progress reports."

"What else?"

"Some people in town asking about you."

"Anyone in particular?"

"So far, just the usual fan club still chasing old scores. Can't bring down senators and generals without upsetting someone," MacPherson wrote, referring to past missions. Even in digital text, the sarcasm came across.

"What about this new situation?"

"No information. DHS and Pentagon are quiet."

"Recommendation?"

"Move quickly; be careful."

"WILCO. Anything further?"

"Return secretary."

"Will contact again in 24," Curran typed. He made a mouse click on the screen, severing the encrypted connection. He immediately turned off the computer, followed by pulling the internet card and returning the laptop to the lead-lined sleeve inside the end cabinet.

"Mac wants his secretary back," he announced to the room.

"Did you tell him about your boat?" Caraballo asked.

"No."

"What does he know?" Caraballo said as he reached Curran with a mug of birch beer.

"Only about Kuvarac."

"Not this other thing?"

"No, but you know how it goes."

"Yeah, he makes James Bond look like a third grader."

"The walls always have ears," Curran proclaimed.

"Roger that."

"Boss wants his secretary back?" Perez asked.

"Yeah, he must be tired of that nimrod temp he has there now," Curran replied. "What's his name? Trevor?"

"Stanley," Caraballo blurted.

"Fillippi still has her in California, right?" Curran asked.

"Last I heard," Caraballo replied. "He doesn't check in and we never check on him."

Curran took a seat on a barstool near the television

"I want to see if anyone has been in the house since we left," he said.

"If anybody wants to mess with it, they'll wait until after midnight," Perez replied.

"Would have to be the back door. The pressure sensor under the front door mat would have alerted us of somebody stood in front of the door," Caraballo said.

"The sensor only works if you weigh more than a buck-twenty," Curran reported.

"Why is that?"

"The girls aren't that heavy."

"How does it alert you?" asked Perez.

"Sends a message to my phone. I want to get Theresa's laptop too. She might not have saved everything on that external hard drive."

The two men simply nod to Curran in the affirmative.

"I know we left it in case they put a locator on it, but I'm kicking myself for not inspecting it and bringing it with us."

Just after 3:00 AM, two dark figures scurry over the sand dune in front of the house on Sea Island. They move steadily through the high dune grass, slip easily through the horizontal pipes of the boardwalk fence, go across the boardwalk in the dim light between the street lights that mark every street, step though the railing on the west side and jump down into the darkness on the south side of the house. They had sat on the upslope of the dune for fifteen minutes surveying the area.

They noticed the usual things; some people trudging home from the bars, no one sitting by themselves watching the area, no one alone in their car, and most houses dark. At a beachfront house two blocks away, the upper deck was full of a group that, judging by their noise level, moved the party from the bar to their deck. All good things. The only thing that noticed them was Caraballo, sitting at the TV in the hangar watching them on thermal imaging as he drank his eighth mug of birch beer.

The difference between breaking into a house you know is empty, and one that you think is empty is the psychological deterrent called "what if." Sure, anybody can watch a house, wait for everyone to leave, then go in an unlocked home and smash-up their fishing gear, write stupid things on mirrors, and ransack the bedrooms. But what if you never saw anyone leave? How do you know the house is empty? What if it's not? What if they made it look like they left but they're waiting for you? What if they know you're coming back? What if there's a dog? What if there's a surveillance system? What if there's a silent alarm? What if the car is in the garage? What if someone sees you? What if someone is watching you watch it? What about the dark spots we can't see? All the questions stack up like sandbags in the guts of a would-be intruder, and the mental risk-verses-reward scale tips heavily in favor of skipping the whole thing. It can't be called using "better judgment" because what is better judgment when it comes to breaking and entering?

"No signs of intruders," Caraballo said, both Curran and Perez hearing the words through an inexpensive Bluetooth earpiece with the annoying blinking light covered by magic marker. No special operational coms required.

"Roger that; moving," Curran replied.

The area is dark; no one around. The only sound is that of the ocean. The two men crouch in their black coveralls and black hoods with their backs to the rough wood of the waist-high bulkhead that marks the end of their property on the east side and the elevated boardwalk behind them. Both men scan the area using their night vision goggles.

They looked for anything out of the ordinary; people, trash cans out of place, stray cats, open doors open that should be closed, broken windows, items to stumble over, or neighbors on their balconies. Curran noticed signs of the insomniac next-door neighbor scurrying around high on her third-floor deck. He pointed her out to Perez.

Without removing the night vision goggles from his eyes, Perez pulled a device roughly the size of a mobile phone from his pocket. Using touch only, he deftly turned it around in his palm, and then pressed a button. In the lower right portion of the view from his goggles, the scene shown from the camera he placed on the neighbor's house appeared, the one trained on the back door.

"We're not in view," he whispered. He clicked the device again and the view changed to the camera mounted on the telephone pole on the boardwalk. He watched it for a moment before clicking again, the view returned to the back door. He nimbly clicked other buttons as he watched the rest of the area in front of him. The device Perez used ran through all the frequencies a surveillance device could use to operate a remote camera. He sees a webcam running on the neighbor's computer, a nanny-cam from the family across the street, a camera in the garage of the Ferrari-driving douchebag two houses over, and the couple in the street-side cottage three houses back from the beach filming their sexual congress. He thought to himself that he's not the only person that can hack a webcam, and what went out on the internet stays on the internet.

Crouched on his right, Perez tapped Curran on the arm. Curran could see him in the night vision so no need for words. Perez pointed two fingers with a black-gloved right hand at his own goggles, then made two slight karate-chop motions in front of his face, followed by one chop to his throat, then a single sliding motion on Curran's thigh with the palm of his left hand, then tapped two left-hand fingertips twice in rapid succession on Curran's thigh. He found no other cameras pointed at the house and gave him the signal to go.

Curran moved slowly, close to the ground, moving like a spider crawling on his hands and feet. He was amazingly fluid, quiet, and stealthy. He moved from the wall, across the small back yard, and disappeared in a shadow cast by the small outdoor shower stall next to the back door. Perez could see him. Curran gave him the signal to move. He went in the same fashion, on hands and feet like a spider.

When he reached the back door, Perez knelt high and peered through the door window into the house. This is where the tension normally rises, the time when the thing they call the "pucker-factor" increases. They know that attached to that door could be all manner of booby traps. Nothing like opening your house door only to catch the doorknob in the gut as it moves at the speed of a cannonball. Nothing like the wallop of the pressure wave created by a military-grade explosive turning your liver and spleen into mush.

Curran un-wrapped a short piece of black duct tape from around the third finger of his right hand; using a thumb, he pressed part of it against the small 8" by 8" window at the bottom of the other small windows in the door. With expeditious use of a multi-tool, he removed the frame around the small window, scored the ancient and weather-beaten bedding compound and with a tug on the duct tape, removed the section of glass. As he carefully set the glass on the concrete, leaning it against the house, he realized that for once he was happy that he decided to wait to install a more secure and energy efficient back door. He thought of the quirky pictures in the office hallway in Crystal City, specifically the one with a picture of a towel draped over a beach chair that says "Procrastination; hard work often pays-off over time, but laziness always pays off now."

In the glow of his night vision, Perez reached a hand through the hole in the back door, made a cursory check of the area around the inside doorknob, unlocked the door, and opened it about two inches. Startled, Curran grabbed a handful of Perez's pant leg. Perez gave Curran the hand-signal to follow him. How did he know the door wasn't rigged?

The two men stayed low, opened the door only enough to slide inside, and closed the door behind them. They knelt silently, listening for any movement or voices inside the house. After a minute or so, Curran swiveled on his feet to stand. Perez stood up next to him.

"Trip wire in the doorway," Perez whispered, indicating the doorway ahead of him marking the hallway from the downstairs utility room to the stairs leading up to the kitchen.

"Trip wire?"

"Yeah. Old-school. That's how I knew there wasn't anything on the door."

"It would be a bit redundant."

Perez moved around Curran and carefully stepped to within reach of the tiny wire stretched across the open doorway about a foot off the floor. He inspected both sides of the wire where it attached to the wooden doorframe. He was surprised at what he saw.

"It's a trip flare," he said in an exasperated whisper.

"Really?" Curran replied in disbelief. "No explosive?"

"Negative." Perez pressed the tripping device against the wall with one finger and disconnected the trip wire with two fingers of the other hand. "Good to go," he said.

The two men moved up the steps to the first floor, checking for more trip wires. Almost on hands and knees, they made their way to the second floor, followed by the third. Curran retrieved Theresa's computer and the two went back downstairs, never turning on a light. Along the way, they set three surveillance cameras in the three stairwells, figuring if an intruder would eventually use a stair. They didn't want to go outside and set-up the cameras on the decks for fear of being seen. The men also checked the other doors, finding them locked but not dead-bolted. They set the dead bolts and make sure the bars were laid in the tracks of the sliding doors. At that point, Curran realized he should have lowered all the hurricane shutters before they moved the girls, making it look like they were leaving for the rest of the summer. It was okay though; the doors would have interfered with their ability to use thermal imaging to detect any bad guys before entering.

Perez never saw such a fast window repair, especially one done in the dark. Curran retrieved a can of glazing compound and rolled the material into four thin eight-inch strips, pressed the material into the grooves of the window frame from inside the house without opening the door, and then the men opened the door enough to exit, closed it, Curran replaced the glass and used a wide putty knife to press the compound into the frame and set the glass. He replaced the trim, and the two men were prepared to leave.

"Tom," Curran heard Caraballo say in his earpiece. Curran scrambled back inside the house with Perez right after him.

"Go ahead," Curran said softly. "Roger that," he said after a slight pause. "I'll be right back," he said to Perez. Curran disappeared up the dark steps. He returned two minutes later.

"You okay Sir?" Perez asked.

"Yeah, I'm good."

Curran and Perez repeated the process of how they came. Spider crawl back to the low bulkhead wall. They put their backs to it, scanned the area for prying eyes.

"All clear. Go," Caraballo advised.

The two men went through the fence overhead, across the boardwalk, through the fence on the other side, over the dune and disappeared in the darkness.

Three blocks over the two men walk up the steps from the beach to the boardwalk. Both are in their regular clothes with their jump suits and night vision gear in Perez' backpack. They reached Curran's Bronco with no issues, got in and drove away.

"Trip flares," Curran said derisively. "Can you believe that?"

"Most of the trip flare type devices for indoor use were replaced with laser long ago."

"Low tech, low cost, or somebody with no connections. Which do you think?"

"Somebody's just trying to piss us off."

"Yep. Imagine if Ma kicked off a trip flare," Curran said, smiling.

"Yeah," Perez replied as he started to laugh. "She'd be madder than a one-legged man in an ass kicking contest."

"Good one. Did you reset the flare on the front door?"

"Yes Sir."

"What am I thinking about right now?"

Perez studies him intently for a moment.

"Silly String," Perez and Curran say in stereo.

Back during the first Iraq war, and into the second, the enemy used old-tech booby traps with trip wires. American soldiers found that silly string helped detect trip wires. Sprayed ahead of them as they entered buildings, it would hang over the wires without setting off the device. It can be said that silly string saved a lot of lives, and there was hell to pay if anyone used the party product for anything else. At one point, troop leaders even had to report when someone used it for other than trip wire detection, classifying such use as an "accidental discharge," just like if someone accidently fired their weapon.

"You know what else?"

"No."

"I know who did it."

Perez sat with his lower lip rolled downward, nodding in approval. He thought about old tech, about infiltrating someone's residence; about scare tactics. About government manipulation. About bullies.

"Why did you have to go back inside the house?" he asked.

"Connie needed clean underwear."

Chapter 18

"How did you do this morning?" Curran said to Perez as he walked to the table with two cups of coffee. Perez sat at his computer running more searches for Curran, but earlier, he performed some field work.

"Proctor has an investigator," Perez reported.

"What's he investigating?"

"Don't know yet. He met with him at the company office, so I went over to his house, tapped his phone and set-up a microphone on his back window."

"Did you put a tracker on his vehicle?"

"Both his and the investigators."

"Okay."

Perez looked at Curran for a minute. He admired his team leader's composure. "You okay?" he asked.

"I'm alright."

"I might call bullshit, sir," Perez declared. "They destroyed your boat, ruined all your fishing gear, scared your woman, almost killed you and your best friend and you're alright?"

"Don't forget exposed you to nerve agent. I can see you're still feeling it," Curran said, noting Perez rubbing his chest.

"Yeah, that too."

"Being pissed about it right now won't help anything."

"No, I guess it wouldn't," he said "You were up late last night. All that pool didn't tire you out?"

"It might have been the *one* beer and *four* cups of coffee, but I had some energy reserves."

"What did you do?" Perez asked.

"Watched four hours of hospital security video."

"Find anything."

"I think I did. I'll show you and Connie later.

Caraballo walked in from the other hangar and proceeded to wash his hands in a sink under the steps to the second floor. Curran could smell the orange scented pumice soap.

"What did you find out?" Curran asked Caraballo.

"Nothing new to report. Nobody was at Proctor's boat, and no one came or left."

"Where was Kuvarac?"

"Not there. Didn't see him."

"Then we lost visibility on him," Curran stated flatly.

"Roger."

"Negative," Perez interjected. "Kuvarac was at the Titan Chemical Company. He arrived before 8:00 am and was still there when I left."

"What was your impression?"

"Kuvarac looked like it was just another day."

"Okay. Connie, anything else?" Curran asked Caraballo.

"The Coast Guard was at the marina with a member of the marine police." They were on the dock talking next to the slip for the Miss Margaret. They looked like they thought an empty spot would tell them something. I heard them with the parabolic antenna."

"Anybody notice you?"

"No."

"What's their game plan?"

"They're going to ask everyone in the tournament if they saw anything."

"The owner of the Miss Margaret wasn't on the boat. He reported it missing two days ago after it didn't return to port," Curran said.

"How do you know that?"

"It was on the news this morning."

Caraballo and Perez gave Curran the same raised-eyebrow look.

"What's with the delay" Caraballo asked.

"It seems he's not the most participatory owner. Did you hear Proctor has an investigator?"

"No. What's he investigating?"

"I have a feeling it's us."

"Probably the one that ransacked the house and set the flares," Perez said.

"That's a reasonable assumption. Problem is, we don't have much freedom to maneuver and make our own opportunities here like we usually do."

"But we still do what we do," Caraballo said assertively. "Starting with Proctor and Kuvarac," he added. Perez just nodded in the affirmative.

Curran paused; mental wheels were turning. He smiled. "Yeah. Time for a little crackback action."

"What do you mean, sir?" asked Perez.

"Like in American football," Caraballo replied. "It's the hit you don't see coming."

"Something I have to do first," Curran said, checking his watch before turning and striding up the steps to the second floor.

Ten minutes later, Curran came down the steps. "Be right back" he said to Perez as he passed before going through the door to the other hangar. He walked around the Cessna as Caraballo looking into the open engine cowling performing his pre-flight checks.

"Where are you off to?" Caraballo asked Curran, noticing his friend passing by.

"Going to see Gracie."

"What for Tom?" Caraballo asked, puzzled. Curran stopped in his tracks and turned back to face him.

"It's bothering me."

"What?"

"Two things Baba said; first was the claim his father was the worst off, so he got airlifted first. Second was the last thing he said."

"Which was?"

"Tell Tommy."

Caraballo felt a twinge of irritation. It manifested itself in a scowl Curran could see clearly.

"He said that?" Caraballo asked abruptly.

"He did."

"Why didn't you tell me?"

"I've been thinking about what it meant. I thought it was regarding the beating he took, but I think it was about something else."

"Want me to come with you?"

"No. I got it."

"What about Oscar?"

"I have him working the internet a bit. I want him looking into the Titan Chemical Company books."

"Okay."

Curran studied Caraballo for a moment.

"So, what's going on?"

"I don't know. You tell me?" Caraballo said gruffly.

"You don't know how to feel about Angelina leaving."

Curran's declaration hit Caraballo like a nail in the forehead. The resulting flinch and bulge in Caraballo's forearms were clear across the hangar. Curran waited for a response. He didn't get one.

"Are you upset, embarrassed, disappointed, feeling abandoned, or what?" he added.

"All the above," Caraballo said after momentarily freezing. Curran waited a moment to respond. Caraballo beat him to it. "I know you're trying to help, Tommy, but I got it."

Curran waited for more. Again, he didn't get it.

"No, you don't," he said.

"How do you know?"

"Because you're acting like a bit of a robot, the way you did for at least a year after Jenny died."

"Okay," Caraballo said dispassionately.

"You can't blame yourself, bro. We sent them off. Well, actually I sent them off."

"But she went without saying anything."

"What? She might not have looked scared, but I think she was. Clamming-up might be her reaction to it. It isn't a slam on you."

Caraballo thought for a moment while he stared at the television mounted on the hangar wall. The TV was tuned to the weather channel with the sound off.

"How did you pay for the cable?" he asked

"Don't change the subject."

"No. How'd you do it?"

"I could have charged it to the account, but I tapped into the hangar next door, who tapped into the airport's cable connection; they never use it at night," Curran said with a smile.

"Good idea."

Curran decided to wait it out. He knew saying anything else at this point was a waste of breath. So, he turned and looked for activity outside the hangar. The airfield was still and quiet. After a moment the Bruce Springsteen song "57 Channels (and Nothin' On)" popped into his head.

"She felt safer away from me than she did around me," Caraballo said. Curran turned to see Caraballo standing behind him.

"That's not it, man."

Caraballo throws his arms in the air wide over his head. "Then what is it, dude?" he asked frustratedly.

"She's an independent woman. She hasn't quite decided that you and she are a permanent arrangement so she's still thinking individually."

"Why is she doing that?"

For a second, Curran thought it was a question he just answered, but realized sometimes emotion thickens Connie's head.

"You've only known her for a bit over a month. Now she knows you're quite the catch…," he said jokingly, "…but the whole thing is still new." It's what I would have done."

"No, it isn't."

"True, but I've known you since we were little. She hasn't so she beat it outta here."

"Yeah, I guess."

"When we're done with this, you can be the one that goes and tells her. She'll be relieved and you two can pick up where you left off.

Caraballo thought for a moment. "Yeah, I guess you're right," he said.

"Don't guess," Curran said playfully. Caraballo smiled. "Who's the elder here, me or you?" he said, slapping Caraballo on the shoulder.

"Depends on the situation I guess."

"Like when our antics piss-off Ma," Curran said. Caraballo smiled back.

"Yep, definitely then."

Curran turned back toward the airfield. He and Caraballo stood shoulder-to-shoulder gazing out at the scene before them. It was a beautiful summer day. The leaves on the trees around the airfield perimeter and the grass on the field was a brilliant green; the blue sky and black tarmac set in contrast. The scent of pines drifted past.

"Reminds me of Bragg," Caraballo said.

"I was going to say Camp Mackall. This area has more oaks mixed in with the pines."

"Yeah."

"Say, when are we getting those ultralights?"

"Should be next week."

"With the floats?"

"Yep."

"Those will be fun."

"As soon as we put them together."

"I found something big," Perez declared, walking hurriedly around the Cessna, laptop held in front of him.

"I know. I kept telling him to live his own life and he said that's what he was doing, but its bullshit, you know," Grace O'Reilly said as she reached under a stack of unopened mail for a pack of cigarettes. The house smelled like hibiscus, not cigarettes. Curran had only been there for ten minutes and already felt his presence had somehow made Gracie nervous. She hasn't been smoking. She lit another cigarette and took a long pull while staring straight at Curran. She squinted as she did so, with crow's feet set beside her eyes. She crossed her legs and draped one arm over the back of the wooden chair. "Shit," she exclaimed, blowing smoke toward the ceiling.

"He blamed his father's death on his being away."

"I know." Gracie exhaled cigarette smoke. Quickly, she fanned the air in front of she and Curran and stood. "Sorry," she said as she moved to the sink, turned on the faucet, doused the cigarette, threw it in the trash can hidden under the sink and returned to her seat. "Sorry Honey, go on," she added, gently gripping Curran on the forearm he had resting on the table.

"I told you he thought he had to support you."

"Yeah. Between the insurance, my hobby, and my side of the family, I'm fine. I volunteer at the hospital just because I want to."

"You like the volunteer work that much?"

"Yeah, I do," she said, a light shining in her eyes. Curran recognized it.

"How long have you been doing it?"

"About six months. Never thought I would like it so much."

"Yeah, I get it. Some people say I missed my calling as a paramedic."

"I remember you used to volunteer on the ambulance in town."

"Yeah, I loved it. Sometimes I'm not sure why I joined the army."

"My Robert thought you would have joined the Coast Guard," she said, the term 'her Robert' referring to her husband.

"Well, life has a weird way of working out; seems I'm pretty good at this army thing. Look, I have something I need to run by you," Curran declared seriously. Gracie stared into his eyes as if bracing for something Curran was about to deliver.

"Go ahead."

"Baba said his father was airlifted off the boat before it went down with all hands. Then he said they told him his father was the worst off so even though he was the captain, he went first."

"Okay," she replied in a tone that was both interested, and dismissive.

"Well, it seems they were referring to a sickness or injury, not the boat sinking. If they said he was the worst-off…" Curran said with air quote fingers. "…that meant it was in comparison to the others, yet it means the others had some sort of affliction as well. If it was an issue with the boat, that would be a common issue with no variation in degree of severity between them. So why just lift *him* off the boat? Why not take them *all* instead of just him? If the boat was sinking, they would have taken everybody."

"What are you getting at?"

"Did he have an illness or heart condition or something that could have happened on the boat?"

"No. He was strong as an ox with the sex drive of an eighteen- year-old," the woman reports adamantly.

"Too much information, Gracie," Curran said playfully, shaking his head and wagging a hand in front of his face. The two shared a brief chuckle. "Seriously though, what drove him off the boat?"

"Why do you want to know?"

"I'll tell you in a minute but suffice it to say the story doesn't make sense to me. If he was sick, I think the other guys could have brought the boat in. The weather was reported as flat calm on that night, and from the float plan they filed with the marina, they were about half-way in from their fishing spot."

"You've been looking into this," she said with an air of suspicion in her voice.

"If something bad happened to him I'd like to know. If it was something devious, I'd like to get to the bottom of it."

"Are you a police officer?"

"Of course not."

"The police closed the case. Why didn't they think something was wrong?"

"Because the explanation made sense in and of itself."

"But it doesn't for you."

"No."

"Then where are we?"

"Thinking about loose ends."

Gracie stared at Curran for a moment.

"Okay. More tea dear?" she said as she stood, simultaneously sliding the wooden chair backward with the back of her leg.

"Yes, please," Curran replied. The woman's trip to the iced tea jar and back gives him time to consider how far he wanted to take this thing. He thought of the information Perez found on the computer, and what he discovered on his own.

She sat back down and folded her hands on the table. It was a sign of rising tension in her. "This next bit of news hits a bit closer," he said. She gave him a slight nod as if saying go. "There is a history of the government dumping chemical weapons and nerve agents off the coast after World War II. We believe that some people were recently exposed to those things. I think they managed to kill the crew of a fishing boat in the tournament last weekend. I've seen what looks like fish kills due to exposure, and what might be a response to a spill or a discovery," Curran reported flatly.

The woman had a grim expression. "How does that involve me?" she said.

"The last recorded location of your husband's boat, and the location where Baba was attacked are very close to each other."

"How close?"

"Within three-hundred yards twenty miles out."

Tears welled in Gracie's eyes. Her cheeks puffed and she lurched forward. She clenched her fists and the vinyl tablecloth bunched underneath her hands. She trembled. "My God I'm cursed," she exclaimed.

"What do you mean?" Curran said, sitting calmly.

"Was my son out looking for his father's boat?" she said as if through gravel. Curran didn't immediately respond.

"What do you know about your husband's sinking?" he finally asked.

"Nothing more than you."

"That's not exactly true," Curran said seriously, setting both forearms on the table. "A friend was able to gain access to the right computer systems and find one report that said the boat was lost with all hands due to fire, and a Coast Guard report saying it was a hazard to navigation. Do you understand the difference?"

"No."

"One means it sank. The other means it was still floating, declared a possible hazard to other vessels and they sank it on purpose."

The woman's eyes glared at Curran as a lump appeared in her throat. When she heard the words "they sank," she bolted upright, gaining about four inches in height. Then she shrank back down to size.

"What?" the woman gasped. "You found the boat?"

"No." I don't think it's out there, but there's a ship out there covering everything within three miles in concrete."

"Concrete?"

"Yeah. Lots of piles of it all over the place."

"That's one way to do it," she said.

"Do what?"

"Oh, you know," Gracie said, clearly distracted, her voice trailing off.

Curran thought for a moment before speaking. He knew what she meant. He knew what she was stopping short of saying. But some of what he discovered wouldn't be proven by accusation alone, so he hit pause on those. "Look, my friend Oscar was nearly killed by an apparent chemical agent out on the ocean and now we want to get to the bottom of it."

"Is he okay?"

"He'll be fine. Did you figure out what Mr. O'Reilly died from?"

"He had a seizure."

"What sort of seizure?"

"I don't know.

"Where do I fit in all this?"

Decision time for Curran; does he divulge more, or leave it alone? Time for a little intelligence gathering.

"You know, the Titan Chemical Company produced thousands of tons of chemical agents for the army in the forties.

"Everybody knows that," Gracie said before shifting gears. "I'm having a beer; you want one?" she announced as she rose, spinning on her heels and stepping to the nearby refrigerator. She didn't wait for a reply.

She retrieved two brown bottles from the fridge, grabs two cold beer glasses from the freezer and returned to the table. She reached past Curran with a bottle in her hand and opened it using an old-fashioned bottle opener mounted on the inside of the kitchen door frame. After repeating the process with the second bottle she set both down on the table. On the label is the picture of a woman's arm holding a beer as if lifting it to take a sip. Above the picture are the words 'Bent-Elbow DGB.' Under the picture reads 'India Pale Ale.'

"You have to try this," she said. "Everybody's always asking 'is it an I.P.A? Yes it's an I.P.A,' blah, blah blah, blah blah," she added mockingly, speaking with a rapid, nasal tone.

"What's DGB mean?"

"Damn good beer. That's what it is, too." She lifted Curran's glass, poured the beer into it, and set it down in front of him. "You know, I never heard any news about people dying on a boat last weekend. I did read about one that was reported missing."

"Same boat, but it's not missing."

"What do you mean?"

"They sank it."

"Who sank it?"

"Whoever can order an F-16 fighter jet to fire a missile at it," Curran said. He decided not to tell her about his boat being blown-up.

"Are you kidding me?" she asked, squinting one eye.

"No ma'am. I was close by," Curran said. He grabbed the beer in front of him and took a slow draw from it. He pulled the glass from his mouth and pressed his lips together, wrinkling his mouth. He nods up and down in approval. "Wow, you're right, that is a 's a damn good beer."

"I told you," she said, staring out the kitchen window. A short silence ensued. Curran tried to gauge her state of mind. Then, she turned her head and stared a steely-cold stare directly at him. "So, you don't think the boat was lost, you think they sank my Robert's boat on purpose."

"I do."

"Why?"

"Preponderance of the evidence."

"Do you think it's down there somewhere?"

"They probably towed it away and sank it, but yeah." Curran said. He waited, thinking it odd Gracie didn't ask who "they" were.

"Could it be covered in a pile of concrete pumped down on top of it."

"Possibly. It would be a really big concrete pile, bigger than any I saw, but if it was blown apart, definitely."

"You think that poor boy Jerry Chivers was buried inside there?"

"I don't know."

"Died with his father on the same day."

"I thought you said Stan was off the boat."

"He was, but when he heard his son was lost at sea, he dropped dead on the kitchen floor right then and there."

"It ruined Silvia," she says matter-of-factly.

"I can imagine it would."

"All this makes you think it was sunk on purpose?"

"This and a couple other things," Curran said. He figured he was finally getting probed for information.

"So, you saw my Robert's boat covered up in concrete and a fighter jet blow-up another one, and you didn't call the police?" she said in a maternal tone like she disapproved of Curran's actions. He automatically made a mental note of the wooden spoons in the clay jar on the counter. Mrs. DeFelice whacked Caraballo with one once as a kid when Connie cursed at the dinner table and he can still recall the slap it made. It was so early in the lives of the inseparable Tommy, Connie, and Jenny that it was during the short period when Mrs. DeFelice referred to him as 'that orphan boy.'

"I saw *something* covered in concrete which *might* be his boat, and I did see a fighter jet blow up another one, but no. I didn't call the police."

"Why not?" Gracie probed.

"Let's just say I have my reasons. Plus, I know a little about the darker side of our government. It's safer for me to look into it on my own rather than call the cops."

"What else is weird out there?"

"They're netting-up schools of dead fish, and we were run-off of the spot where the boat is."

"Run-off?"

"Well, not really," Curran grumbled. "They tried once and we reacted, and another time we just ran off. "You know, Baba should have been with us during the tournament last weekend."

"How did you guys do?"

"We took first on Dennis Draper's boat."

"Congratulations!"

"Yeah, that chemical company guy still can't fish," Curran said, thinking of an end-around.

"Blanton Proctor?"

"Yeah."

"You know he has that boat just to get away from his wife."

"I heard that."

"Did you hear he has the largest eel breeding program in the United States?"

"No, I didn't!" Curran blurted, flabbergasted. His ongoing opinion of Proctor was one of worthlessness even less desirable than the legendary "tits on a bull."

"Is he doing it for the money or the recovery of the species?"

"Both. We installed all the holding tanks for his fish farm over on that old chemical yard where he works."

"At the chemical plant?"

"Yeah, and he still has poachers breaking in to get at the glass eels."

"How do you know that?"

"He tells me. We do the maintenance on the pumps, tanks, and PVC pipes. It's all inside warehouses but wintertime is especially hard on that stuff."

"Who does the maintenance?"

"I take a couple of the local Pineys from down the street with me."

"Did Baba ever go with you?"

"Every once in a while."

"What did Proctor do about the poachers?"

"He didn't say. He has a fisheries biologist from Albania or somewhere; scary guy until you get used to him; maybe he handles the poachers."

"What's that guy's name?"

"He goes by Roddy," Grace replied.

"Is he one of the mates on Proctor's boat?"

"Yep."

"How did you get hooked up with that gig?"

"We've done hatchery set-ups for a few other companies and the Proctors are second cousins, you know."

"I didn't know that.

"Yeah. Blanton's also starting striped bass breeding this year.

"Awesome."

"So, what did you think about that beer?"

'It was really, really good," Curran proclaimed. Why use a big word when two smaller ones will do? "Had a great flavor and a nice little bite to it."

"Glad you approve. They serve it at four places in the area, one on Sea Island."

"No way!" Curran barked, absolutely astounded by her abilities. "Volunteering, building fish farms, brewing beer! Gracie, you have skills!"

"Would you like to see the brewery?"

"Brewery?"

"Well, it's in the building around back, but I'm almost ready to rent a space in the industrial park."

"Awesome. I'd love to see it."

Curran eventually said goodbye to Grace O'Reilly, got in his Bronco and pulled out of the driveway. He drove west about half a mile down the road leading back to the airport and turned off onto an overgrown dirt road at the bottom of the power company high tension line. He shifted the truck into four-wheel drive and bounced down the overgrown path headed southeast. About half a mile down the line he turned off and tucked the truck out of sight in the woods.

Curran say in the truck with the window down. He breathed in the aroma of the pine forest as he sat silently, listening to the sounds of the woods. The pine boughs rustled overhead. Birds chirped. Curran's slight tinnitus rang in his right ear. He checked his watch. Time to go.

He stepped out of the truck, went to the back, swung the spare tire out of the way, popped the hatch, and retrieved a pair of camouflage pants. After putting them on over his black surfing shorts, he grabbed a pair of well broken-in, light brown hiking boots. He slipped on the socks stashed inside the boots and then the boots. He tied them and stood erect, smiling. He shifted his weight from one foot to the other a couple times and whispered, "that's what I'm talking about." After closing the truck, Curran set out through the woods headed east.

Fifteen minutes later, after moving slowly, he crouched in the high foliage fifty yards from the south corner of Grace O'Reilly's house. He got there right on time to see her leave for her volunteer job at the hospital. He waited the appropriate amount of time to be sure she didn't return for something like a coffee go-cup, a snack she might have made for work, etc. Then Curran went to the back door, took the door key from under the mat (which he knew was there because Caraballo did his normal recon the last time they were there) and went inside. Curran knew there would be no alarm system, no video surveillance, no guard dog, and no one else in the house.

Curran spent a few minutes looking around before he settled into the chair behind Gracie's desk. He went through her computer, receipt book, checkbook, and the management software for the budding brewery. He ran though the files for the work she did setting up fish hatcheries and plowed into the pile of bank statements she had still in the envelopes in a basket on the nearby window seat.

After that Curran found the steps leading down to the basement. There, he found a tall five-drawer file cabinet full of Mr.

O'Reilly's business records. He sifted through the top two drawers. He opened the third and the sight of what lay inside sent a bolt of adrenaline up his spine and the hairs on his arms stood up. It was a medical record folder from the hospital. He pulled it out, opened it, and set it on top of the other files. Using a finger as a guide, he scanned down the first page. He flipped it over and scanned down the second page. He stopped, staring at one entry. "Oh shit," he whispered breathlessly. He retrieved the phone from his pocket and snapped a picture of the page. After carefully returning the file to the drawer and closed the drawer slowly. He opened the fourth drawer and spied something inside. The item caught his eye. A black and white picture in a 5"x 8" frame. He pulled it out and held it up to the light. In the picture a tall, thin man stood on a barge wiping his forehead with a small towel. After a moment, Curran once again retrieved his phone and took a picture of the picture in his hand.

Curran made sure the basement was as he found it before returning to the first floor. On his way past the kitchen, he noticed his half-finished glass of iced tea on the counter. Good iced tea is hard to waste. After momentary pause, he left.

Chapter 19

Curran returned to the hangar to find the Cessna was not there and both Caraballo and Perez were out. He got back on his computer and wrote down his thoughts on his meeting with Grace O'Reilly. After that he fed a couple pictures into his computer and contacted MacPherson, the boss. The first picture regarded their last conversation.

"Is this someone asking about me?" he asked with the first picture.

"Affirmative," was MacPherson's reply.

"Please have your office kid run this through facial recognition and identify subject in the foreground," Curran wrote with the second photo.

"WILCO. When will you be ready for follow-on assignment?" Mac replied.

"Five days. Project here will conclude and two team members will return from leave."

"Keep me informed."

"Will do."

Curran went for a forty-minute run around the perimeter of the airfield and was cooling down laying on a slanted board set-up at the start of a fitness trail near the tiny airport office building right as Caraballo and Perez landed and taxied to the gas pump. Caraballo turned off the engine and the area went silent as the prop stopped.

He and Perez stepped out of the plane. The only sound was from the yellow banner towing airplane diving to retrieve another banner in the middle of the airfield.

"Get up you lazy bastard," Caraballo joked as he reached the gas pump.

Curran smiled but said nothing as he walked to the perimeter fence. He put his finders through the chain link and let his arms hang as he watched Caraballo refuel the plane. Minutes later, Caraballo jammed the fuel nozzle back into its space on the side of the 100LL fuel pump. "We got some good chow, Tommy" he said as he looked over at Curran.

"Oh yeah? Like what?"

"Osso Bucco, Insalata Caprese, and some nice Cannoli for dessert from the place in Millville."

"Broccoli Rabe too?"

"Yes, Broccoli Rabe too," Caraballo replied with a hint of an Italian accent.

"Awesome. It pays to have an airplane."

"It sure does."

"Meet you at the hangar," Curran said before running off.

After dinner upstairs, the three men went back downstairs to discuss current events. All three poured themselves a mug of birch beer and took chairs around the circular resin table that held their laptops and other items.

"This is my new favorite beverage," Perez declared.

"Can't believe it took this long to discover, eh?" Caraballo replied.

"Like the first time you drink Bacchus in Korea," said Curran. "Like *whammo!*" he added, hands on either side of his head.

"Yeah, and that Bacchus stuff puts lead in the pencil," Caraballo reported.

"Bonus," Perez added.

"Yep. Nothing like a giant dose of niacinamide. So, Connie what did you see on the flight?" Curran asked.

"Same stuff. Salvage boat pumping concrete. Black RHIB running around."

"Any dead fish?"

"Yeah. In the exact same spot."

"That's actually good. It's not spreading. But I'd love to get a look at what's om the bottom. Check this out," Curran said as he tapped on his computer before turning it to face Perez and Caraballo. "There we go," he said. On the computer screen are entries in a file relating to the salvage vessel. "There's a written order for the salvage vessel from five months ago. Look at the assignment detail. It shows the location of their target and description as the 'MV Gracie Ann.' Look next to it. There's a task order for the research boat."

"Survey MV Gracie Ann," Caraballo said, reading off the screen.

"The boat owned by Robert O'Reilly Senior. Named after his wife. Underwater survey of a sunken boat," Curran said. "Then look at this," Curran added before clicking on another file. It's a receipt from nine months ago from the Titan Chemical Company of South Jersey. Caraballo and Perez scan the computer screen.

"Says it's for services rendered," Caraballo read.

"The recipient is Gracie Ann. "Is that the boat or the wife?" asked Perez.

"I think it's the wife. I think it's only a receipt and she got paid in cash."

"Why would she get paid under the table? The check is for over $8000 dollars Tom," Caraballo asked.

"Eel tanks?"

"Eel tanks? The money was for eel tanks?" blurted Caraballo suspiciously.

"It could be." Curran replied. "She has a business installing the tanks and systems for fish hatcheries."

"Grace O'Reilly?"

"Yes. Grace O'Reilly. She also has her own microbrewery."

"It doesn't mean something else didn't happen but if she was in on it, I sure would be disappointed."

"We have to verify these eel tanks," Perez quietly announced.

"Did you verify the microbrewery?" Caraballo asked.

"Sure did."

"Good man."

"It's sold around the island too."

"No shit?"

"Zero shit. But there is something else," Curran announced as he clicked on his computer. "That's a copy of the cause of death for Mr. O'Reilly."

"Exsanguination due to penetrating wound of the upper right thoracic cavity," Caraballo said, reading the abbreviated medical language. "You know what that sounds like?"

"Bullet wound," Curran and Perez said in unison.

"Now why would she keep that from you?" Caraballo snorted contemptuously. "Weren't her son's last words 'tell Tommy'?"

"That's a million-dollar question. In fact," Curran said as he moved the mouse on the computer. He clicked on a file. "It's two-million," he added as he sat back in his chair. Caraballo and Perez peered at the screen. "A few months ago, she had $250k in debt and another thirty-five in medical bills. Now she's debt-free with $1.75 million in mutual funds. This is what Oscar found this morning, and I verified at her house."

Curran let that soak-in as he grabbed the three birch beer mugs and walked over to refill them.

"For services rendered," Caraballo said flatly.

"Oscar, your computer skills are better than mine." Curran said as he poured three mugs. "You find the source of that money and we might be able to figure out the reason behind the eventual demise of Robert O'Reilly Senior, and what involvement, if any, his wife had in the whole thing. But there is another thing that begs a question."

"What's the thing?" asked Caraballo.

"What I saw on video last night," Curran said as he approached the table carrying the soda mugs.

"Which was?"

"Grace Ann O'Reilly taking her husband's medical record out of the hospital record room and replacing it with an empty file," Curran said as he remained standing.

"And the question being?" Caraballo said.

"Was it, to use terms I heard on TV, of her own free will and volition with malice aforethought, or because she was forced to do it against her will?"

"Is that it?"

"Well, I sent a couple pictures to Mac. Oscar, click on that picture file," Curran directed. Perez leaned up and clicked on the computer. The picture of a man's face came into view. "I asked if he might be one of the people asking about us, like Mac said the other day. The answer was yes."

"Why him?"

"I don't know, but I'm on to something I'll tell you about if it develops further. Click on the next one."

Perez opens the next picture.

"Who's that?" asked Caraballo as he leaned closer to the computer. "You know who it looks like," Caraballo said, not really a question.

"Yeah, it looks like Baba, but it can't be him or his old man. Look at the old tractor in the background. Steel wheels. It's probably his grandfather."

"Where'd you get it?" asked Perez.

"In the same file cabinet where I found the medical record."

"Then next in the hopper is what?" Caraballo asked.

Curran thought for a moment. "Put on your tactical gear," he said. "Then we'll do some mission planning."

Chapter 20

Curran felt the rain run down his back as he crouched in the high straw at the edge of the pine forest. He didn't care about being wet. He was cool. It was better than sweating. Besides, the cool rain would help Caraballo see warm objects around him as Caraballo circled overhead in the Cessna wearing the latest generation thermal imaging/night vision goggles.

Perez had pulled into the parking lot of an old, run-down motel on the road to Millville, New Jersey. He came almost to a stop when Curran stepped out of the passenger side and made his way quickly to the darkness of the woods behind the hotel. Perez glided back out onto the street and headed into the town. Curran crouched in the woods for ten minutes after Perez was gone, adjusting his senses to the darkness and sound of the woods, and to be sure no one noticed him. The rain softened the leaves on the forest floor and masked any sound of Curran's movement through the area. He traveled though the dark forest to the other side where it met the field behind the rear lot of the Titan Chemical company.

"Six, this is one," Curran heard Caraballo say through his earpiece. "I have you in sight," he added. Curran could hear the aircraft flying its track around the area but couldn't see it. "Three deer between you and the fence. No one in sight inside the perimeter." He verified what Curran saw in his own night vision goggles. Curran tapped on his throat microphone three times in reply.

"By the way; what song am I thinking of right now?" Caraballo quipped. Curran didn't answer.

"Six, this is three," Curran heard Perez say. "Titan parking lot is empty. All the lights are out."

Curran tapped his throat microphone again. He started moving slowly across the field directly at the rear perimeter fence of the giant chemical company yard. Caraballo and Perez' earlier aerial recon/food run revealed the three newest items on the chemical company compound were three steel warehouses set end-to-end along the fence at the rear of the property, placed between the perimeter fence and three enormous gaseous chemical storage bladders enclosed in rusted round steel frames. No eel tanks were readily visible from overhead.

Curran got within fifteen feet of the three deer standing in the field before they noticed him. He stopped, letting them slowly walk away instead of becoming alarmed and fleeing, possibly drawing some attention. He continued moving until he reached the eight-foot high, rusted chain link fence that was the only perimeter barrier to the chemical company yard. He felt both irritation and relief that the wind was behind him. Irritated for the fact you never approach a potentially dangerous area from upwind. Relieved he wasn't downwind from the aroma of the chemical company. He figured it wasn't as bad as the smell of the sewerage pond in the middle of the housing area at Kandahar Airfield in Afghanistan, but still objectionable. At least the shit pond in Afghanistan had a fountain in the middle. No matter, whatever caused the odors at the chemical company caused a slight layer of cloudy vapor visible at night. Curran could see it hanging over the area.

"Six, I see you at the perimeter. You're clear to proceed," Caraballo said over the radio.

Silently, Curran crept down the fence line. It was only a few feet until he noticed a bare spot on the ground in a slight depression under the fence. It was a possibly ingress point. Curran thought it would have to be a small person, but someone could make it.

"Why wouldn't they fix this?" he thought. Then something dawned on him. Poachers. Gracie said they were having a problem with poachers. What would someone with a poacher problem do? Curran backed up a few feet and laid prone on the ground. He moved laterally about a foot, trying to let the dim illumination of a distant flood light help him see the bottom of the fence. It was no use. He flipped the night vision goggles down from their perch on top of his skateboard-style helmet and flipped the switch from thermal to infra-red.

"And there we go," he said in his head. He could see the tiny canister of a trip flare. Old school. M49 type like the ones back at the house. 35,000 candlepower of NVG blinding goodness. Curran got back up and moved further down the fence. He anticipated this situation and was ready. In the darkness behind the warehouse building farthest to the left, he pulled a rolled-up army laundry bag out of his pants cargo pocket and threw it over the three strands of barbed wire at the top of the fence. He was traveling light, only a sidearm instead of a carbine and no plate armor, so he just climbed over the fence as easily as a cat climbs a kitchen counter. One hop to grab the top, gymnast roll over it like going over a parallel bar and a short fall back to earth. He deftly stepped the three remaining feet to the side of the warehouse and froze, crouching motionless. He tapped his throat microphone three times.

"Area still clear," Caraballo reported.

You couldn't see the grin on Curran's face, but it was there. It wasn't for his athletic ability. He was digging the action and the potential danger of who might be lurking on this side of the fence of this fuming fart factory. He circled around the first corner and moved down the wall of the warehouse. He stopped at the front and scanned the area, first with the naked eye, followed by night vision and thermal imaging. Nothing there. He adjusted the gloves on his hands, and then rounded the corner and reached the door of the warehouse.

He carefully tried the door. Locked. He was prepared. Curran reached into his pocket and retrieved a lock-picking device resembling a little hand grip exerciser with an upside-down hole saw on top. He inserted it into the deadbolt lock over the knob. With two rapid gripping motions he operated the device, and then turned the lock. Then he inserted it into the lock within the doorknob. After three rapid gripping motions, Curran turned the knob and opened the door about an inch. A dim green light reflected off his face. He checked the area outside once again. Then he opened the warehouse door wide enough to go inside. He flipped his night vision goggles down for a look by thermal. A moment later he flipped them back up, stepped inside, and shut the door behind him.

Curran crouched low inside the warehouse. Around him hummed the sounds of water pumps. It made him think of the pool at the DeFelice home in Florida. The air was moist and smelled like saltwater algae. For a second, Curran felt stupid for tactically sneaking into an aquarium. Five steel tanks the size of large home hot tubs lined the near wall. Six more rows of tanks just like those filled the rest of the building. Lights inside fed a shaft of greenish light out of the small windows in the sides of the tanks. Curran crept to the first tank. Peering into the window, he was swimming creatures mostly collected at the bottom.

"Those are definitely eels," he thought. One by one, he looked in the tanks. First the tanks along the wall, followed by the next row, then the next. As he rounded the final row, something caught his eye. On the far wall, a workbench sat in the middle flanked by two tanks on either side. On the wall over the workbench were five pool chemistry controller modules, with wiring leading down to chemical canisters mounted under them. On the workbench sat a large digital water sample analyzer, a collection of water vials and various bottles of testing agents, a stack of three-ring binders

and a couple notebooks, and a small television screen playing the Phillies baseball game. Under the workbench were two small square refrigerators, and in front, was a barstool. Sitting on the barstool was a man.

A bolt of adrenaline coursed through Curran's veins as he silently pulled the .40 caliber handgun from the holster on his thigh. He took a tight two-hand grip close to his chest. He squared himself to his target and pressed his arms forward, extending the weapon in front of himself. Moving forward deliberately, he closed the distance to the man. He stopped roughly five feet away. He was close enough to speak softly, but far enough away to react if attacked. He didn't like closing the distance too soon. This wasn't a movie. You don't stick your gun in someone's back and say, "hands in the air." As soon as someone is touched, they react. You also don't sneak-up and grab them. They always fight and you just gave them one of your arms. Either drop them without any attempt to communicate or keep your distance.

"Don't move," he said smoothly just loudly enough for the man to hear him over the sound of the pumps.

The man sitting on the barstool froze. He was holding a small vial and a tiny bottle of water testing fluid, putting one drop at a time in the vial. He turned his head slowly. When he saw Curran's green and black camouflaged face, he smiled.

"Tom Curran," the man said happily. He set down the items in his hand and stood. Standing about 5'10" tall he was about three inches shorter than Curran.

"God damn, shit bird," Curran said, standing and holstering his pistol. The two men hugged. When the hug concluded, they separated themselves but kept one arm each on a shoulder. "Radomir, how's your mother?" Curran added.

"She's fine. Asks about you," Kuvarac said in a gravelly voice.

"Did you ever move her to Zagreb?"

"Yes, but now she lives in Split."

"Man, it's nice there. Small world, right brother?" Curran stated.

"It sure is. Do your guys still think I'm a mass murderer?"

"They sure do," Curran replied.

"Good. What they don't know won't kill them," Kuvarac joked.

"And the story about raping women in front of their husbands before you killed them.

"Ah, that old gem, eh?" Kuvarac said raucously. He turned and crouched in front of one of the small refrigerators. He retrieved a bottle and stood. Kuvarac had Curran by a good fifteen years, and the wear and tear was obvious. He moved stiffly and didn't appear to stand completely erect. "We have to have some rakija," he declared, facing Curran.

"Ugh, only one," Curran said, smiling. "I remember the last time. My head felt like a pumpkin for two days."

"Just like drinking tequila, but better tasting," Kuvarac replied. He retrieved two shot-sized glasses from a space on top of one of the controller modules on the wall. He poured the liquid and handed one of the glasses to Curran. The two men clinked glasses. When Curran brought the glass to his mouth, he paused and smelled the aroma of the liquor before drinking half of it.

"My mother wondered if you still did that?" Kuvarac said.

"Did what?"

"Smelled everything you ate and drank."

Curran smiled. "Old habit my friend. Saved my bacon a couple times."

"You're wise to do it."

Curran drank the rest of his shot. "Radomir, tell me what's going on?" he said.

Curran and Perez arrived back at the hangar shortly before dawn, in what military people call "morning nautical twilight." The door to the airfield was open and Caraballo was cleaning the Cessna's windshield. Perez walked past the aircraft headed toward the other hangar as Curran walked up to Caraballo.

"You ready?" Curran asked.

"Yep. What's the plan?"

"Other side. We have to take the truck."

"Okay."

The two men got into Curran's blue Bronco and drove around the hangars to the other side where people parked airplanes out on the tarmac. They traveled slowly toward the airfield gate.

"You tell Perez the truth about Kuvarac?" Caraballo asked.

"Need to know, my brother, need to know," Curran droned as he stopped at the gate. "By the way," he added, looking at Caraballo. "All veiled and misty, Streets of Blue," Curran sang loudly, the first two lines of the song *Mystify* by the 1980's band INXS (pronounced In-Excess).

"What?" asked Caraballo, startled but amused.

"The song you were thinking of last night. You asked me."

"Jeez, Louise," Caraballo exclaimed.

"I need perfection," Curran sang, skipping ahead in the song. Caraballo joined in for more.

They went through the airfield gate, singing along. Then they drove along the airport entrance and rode past the small airport FBO building. They traveled past another set of hangars and went through another gate back onto the airfield on the other side of the airport. Dawn had broken and the low summer sun cast long shadows across the airfield. Curran heard a sound coming from the north, over the trees past the airport perimeter. "Here we go," he said.

Curran and Caraballo got out of the truck, both carrying large zippered duffel bags. Curran reached into his pocket and retrieved a pair of orange, soft foam ear plugs.

Suddenly, a Coast Guard helicopter appeared over the trees at the edge of the airfield, the down-blast from the rotors rustling the leaves on the tall oaks near the perimeter. It flew over and landed eastern end of runway 31. It turned and taxied about one-hundred feet and stopped.

"A Blackhawk by any other name," Curran said over the rising din of the rotor blades.

"Is still a Blackhawk," Caraballo answered.

The side door of the helicopter slid open and the crew chief hopped out. He pointed at Curran and Caraballo with a straight hand, fingers together like a Jamaican traffic cop, and motioned for them to come to the aircraft. They walked swiftly over to it, climbed in, and found their seats. Curran slapped the man sitting next to him on the thigh.

"Hey Rock," Curran said over the din of the jet engines and rotor transmission.

"Hey Tommy."

Curran motioned toward the front of the aircraft. He noticed the ship had a crew of three with no rescue swimmer. "Friends of yours?" he said.

"Friends of ours. You always dress like that?" Zanni replied, referring to Curran's dark green t-shirt, combat boots, M-81 woodland camouflage pattern fatigue pants, and the gun he had tucked inside the right waistband in an IWB holster. There was still a trace of camouflage paint on his neck and at his hairline.

"Had something to do last night."

"Quick out and back, right?"

"You got it." Curran said.

"Well you're crazy for doing this?"

"Not me," Curran stated. "Him," he added, motioning to Caraballo.

"How'd you get him to do it?" Zanni asked.

Caraballo looked at Zanni and made the closed fist motion that starts the game "rock, paper, scissors." Zanni laughed out loud.

The Coast Guard helicopter made a beeline straight from the airport, across the countryside and saltwater marsh, over Sea Island and out to sea. When the pilot turned the aircraft and started circling one area, Curran knew they were at the place where on two different occasions they spotted a fishing trawler netting a school of dead fish.

The aircraft stopped forward progress and started a very slow descent toward the water. In back, Curran helped Caraballo get into his military underwater rebreather scuba gear. Caraballo held-up his big dive watch to Curran for both to see. This one was a little different. It showed a bearing and distance to a target. The two men gave each other the "okay" symbol. They had already discussed the operation. Curran wanted to go along, but just to be sure the helicopter didn't leave them stranded twenty miles out, he was going to stay aboard.

The aircraft's rotor blast deflected the surface water as the aircraft reached low hover. The crew chief signaled to Curran they were as low as they would get. Curran tapped Caraballo on the shoulder. Both men found the vibration, noise, smell of aviation kerosene and swirling blades of the helicopter oddly reassuring, but no time to waste. Caraballo slid toward the open door, hanging his lower legs over the sill. He waited as Curran tossed a small dark blue scuba scooter roughly the size of a watermelon out the door. He watched it plunge into the water and then bob to the surface before sliding his body out the rest of the way and dropping into the water, legs crossed, arms hugging his swim fins, one hand holding his mask and regulator in place.

Caraballo quickly donned his fins. Water sprayed all around him as the helicopter hoisted itself into a higher hover. He swam about twenty feet to the scooter, grabbed it by the handles, checked the dive computer on his wrist, twisted the scooter's hand grip activating the tiny propeller at the rear, and down he went.

The pilot started a low orbit around the area. After a few minutes, as Curran, Zanni, and the crew chief watched out the open side door, their eyes focused on the spot where Caraballo dove under, Zanni tapped Curran on the leg. He had a folded yellow envelope in his hand, the kind with the metal clasp. Curran noticed it, looked at Zanni, then took the envelope and slid it into his cargo pocket.

"Read it later," Zanni said flatly. Curran simply nodded in the affirmative.

Ten minutes later Curran pointed at something out the door. "There he is," he shouted over the noise of the aircraft. The crew chief relayed the news to the pilots and the aircraft swooped in to pick up Caraballo. They hoisted the small scuba scooter up first, then sent a sling down for Caraballo. Curran felt a strange sense of alarm. He sat in his seat on the opposite side of the aircraft from the open door, pressing his back into the nylon webbing of the seatback. He had one hand on the gun on his side while the other held a vice-like grip on the frame of the seat next to his left thigh. His eyes scanned from Zanni on his left to the front of the helicopter to his right, and back.

As the crew chief operated the hoist, Caraballo cleared the door sill and swung inside the aircraft. He stood as tall as he could in the limited space of the compartment and grabbed an overhead handle with one hand. Right away he spotted the tension in Curran. He looked at Zanni, who seemed to be more interested in eating a Slim Jim and looking at him than anything else, and then back at Curran. Caraballo turned around and slid the aircraft door closed. He moved over and put his head on the side of Curran's opposite Zanni.

"What's wrong?" he asked, close to Curran's ear.

"Nothing. I just got paranoid."

Caraballo simply pursed his lips and nodded. He understood. The ocean near Southern New Jersey hadn't been particularly friendly to the two men in recent days. Bullies, nerve agents, fighter jets, a dead friend. Caraballo turned and slumped into the seat next to Curran. Looking around, he noticed the crew chief holding two water bottles close enough for him to grab. He took them and gave one to Curran. The crew chief threw one to Zanni, who caught it and chugged the whole thing.

After the two men opened the bottles and drank some water, they looked at each other. Caraballo made a hand motion like pointing down with one finger with his hand in front of his chest. Curran caught it and looked him in the eye. Caraballo nodded a small affirmative north and south. He found something under the water. Curran knew what he meant.

Twenty-minutes later the aircraft set down back at the Woodbine airport and rolled back to the same place it picked up Curran and Caraballo. Having said thanks and goodbye to Zanni and the crew, they hopped out, grabbed their bags, and walked away. Caraballo was back in his street clothes. The Coast Guard wasted no time in taking off and moving out of sight, headed back to the Coast Guard air base at the Atlantic City International Airport in the woods behind Atlantic City.

The guys got in Curran's truck and started back toward the other side of the airport to their hangars. Fresh from their trip, but keeping quiet until they had some privacy, Curran asked Caraballo a question using the half-question format he learned from watching Mrs. DeFelice. You normally know the answer.

"So, what you saw out there on the bottom," Curran asked.

"Was exactly what you expected." Caraballo answered, finishing a sentence Curran started.

Chapter 21

Curran and Caraballo cleaned up, took a couple hours down time and were back up by 11 AM. Caraballo resumed his maintenance on the Cessna as Curran grabbed the envelope Zanni gave him and walked out the open hangar door. He leaned back against the outside of the hangar and watched the banner airplanes drop and pick-up advertising banners before opening the envelope. He pulled out a large piece of paper and read through it. As he did, you could see the words on the page affect him. He shrank slightly, like letting some air out of a rubber raft. He returned the paper to the envelope and retrieved a picture roughly 4" by 6". When he looked at the photo, it was like he was punched in the gut by an invisible fist. He bent at the waist and put his hands on his legs above the knees, propping himself up.

Caraballo noticed his posture and walked over to Curran. He reached his friend as Curran resumed his upright position with his back against the hangar. "What it is it?" he asked.

Curran didn't say anything. He looked at Caraballo and handed him the photograph. Caraballo grabbed it and held it up for a look.

"No shit?" he said, his voice slightly elevated in tone.

"No shit," Curran said bluntly. He put his hands on his hips and stared out at the airfield.

"Is it priority one?"

"No. First things first."

"You know what this calls for?"

"No. What?" Curran asked.

"Café Cubano."

Curran thought for a second. "You know. You're right!" he said breathlessly.

Although the day was bright and beautiful at the Jersey Shore, it was pouring rain in center city Philadelphia. The scene from a week ago repeated itself almost exactly. Later in the afternoon, a slim, white-haired old woman was led into the lobby of the Doubletree Hotel on South Broad and Locust streets in Philadelphia. Her dark, rather enormous bodyguard stayed at the door as she moved toward a red velvet, kidney-shaped settee nearby. Her royal blue dress hung on a bony body weathered by the years, but her regal walk suggested a woman of stature. She wore a necklace of large white pearls shaped like macadamia nuts and carried a small, black patent leather clutch that matched her short black patent leather pumps. She sat and waited, hands crossed, placed on her lap atop her purse.

A short while later, a nondescript black Lincoln town car with deeply tinted windows pulls to the curb out front, the door opened immediately by a waiting bell captain. A rather unimpressive man emerged, grey haired, dressed in a black suit, white shirt, pale blue tie; gold ring on his finger with a Masonic symbol in a black field, matching cuff links, gold Rolex that looked real enough. He moved casually into the expansive lobby, hardly noticing the gargantuan bodyguard standing at the door. He walked directly to the settee where the old woman sat. He sat next to her, about two feet separating them, and retrieved a copy of the USA Today newspaper from the small coffee table in front of him. He opened it to the middle, glanced at the page, casually crossed one leg, and turned the paper to the next page as he scanned the room from behind it.

"Our situation has taken a bit of a turn," the man said into the newspaper. The woman waited for him to continue. "The situation's been neutralized. Your items have been covered or removed, but there were some over-zealous individuals who drew unwanted attention to the project."

"*My* items?" the woman said, irritated at the man's attribution.

"Your company produced two-thirds of them. They took your grandfather, father, uncle, and one brother. I would say they're yours."

"Why not eliminate the attention."

"Because of the possible collateral damage."

"What is it you really came to tell me?"

The man thought a moment. "We're assessing our end-game," he said bluntly.

"Meaning?"

"Some believe the solution is a coordinated effort to fix the problem. A great deal more believe it's most expedient to fix the blame."

The hairs on the woman's arms stood-up, but she maintained her calm demeanor. The man already said 'your' items, and now he was talking about blame.

"It's a big ocean out there," she said.

"True, but things were a lot more controllable before the internet."

The woman deliberately waited to respond. "Which side are you on?" she asked.

"I'm only the messenger."

"In that case, does this message come with a warning?"

"It does."

"Then give it, and be on your way," she directed, trying to sound authoritative.

"There is no longer any interest in covering for this situation, but we can offer some help for you to do it."

The woman paused, contemplating the man's words.

"Do you have any information for me?"

The man placed an 11x14 yellow flip-top envelope on the seat between them.

"Now take something back for me," she said bluntly

"This is unusual," the man replied.

"Tell them I have enough dirt on most of them to ruin them whenever I choose, so they should look for a win-win solution, and the next time they decide to threaten me, they should do it themselves."

"Are you sure you want me to deliver the message?"

"I am."

"Very well. Good day, madam," the man said. With their conversation ended, he left.

The woman grabbed the large envelope beside her and set it on her lap, holding the outer edge in both hands. A moment later, she reached for her purse, only to stop, her hands trembling. Seeing her obvious distress, her bodyguard walked to her. He stopped three feet in front of her, noticing her cheeks starting to flush. A look of concern came to his huge, swarthy face. She looked up at him.

"They have a bar in here, right?" she said.

The old woman rose and padded slowly across the lobby to the stairs leading to the bar, up five steps with an elevated view of the lobby and the street outside the hotel. She sat at a small table on a long leather padded leather bench against the wall as her bodyguard went to retrieve her drink at the bar. As she checked out her view of the lobby from the table, two men seated at the bar rose and walked toward her, carrying their draft beers with them. They sat at a table made for two next to her, one man on the leather bench seat with the other man across the table from him.

The woman sat waiting for her bodyguard to return. Her hands trembled as she tentatively touched different objects near her. The napkin on the table. The rim of the tiny candle in the middle. Shakily, she drew the brown envelope from her lap and placed it on the table. She pried open the tiny metal clips and opened the envelope. After drawing it closer to her, she reached in and slid the contents out about half-way. On top was a note. She extracted the note by itself and slid the other items back in. After lifting her reading glasses to her eyes, she read the note:

"If there is a man sitting next to you with dark hair and green eyes, close the envelope and give it to him."

Startled, she returned the note to the envelope. She set it on the table and looked at the two men at the table next to her.

"Good afternoon, gentlemen," she said in a businesslike manner. The two men turned their heads to address her.

"Good afternoon, ma'am," they said cordially, in stereo.

She stared at the one sitting on the leather bench. She picked-up the envelope and handed it to him "I think this is for you," she said.

"Tentatively, Curran accepted the envelope, taking it from her. He looked inquisitively, yet playfully at Caraballo. "Imagine that." he said.

"And you said nobody knew you here," Caraballo jibed, smiling.

"My reputation must have preceded me."

"And you are?" the woman asked Curran.

"Nobody special."

The bodyguard returned to the table.

"Any problems madam?" he rumbled lowly as he set a drink in front of her.

"No problem. These boys are harmless," she exclaimed.

"Man, busting our chops already. We just met," Caraballo proclaimed.

Curran didn't react. Instead, he took a pull off his beer long enough to survey the area. The government guy was gone. The bodyguard was walking away. The concentrated dose of morphine he had was still in his pocket. It was enough to incapacitate or kill her. His 9mm carry gun was tucked in its appendix carry holster in the front of his waistband facing directly down at his private parts. It was enough to incapacitate or kill him.

He decided to take a quick look at the contents of the envelope. Just as she had, he bent the clips to open the flap, stuck his hand inside and pulled the contents out about half-way. He noticed a letter on top. He pulled it out. It was addressed to him. All it said was "Tom." He opened the letter. Unfolding the paper, his eyes came on something in the middle. It had only one word. "Don't." He looked at Caraballo, then handed him the paper. Caraballo read it and looked back at him, nodding.

"So don't," he said.

Both men nodded, took long draws from their beer glasses, and set the glasses down. They both looked at the woman, each ready with a witty remark. They both skipped it. Instead, they simply got up and left.

As they reached the rotating front door to the hotel, Caraballo looked over at the bodyguard, standing nearby trying to look casual. Caraballo puffed up his chest."

"Me Hulk, smash!" he growled like the cartoon Hulk. The two men kept moving, going out the revolving door and turning south, out of sight. Outside, Curran and Caraballo walked quickly down the street while keeping an eye out for Perez in the team's black Chevy Suburban.

"You had to say it didn't you," Curran said.

"Couldn't help myself," Caraballo replied.

Perez swooped up and stopped next to the car parked on the street separating Curran and Caraballo from the black suburban. The two men went around the car and got in, with Curran in back.

"You want to make a quick stop home?" Caraballo asked. "We're close."

"No. I want to get this done. But first, 1237 East Passyunk," Curran replied.

"Roger. Did you hear that?" Caraballo asked Perez.

"Got it."

"Turn right here on Locust." Caraballo directed.

"What's down there?" asked Perez.

"Pat's Steaks."

The three men found their sandwich restaurant. Caraballo got out of the truck and ran over to the window.

Three cafones," he said to the man behind the small window in front. The man turned and yelled "three cafones." A cafone (pronounced ga-vone in South Philly) in Italian is an ill-mannered person, but here it meant a cheese steak sandwich with fried peppers and onions.

They got their food and continued their way back to South Jersey. All three decided to wait until they returned to the hangar so they could have a beer with their steak sandwich. In back, Curran opened the envelope. He came on a picture of two men, single headshots like passport photos with their name underneath. Nothing remarkable. The next picture was of a vehicle crash, a pickup-truck sent into a telephone pole and demolished. Both men in the first photograph were visible in the second. The next picture was of the two men in a black rigid-hull inflatable boat.

"Remember these two guys?" Curran said, passing the boat picture forward to Caraballo.

"Yeah. What about them?" Caraballo replied, showing the picture to Perez.

"Here's what they look like now," Curran replied, handing Caraballo the picture of the crash.

"They've looked better."

"That was in that envelope?"

"Yep. That's one issue solved for us."

"Yeah," Caraballo replied, showing the picture to Perez.

"They might be the same guys that beat-up Baba. They may not," Curran said.

"We'll just have to be satisfied with that outcome. Otherwise we'll be on this thing forever."

"Roger that," Curran said, looking out the window as they crossed the bridge into New Jersey.

After that, the trio sat mostly in silence until after they arrived back at the hangar and were sitting eating their food.

"You know what's been bothering me?" Curran asked? Perez and Caraballo just shook their heads. "It's been the lack of government intervention. We've been looking into a history of chemical agent dumping in the ocean, a current chemical agent situation, ran into a known bad guy from the Bosnian War, been chased by fighter jets, blown-up by fighter jets, run off by bad guys, a silver-star winner is dead, his father is dead under dubious circumstances, we got assistance from a CIA spook and some questionable Coasties, the house was broken into, and nobody's come looking for us."

"That is odd," Caraballo replied.

"At the least, MacPherson would have shown-up by now to stick his nose in things," Perez assed, never really a fan of MacPherson.

"But this show's they're watching," Curran said, tapping his finger on the envelope on the table.

"They're letting it play out," Caraballo asserted. "So why didn't seven eights just come over and hand the envelope to you himself?" he added. "That *was* your contact that met with the woman in the hotel."

"Yes, it was. I think he did that more for dramatic effect on her, not us."

"Then he outed us for his own purposes." Caraballo said, not a question.

"Yes and no. If they were truly involved, a black helicopter would land outside, or a fleet of black SUV's would roll up to the door."

"What's next?" Perez asked.

"We play it out."

Chapter 22

"Gracie, I have to talk to you," Curran said, standing in the rain on Grace O'Reilly's front porch. The stare he was getting back through the window wasn't good. And she wasn't budging.

"I found your husband's boat," Curran said. He stood and waited. He felt a chill as the rain soaked through his black t-shirt. Goosebumps jumped up on his arms. The outline of the gun in his waistband became visible. "Grace," he said admonishingly.

Reluctantly, Grace unlocked the door. Without opening it as she usually does, she walked away.

Curran let himself in. He watched her walk slowly into the kitchen. She hung a half-folded bath towel over the chair where she expected Curran to sit. Like a person with no energy she poured two glasses of iced tea, set them on the table, and sat. Curran finally approached. He took the towel, dried his face, neck and arms, draped the towel back over the chair and sat. The two sat motionless. Grace looked down. Curran looked directly at her.

"Why Gracie?" Curran asked. She didn't respond. I know you took the medical records from the hospital. I know your husband was out recovering chemical agents illegally dumped only twenty miles out." The woman sat as still as a statue. She didn't blink. She didn't move. "I also know he didn't know it was your father that dumped them out there, and he didn't expect to get killed for it," Curran added. These words made Gracie flinch; her eyes squint. "But he wasn't killed by a chemical leak. He was shot," Curran declared. The woman grimaced. Tears streamed down her pale cheeks. "His wounds were from projectiles either fired at him or flying at him as a result of their impact elsewhere. The boat was shot to pieces. They towed it out of the area but just like they got lazy with dumping the chemicals, they didn't tow it far enough. Barrels left on board leaked nerve agent for months. What do you have to say for yourself?

Gracie shook her head slightly, never taking her eyes off the glass on the table in front of her. She rolled her shoulders inward, shame driving her toward despair. "I don't know what to say," she whispered.

"When you said 'your side of the family' would provide for you, I didn't know that meant the actual owner of the Titan Chemical Company. The old woman. Abigail DuMont, your aunt. Her married name. Your father's sister. The driving force behind the whole company. The same company that supplied most of the chemical agents for the war. *Also,* the same company that dumped most of the chemical agents *after* the war. They created something so powerful and so deadly they didn't know how to get rid of it, so they just dumped it in the oceans," Curran said emphatically. He pressed his hands into the table and leaned forward as he spoke. It was clear he was getting angry. "Some of the little worker bees were too lazy to do as they were directed. Instead of going past the continental shelf, they waited until they were barely over the horizon. Now, when people find out, people get dead. It almost happened to me. They shot my boat out from under me. They killed your husband, and they killed your son. The only thing that makes this worse, is you knew about it, and you covered it up. For what? For money?"

The woman started crying in earnest. Her back throbbed rhythmically off the back of the chair as she sobbed into her hands.

"How much was your son's life worth? What did you get for *services rendered*?" Curran said insultingly. The words made her recoil. "I can tell you what your husband's life was worth. I saw the payoff. It was all lies. Your aunt's been hiding things for the government for years. They came with F-16's when she called! The only thing that's been true is the eel tanks. Blanton Proctor's just a family stooge."

Suddenly a bang! A gunshot from outside. Curran jumped from his chair, spun a one-eighty, and moved about ten feet toward the front door. He stopped and bent slightly, parting the thin white curtains to see outside. A black Cadillac sat in the driveway. A big body guard laid face-down on the ground behind it, his body laying half in the dirt and half on the hardtop surface. Caraballo leaned back against the side of Curran's truck in the rain, a gun in his right hand held down at his side.

Curran stepped quickly to the door. He opened it and went outside. Caraballo turned his head toward Curran. "He had a gun," Caraballo remorsefully declared, pointing at the bodyguard as rainwater streamed down his face. His voice shook a bit. Not his first kill by far, but it was a civilian.

Curran raised his hand, giving Caraballo a calming gesture. He saw Caraballo's eyes averted from him.

"Tommy look out!" Caraballo yelled.

Curran turned around. Grace was coming at him. He saw the barrel of a very large gun. A shotgun being marched right at him. He dove to the side off the porch. Grace continued moving forward, butt stock of the shotgun under her right arm. Straight ahead she went, blank expression on her face, paying no attention to Curran or Caraballo. She fired. The rear passenger window of the Cadillac exploded, exposing the old woman in the back seat. She caught some of the shot from the blast. Grace fired a second time. Direct hit on the face and chest of the old woman. It threw her sideways into the driver's side door. Grace fired a third time. Then she dropped the gun on the ground, stood with her hands up about head high and froze. You could practically see the tension building in her body. She bent slightly at the waist and rocked back and forth. She clenched her fists and tightly shut her eyes. Then she screamed at the top of her lungs. It was a gushing sort of wail as if all the weight of the world was coming out at once. Cleansing. Releasing all the pent-up emotion at once. When it was over, she looked ten pounds lighter and five inches shorter.

Curran had gotten back on one knee before she fired and pulled his weapon. It was pointed at her, but he decided not to fire.

Same for Caraballo, who held his own gun on her. Curran stood and returned his weapon to its holster in the front waistband of his black pants. Caraballo saw it and did the same. And then the unexpected happened. Gracie simply turned around and went silently back in the house, calmly shutting the door behind her as she did. Curran and Caraballo stood, dumbfounded, drenched in the rain. Caraballo lifted his arms, hands palms-up, about half-way, and then dropped them back to his sides, slapping his wet cargo shorts.

Curran walked toward the front passenger door of the Cadillac. He knew this type of vehicle has the trunk release inside the glove compartment door. He opened the car door, found the button, then turned toward the back of the car. "Grab his legs," he said, directing Caraballo toward the feet of the dead bodyguard.

Curran reached into the trunk and retrieved a small towel. He grabbed the bodyguard's gun and threw it in the trunk making sure to not touch it with his own skin. After that, they hoisted the dead man up and heaved him inside the Cadillac's expansive trunk. "Still room for another," he said.

"Anybody specific?" Caraballo replied.

"Wait for it," Curran directed. He let a few seconds pass.

The sound of a car door shutting ended the wait. Curran nodded to Caraballo as he reached for the trunk lid. As he did, the Cadillac's engine started. Curran shut the trunk right as Grace shifted the car's transmission into drive. Then she pulled away. The two men stood and watched.

"We gonna stop her?" Caraballo asked.

"What for? Where's she gonna go?"

"I didn't want to shoot an old lady anyway."

"Neither did I. All she needed was for somebody to point out what she did."

"She even took the gun with her," Caraballo said.

"Yep."

"Good thing she didn't try to use it on us."

"How could she? It was her husband's three-shot autoloader. I saw him use it a bunch of times."

"Where do you think she'll go?"

"Probably to the landfill. She can't bring Proctor's aunt down to the chemical plant"

"Probably not."

"Okay, let's go."

Chapter 23

Curran and Caraballo collected Perez at the airport hangar and returned to the house on Sea Island. The rain ended and the afternoon sky was clear and blue. People were slowly making their way back to the beach. Inside the house, they removed the trip flares found a few days ago, straightened-up a bit, then made a trip north to a tackle shop just outside Atlantic City. There, Curran replaced much of the fishing equipment destroyed by the intruders.

"Tonight, we're forgetting about all this stuff," Curran said as they arrived back at the house.

It had been a stressful week. After dark, the three men found themselves on the boardwalk in Ocean City, New Jersey. Curran handed Caraballo and Perez two rolls of quarters each, and the threesome spent a few hours playing pinball, eating pizza, drinking birch beer, and enjoying being lost in the sights, sounds, and smells of the seashore boardwalk in the summertime.

"The killer awoke before dawn," Curran said, wrapping Caraballo on the soles of his feet.

"He put his boots on," Caraballo replied.

"Don't tell me you're groggy," Curran exclaimed, noticing his bleary-eyed friend. "You didn't even have a drink last night."

"Apparently I find normal life somewhat tiring."

"Come on. Coffee time."

"I'm on it."

Curran and Caraballo arrived at the marina and made their way down to the Comedor De Serpiente, the "Snake Eater."

"Come on boys, you're dragging ass!" Deke shouted from the flybridge.

The guys jumped on the boat as the mates untied the lines and the boat pulled out of the slip. They made their way out to some fishing grounds 28 miles out where a hump on the bottom attracts bait, which in turn attracts numerous varieties of fish. They set-up and trolled around the area for an hour or so. Having little luck, Curran and Deke mounted the tuna tower high above the flybridge in search of signs of fish. It was a beautiful day. Glassy seas, deep blue skies, calm winds. Far below Curran and Deke, the hum of turbocharged diesels pushed the boat effortlessly. But something was different. Curran kept noticing Deke watching him. He did it often, like how a father watches his kids, awestruck with how they're growing or how talented they are.

Curran reached into a storage compartment under the tower's helm station and retrieved a pair of binoculars. He thought they would help him spot birds or some other sign of fish in the area. He was wrong. After about fifteen minutes he put the binoculars away.

"Maybe try southwest a bit," he suggested.

"Deke slowed the boat to idle speed and looked at Curran. "What are you waiting for Tommy?" he asked.

Curran looked at him. You couldn't see his eyes behind his blue mirrored sunglasses, but you could tell he was serious. "Why did you do it, Deke?"

"For the money," Deke said, responding instantly. He was smiling as if proud of himself. Curran felt a combination of regret, guilt, and anger.

"I don't believe you," he said.

"How did you figure it out?"

"I know people, and I have half a brain," Curran said sarcastically.

"I know you do, but how?" Deke asked again. The boat made a big roll over a swell, high in the air, the tower made a significant swing. The force caused Deke to reach out and brace himself with a straight arm on Curran's shoulder. It wasn't an aggressive move. Curran didn't react.

"I would have to be a moron to not figure it out. First, Proctor would have never been so casual with your antagonizing him during the tournament unless you were associated in some way. He didn't react at all when we circled him and watched him transfer people from the commercial boat. We traced bills of lading for salvage companies and tugboat operators back to a woman named DuMont. Then we figured out her recent travels and surveyed all video cameras in a twenty-mile radius around her home. Eventually that led us to a meeting between she and a government spook I happen to know in a hotel on Broad Street in Philadelphia."

"Sounds complicated."

"No, it doesn't," Curran said irritatingly. "You know all about the capabilities of the government. Ironically, It's funny. You know who Mrs. DuMont looks like? She looks like you. I saw Mrs. DuMont at Grace O'Reilly's house. She's Gracie's aunt. You know Gracie, right?" Curran asked. "You know. Your *sister*? I found a picture in her basement. MacPherson confirmed the identity of the man in the picture as her father, but the facial recognition came back as a familial match on you. I didn't need a computer to tell me. I recognized the resemblance right away."

"So what?"

"My guy was able to figure out the big salvage boat covering everything with cement was leased by a company you use as a front for transferring technology and arms to foreign countries. The guys you paid to keep people away from the area beat your nephew to death."

Curran stared at Deke as Deke held the wheel and kept his gaze straight forward. Curran's jaw muscles started flexing, which is normally a sign he's about to strike.

"You and Connie took care of those two."

"Meaning what?"

"They went a bit too far and they were a loose-end."

"They were scapegoats," Curran said bluntly.

"So what."

"So, you have at least twelve people's blood on your hands."

"How do you figure that?"

"I found the Gracie Ann. It was all shot to shit, but just as the people that dumped the chemicals got lazy and dumped them too close to shore, they did the same with towing away the sunken boat. I also witnessed an F-16 destroy the Miss Margaret. They were all dead from nerve agent exposure. That's nine or ten people right there. We had to cap Mrs. DuMont's bodyguard yesterday and Grace did her aunt with a shotgun, so that's at least twelve. I wouldn't be surprised if she went and did the same to Blanton Proctor yesterday afternoon."

"Is that it?"

"No. You know an F-16 blew my boat out of the water with Connie and me on it. You know because the pilot was a government spook that works under another company of yours that tests the UAV guidance systems your family developed. Well, actually, the systems your father killed to obtain."

"That's pretty good, Tommy," Deke muttered, grinning.

"And the topper is Radomir Kuvarac. It's not his real name, but I've known him for over twenty years. I can't tell you who he really is, but he isn't a mass-murdering Balkan madman like people like to say. Right now, he really is just a fish biologist. He raises eels and striped bass and helps other Balkans enter the country to work on fishing boats."

"That's pretty good," Draper repeated, his voice trailing off.

"*Pretty good,*" Curran whined. "Deke, twelve people are dead. Your sister killed her aunt and is probably going to kill her cousin. You're selling chemical agents, covering it all up in a criminal conspiracy, the government is cutting you loose, and on top of all of it, you ordered somebody to kill Connie and me! What the hell, man?"

Deke looked off in the distance to the right of the boat for a moment, and then turned and stared at Curran. Suddenly he turned and jumped over the rail. As deftly as a trapeze artist, he grabbed the outside of the tower, locked his feet onto either side of the side ladder and slid down the tower to the bottom. He swung off the bottom and landed on the deck of the stern cockpit even before Curran was able to react.

Curran was surprised by Deke's actions. Even though he was getting increasingly angry and ready to exact some punishment on him, Curran was reluctant to really bring the wrath on this man. He loved and admired Deke. He considered him a father figure. However, doing evil is doing evil.

A rush of energy surged through Curran. He was prepared to pursue Deke. Curran swung underneath the railing at the top of the tuna tower, turned and put his foot on the top rung of the ladder. He descended as fast as he could, reaching the flybridge in only about fifteen seconds. He rounded the raining to the ladder well and rushed down into the cockpit.

Curran froze at the bottom of the steps to the cockpit. Two men rushed past him toward the stern. It was Deke's two mates abandoning the boat, each carrying an armful of life jackets. Curran saw them jump off the stern and into the water. Turning back toward the cabin he noticed Caraballo walking backwards out the cabin door with his hands up about head high. Curran had just enough of an angle to see Deke holding a gun on Caraballo while using a satellite telephone with the other hand.

"Deke, what are you doing?" Curran shouted.

"We gotta go?" Caraballo declared, staring at Curran wide-eyed. Caraballo had his bag over his shoulder.

"Go where?" Curran asked. He saw something in his peripheral vision. He didn't get the chance to recognize it before the thunderous roar of a jet engine passed overhead. "Oh, okay," Curran added.

Curran and Deke made eye contact. Deke was sweating. His eyes held a look of despair Curran had never seen. He nodded to Curran. Without responding, Curran and Caraballo turned, ran across the deck and jumped off the transom into the water. Floating in the water, they turned and saw Deke run up the ladder to the flybridge as the boat moved away from them. Deke hit the throttles and the boat darted off as the engines threw black diesel smoke behind it. They were riveted to the sight. They couldn't look away.

About a mile away, the two saw a bright flash of light appear, obscuring their view of the big sportfishing boat. Suddenly, the boat exploded. A boom came across with water along with the shock wave from the blast. The tower folded forward as the rest of the boat blew apart, stopping a short distance from the point of impact.

"Dumb bastard," Caraballo blurted disgustedly, watching the boat burn.

"Yep." Curran responded. Caraballo turned around to face Curran.

"No. I mean you."

"Me?"

"You had to confront him all the way out here," Caraballo said frustratedly.

"He brought it up."

"He did?"

"Yeah. He asked me what I was waiting for."

"Maybe you should have said waiting for him to get closer to shore."

Curran smiled. He noticed Caraballo's gym bag. "You put the sat phone in the waterproof bag, right?"

"Sure did."

Curran and Caraballo heard the two mates yelling from about three hundred yards away. They yelled back and waved. Caraballo laid back and used the bottom of his t-shirt to catch some air, using it as a flotation device. He started smiling.

"What," Curran asked.

"Seems like we've been in this position before."

"Yeah," Curran replied, chuckling.

"So, what song am I thinking of?"

"Cake. The Distance."

"How do you know?"

"Bowel shaking earthquakes of doubt and remorse. Assail him, impale him, with monster truck force.

"Not really," Caraballo said.

"Really?"

"No. You've seen Jaws."

"Yeah," Curran replied. Caraballo looked around, then back at Curran.

"Show me the way to go home," Caraballo started to sing.

Curran smiled. Then he joined in.

Information on Ocean Dumping:

All the descriptions of government dumping of chemical weapons, nerve agents, explosives, etc., are <u>real</u>…and should scare the hell out of you. For more information, I used the following links for information on the topic:

http://www.nytimes.com/1987/08/31/nyregion/new-concern-raised-by-waste-dumping-in-atlantic-off-li.html

http://www.dailypress.com/media/acrobat/2005-10/20226301.pdf (1)

http://www.nuc.berkeley.edu/forum/218/deadliness-belowweapons-mass-destruction-thrown-sea-years-ago-present-danger-now-and-army-

http://www.stripersonline.com/a/new-york-dumping-of-toxic-waste-3-miles-off-new-jersey-shores

http://www.northjersey.com/news/124555754_Undersea_mission.html

http://www.foxnews.com/tech/2012/10/08/millions-unexploded-bombs-lie-in-waters-off-us-coasts/

http://en.wikipedia.org/wiki/Marine_Protection,_Research,_and_Sanctuaries_Act_of_1972

http://articles.philly.com/1992-11-12/news/26010001_1_sewage-sludge-cindy-lee-van-dover-largest-sludge

http://www.naturalnews.com/037644_mustard_gas_Gulf_of_Mexico_dumping.html

http://usatoday30.usatoday.com/news/nation/2005-11-01-weapons-ocean_x.htm Holy shit!

http://www.northjersey.com/news/124555754_Undersea_mission.html

http://www.bookrags.com/research/ocean-dumping-ban-act-1988-enve-02/

http://archive.gao.gov/f0302/109826.pdf

http://usnews.nbcnews.com/_news/2012/09/28/14141378-world-war-ii-bombs-mustard-gas-in-gulf-of-mexico-need-to-be-checked-experts-warn?lite

http://www.dotandcalm.com/calm-archive/index/t-13305.html (2)

http://www.dotandcalm.com/calm-archive/index/t-13305.html (3)

http://cns.miis.edu/stories/090806_cw_dumping.htm

Made in the USA
Monee, IL
03 December 2020